THE
SAVAGE
GARDEN

By the same author

The Whaleboat House

THE
SAVAGE
GARDEN

MARK MILLS

HarperCollins*Publishers*

HarperCollins*Publishers*
77–85 Fulham Palace Road
Hammersmith, London W6 8JB

www.harpercollins.co.uk

Published by HarperCollins*Publishers* 2007

2

Copyright © Mark Mills 2007

Mark Mills asserts the moral right to
be identified as the author of this work

Lines from 'Little Gidding' by T.S. Eliot are reproduced
by permission of Faber and Faber Ltd.

A catalogue record for this book
is available from the British Library

ISBN-13 978-0-00-716191-1
ISBN-10 0-00-716191-3

Set in Sabon by
Palimpsest Book Production Limited, Grangemouth, Stirlingshire

Printed in Great Britain by
Clays Ltd, St Ives plc

This book is proudly printed on paper which contains wood
from well managed forests, certified in accordance with
the rules of the Forest Stewardship Council.
For more information about FSC,
please visit www.fsc-uk.org

Mixed Sources

Product group from well-managed
forests and other controlled sources
www.fsc.org Cert no. TT-COC-2139
© 1996 Forest Stewardship Council

FSC

Acknowledgements

My thanks, as ever, go to my inimitable agent and friend Stephanie Cabot for – well – being Stephanie Cabot, to my editors Julia Wisdom and Rachel Kahan for their enthusiasm, wisdom and guidance, and to my wife Caroline for her tireless patience and encouragement.

I am also extremely grateful to Francis and Rachel Hamel-Cooke, Anne O'Brien and Jane Hall, as well as Charles and Angela Cottrell-Dormer, whose hospitality and generosity of spirit account for much more of this book than they are probably aware.

For Caroline, Gus and Rosie

We shall not cease from exploration
And the end of all our exploring
Will be to arrive where we started
And know the place for the first time.

T.S. Eliot, 'Little Gidding', *Four Quartets*

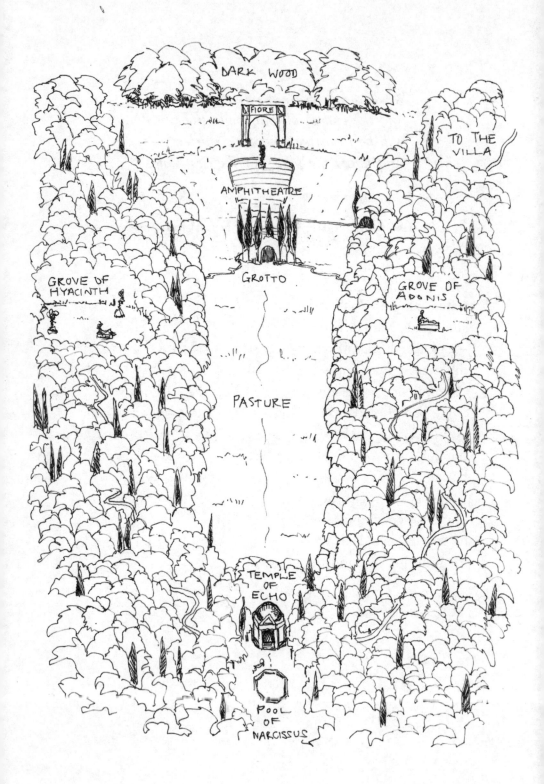

August 1958

Later, when it was over, he cast his thoughts back to that sun-struck May day in Cambridge – where it had all begun – and asked himself whether he would have done anything differently, knowing what he now did.

It was not a question easily answered.

He barely recognized himself in the carefree young man cycling along the towpath beside the river, bucking over the ruts, the bottle of wine dancing around in the bike basket.

Try as he might, he couldn't penetrate the workings of that stranger's mind, let alone say with any certainty how he would have dealt with the news that murder lay in wait for him, just around the corner.

1

He was known, primarily, for his marrows.

This made him a figure of considerable suspicion to
the ladies of the Horticultural Society, who, until his
arrival on the scene, had vied quite happily amongst
themselves for the most coveted award in the vegetable
class at their annual show. The fact that he was a
newcomer to the village no doubt fuelled their
resentments; that he lived alone with a 'housekeeper'
some years younger than himself, a woman whose cast
of countenance could only be described as 'oriental',
permitted them to bury the pain of defeat in malicious
gossip.

That first year he carried off the prize, I can
recall Mrs Meade and her cronies huddled together at
the back of the marquee, like cows before a gathering
storm. I can also remember the vicar, somewhat the
worse-for-wear after an enthusiastic sampling of the
cider entries, handing down his verdict on the marrow
category. With an air of almost lascivious relish, he

declared Mr Atherton's prodigious specimen to be
'positively tumescent' (thereby reinforcing my own
suspicions about the good reverend).

Mr Atherton, tall, lean, and slightly stooped by his
seventy-some years, approached the podium without the
aid of his walking stick. He graciously accepted the
certificate (and the bottle of elderflower cordial that
accompanied it) then returned to his chair. I happened
to be seated beside him that warm, blustery afternoon,
and while the canvas snapped in the wind and the vicar
slurred his way through a heartfelt tribute to all who
had submitted Victoria sponges, Mr Atherton inclined
his head towards me, a look of quiet mischief in his
eyes.

'Do you think they'll ever forgive me?' he muttered
under his breath.

I knew exactly who he was talking about.

'Oh, I doubt it,' I replied, 'I doubt it very much.'

These were the first words we had ever exchanged,
though it was not the first time I had elicited a smile
from him. Earlier that summer, I had caught him
observing me with an amused expression from beneath a
Panama hat. He had been seated in a deck chair on the
boundary of the cricket pitch, and a burly, lower-
order batsman from Droxford had just hit me for 'six'
three times in quick succession, effectively sealing
yet another ignoble defeat for the Hambledon 2nd XI.

Adam turned the sheet over, expecting to read on. The
page was blank.

'That's it?' he asked.

3

'Evidently,' said Gloria. 'What do you think?'

'It's good.'

'Good? "Good" is like "nice". "Good" is what mothers say about children who don't misbehave. Boring children! For God's sake, Adam, this is my novel we're talking about.'

Probably best not to mention the over-zealous use of commas.

'*Very* good. Excellent,' he said.

Gloria pouted a wary forgiveness, her breasts straining against the material of her cotton print dress as she leaned towards him. 'It's just the opening, but it's intriguing, don't you think?'

'Intriguing. Yes. Very mysterious. Who is this Mr Atherton with the prodigious marrows?'

'Ah-ha!' she trumpeted. 'You see? Page one and you're already asking questions. That's good.'

He raised an eyebrow at her choice of adjective but she didn't appear to notice.

'Who do *you* think he is? Or, more to the point: *What* do you think he is?'

She was losing him now. The wine wasn't helping, unpalatably warm in the afternoon heat, a wasp buzzing forlornly around the neck of the bottle.

'I really don't know.'

Gloria swept the wasp aside with the back of her hand and filled her glass, topping up Adam's as an after-thought.

'He's a German spy,' she announced.

'A German spy?'

'That's right. You see, it's wartime – 1940, to be precise – and while the Battle of Britain rages in the skies above a small Hampshire village, an altogether different battle is about to unfold on the ground. As above –'

'– so below.'

Were they really quoting Hermes Trismegistus at each other over this?

'And who or what is Herr Atherton spying on?' he persevered, regretting the question almost immediately.

'A secret submarine base in Portsmouth harbour.'

So this was where two years of English literature studies had led her, all that Beowulf and Chaucer, and Sir Gawain and the Green Knight: to a secret submarine base in Portsmouth harbour.

'What?' demanded Gloria warily.

'I was just thinking,' he lied, 'that your narrator's a man. Unless she's a woman who happens to play cricket for the village team.'

'So?'

'It's a challenge, I imagine, writing a male narrator.'

'You don't think I'm up to it?'

'I didn't say that.'

'Four brothers,' she said, holding up three fingers. 'And it's not as if you're the first chap I've ever stepped out with.'

This was a truth she liked to assert from time to time, dishing out unsavoury details to drive home her point, although she was too angry for that right now.

She tossed the remainder of her wine away, the liquid crescent flopping into the tall grass. She got to her feet a little unsteadily. 'I'm going.'

'Don't,' he said, taking her hand. 'Stay.'

'You hate it.'

5

'That's not true.'

'I know what you're thinking.'

'You're wrong. I could be jailed for what I'm thinking.'

It was a crass play, but he knew her vulnerability to that kind of talk. Besides, this was the reason they'd skipped their lectures and come to the meadow, was it not?

'I'm sorry,' he said, capitalizing on her faint smile, 'I suppose I'm just jealous.'

'Jealous?'

'I couldn't do it, I know that. It's great. Really. It hooked me instantly. The drunken vicar's a great touch.'

'You like him?'

'A lot.'

Gloria allowed herself to be drawn back down on to the blanket, into their sunken den, out of sight of the river towpath where the stubby willows bristled.

His fingers charted a lazy yet determined course along the inside of her dove-white thigh, the flesh warm and yielding, like new dough.

She leaned towards him and kissed him, forcing her tongue between his lips.

He tasted the cheap white wine and felt himself stir under her touch. His hand moved to her breasts, his thumb brushing over her nipples, the way she liked it.

Sexual favours in return for blanket praise. Was it really that simple?

He checked his thoughts, guilty that his mind was straying from the matter in hand.

He needn't have worried.

'You know,' said Gloria, breaking free and drawing

breath, 'I think I'll give Mr Atherton a granddaughter. My hero needs to lose his heart.'

The note was waiting for him in his pigeonhole when he returned to college. He recognized the handwriting immediately. It was the same barely legible scrawl that adorned his weekly essays. The note read:

Dear Mr Strickland,
Apologies for making this demand upon your busy schedule, but there is a matter I should like to discuss with you regarding your thesis.
Shall we say 5 p.m. today in my office at the faculty? (That's the large stone building at the end of Trumpington Street, in case you've forgotten.)
Warm regards
Professor Leonard

Adam glanced at his watch. Fifteen minutes to get across town. The bath would have to wait.

Professor Crispin Leonard was something of an institution, not just within the faculty but the university as a whole. Although well into his seventies, he was quite unlike his elderly peers, who only emerged from their gloomy college rooms at mealtimes, or so it seemed, shuffling in their threadbare gowns to and from the dining hall across velvet lawns whose sacred turf it was their privilege to tread. Few knew what these aged characters did (or had ever done) to justify the sinecure of a college fellowship. Authorship of a book, one book, any book, appeared to suffice, even if the value of that work had long since been eclipsed. For whatever reason, they were deemed to have paid their dues, and in return the colleges offered them a comfortable dotage unencumbered by responsibilities.

Professor Leonard was cut from a far tougher cloth. He lectured and supervised in three subjects, he continued to offer his services as a college tutor, and he remained involved in a number of societies, some of which he had also founded. And all this while still finding time not only to write but to be published. By any standards it was a remarkable workload, and one he appeared to shoulder quite effortlessly.

How did he manage it? He never hurried and was never late; he just loped about like a well-fed cat, giving off an air of slight distraction, as if his mind was always on higher things.

He was deep in slumber when Adam entered his office. The first knock didn't rouse him, and when Adam poked his head around the door and saw him slumped in an armchair, a book on his lap, he knocked again, louder this time.

Professor Leonard stirred, taking his bearings, taking in Adam. 'I'm sorry, I must have nodded off.' He closed the book and laid it aside. Adam noted that it was one of the professor's own works, on the sculpture of Mantegna.

'No court in the land would convict you.'

Professor Leonard invited irreverence, he actively encouraged it, but for a moment Adam feared he had overstepped the mark.

'That might be funnier, Mr Strickland, if you'd ever bothered to read my book on Mantegna. Which reminds me – how *is* your serve?'

'Excuse me?'

'Well, the last time I saw you, you were cycling down King's Parade in something of a hurry. You were gripping two tennis rackets, and the young lady riding side-saddle was gripping you.'

'Oh.'

'Has it improved?'

'Improved?'

'Your serve, Mr Strickland. We would all feel so much happier if you at least had something else to show for your absence.'

'I work hard,' bleated Adam, 'I work late.'

Professor Leonard reached for some papers stacked on the side table next to his chair. 'Since you're here, you might as well take this now.' He flipped through the pile and pulled out Adam's essay. 'I probably marked you lower than I should have done.'

'Oh,' said Adam, a little put out.

'Thinking about it, you might have had more of a point than I credited you with at first.'

'Which point was that?'

'Don't flatter yourself, Mr Strickland. To my knowledge – and I read it twice – you only made one point. The others were lifted straight from the books I suggested you read.' He raised a long, bony finger. 'And some I didn't suggest . . . which, I grant you, displays more initiative than most.'

He handed the essay over.

'We'll discuss it at greater length another time. Now, your thesis. Have you had any further thoughts?'

Adam had flirted with a couple of ideas – Islamic icon-ography in Romanesque architecture, the use of line in early Renaissance drawing – but the professor would recognize them for what they were: lazy speculations on some well-trodden fields of study. No, best to keep quiet.

'Not really.'

'You still have a year, of course, but it's advisable to start applying yourself now, certainly if you wish to show us something of your true colours. Do you, Mr Strickland?'

'Yes,' said Adam. 'Of course.'

'How's your Italian?'

'Okay. Rusty.'

'Good, then I might have something for you.'

The professor explained that he had recently been contacted by an old acquaintance of his. Signora Docci, the lady in question, was the owner of a large villa in the hills of Tuscany, just south of Florence. 'An impressive, if somewhat pedestrian, example of High Renaissance Tuscan vernacular,' was how the professor described the architecture of the building. He saved his praise for the garden, not the formal arrangement of Renaissance terraces abutting the villa, but a later Mannerist addition occupying a sunken grove nearby. Conceived and laid out by a grieving husband to the memory of his dead wife, this plunging patch of woodland was fed by a spring and modelled on Roman gardens of the period, with meandering pathways and rills, statues, inscriptions and neo-classical structures.

'It's a very unusual place,' the professor said. 'Extremely arresting.'

'You know it?'

'I did, some years ago. It has never been altered – which is rare – and I know for a fact that no proper study has ever been conducted of it. Which is where you come in, if you want to, that is. Signora Docci has kindly offered it as a subject for one of my students.'

Mannerist was bad, too overblown for Adam's taste, and he'd have to do a lot of reading up. Italy, on the other hand, was good, very good.

'Maybe a garden isn't quite what you had in mind, but don't dismiss it . . . Art and Nature coming together to create a whole new entity – a third nature, if you will.'

Adam didn't require any more encouragement. 'Yes,' he said. 'Yes please.'

2

Exams were upon them before they knew it, and gone just as quickly. They celebrated, got drunk, punted off to Grantchester with picnics, danced at college balls and hurled themselves fully clothed into the river – memories irreparably tarnished for Adam by Gloria's decision to end their relationship on the last night of term. The situation was non-negotiable and, true to character, Gloria made no attempt to feign a remorse she clearly didn't feel. She did manage, however, to offer him one scrap of consolation: as he would no longer be coming to stay at her family's pile in Scotland, he would be spared the maddening attentions of the summer midges.

'Cattle have been known to hurl themselves off cliffs because of the midges.'

These were her last words to him before he stormed out on her, slamming the door behind him.

The following day everyone trickled back to their real lives. For Adam, this was a faceless suburb to the south of London, and a Tudor-style villa with Elizabethan yearnings. Thrown up just after the war, the house only existed because a German air crew had taken one look at the lethal hail of flak over the city and promptly jettisoned their payload before running for home.

Adam and his brother had once dug a trench at the end of the garden – the first line of defence against invasion by some imagined enemy force – only to find themselves unearthing the remains of the terraced houses that had previously occupied the plot. Harry had taken those fragments of brick and tile and glass, sinking them in plaster of Paris, producing a mosaic in the shape of a house: the first tell-tale sign of his calling that Adam could recall.

Adam searched out old friends from the neighbourhood. They drank beer together in the garden of the Stag and Hounds, trading stories and trying their best to ignore the inescapable truth – that the ties that once bound them were loosening by the year and might soon be gone altogether.

His mother was delighted to have him home and keen to show it, which usually meant she was unhappy. Whenever she smothered him with affection, he had the uneasy sensation she was using him as a rod with which to beat his father: You see what you're missing out on? His father was more withdrawn than ever, and not best pleased. He had wanted Adam to give the summer over to work-experience – a placement with an acquaintance of his at the Baltic Exchange. It was a wise thing to develop a working knowledge of the Baltic Exchange before a career in marine insurance at Lloyd's. It was a wise thing to do, because that's exactly what he himself had done. In the end, though, he conceded defeat.

The arrangements had gone without a hitch: a letter to

Signora Docci, her reply (typed and in impeccable English) saying that she had secured a room for him at a pensione in the local town. Aside from rustling up a bit of funding for Adam from within the History of Art Department, Professor Leonard had not needed to involve himself. He did, however, suggest that Adam meet up with him in town before leaving for the Continent.

The proposed venue was a grand stone building close by Cannon Street station in the City. Adam had never heard of the Worshipful Company of Skinners, although he wasn't unduly surprised to discover that the professor was associated with a medieval guild whose history reached back seven centuries. They passed through panelled chambers en route to the roof terrace, where they took lunch beneath an even layer of cloud like a moth-eaten blanket, the sun slanting through at intervals and picking out patches of the city.

They ate beef off the bone and drank claret.

The professor had come armed with a bundle of books and articles for Adam's mental edification.

'Read these right through,' he said, handing over copies of Ovid's *Metamorphoses* and *Fasti*. 'The rest are for reference purposes. You'll find the family has an impressive library, which I'm sure you'll be given access to.' The professor was reluctant to say any more about the garden – 'You don't want me colouring your judgement' – although he was happy to share some other background with Adam.

Signora Docci lived alone at Villa Docci, her husband having died some years before. Her eldest son Emilio was also dead, killed towards the end of the war by the Germans who had occupied the villa. There was another son,

14

Maurizio, soon to take over the estate, as well as a dissolute daughter, Caterina, who now lived in Rome.

The rest of lunch was spent talking about the professor's imminent trip to France. He was off to view the Palaeolithic cave paintings at Lascaux – his third visit since their chance discovery by a group of local boys back in 1940. He recalled his frustration at having to wait five years for the war to end before making his first pilgrimage. Thirteen years on, he felt it was now possible to trace the influence of that primitive imagery on the work of contemporary artists. In fact, it was to be the subject of an article, and possibly even a book.

'Europe's greatest living painters drawing inspiration from its oldest known painters, seventeen thousand years on. If that isn't art history, I don't know what is.'

'No.'

'You don't have to humour me, you know.'

'Of course I do,' said Adam. 'You're buying lunch.'

Later, when they parted company out on the street, the professor said, 'Francesca . . . Signora Docci . . . she's old now, and frail by all accounts. But don't underestimate her.'

'What do you mean?'

Professor Leonard hesitated, glancing off down the street. 'I'm not sure I rightly know, but it's sound advice.'

As Adam sat slumped and slightly inebriated in the deserted carriage on the train journey back to Purley, he was left with the uneasy sensation that the professor's parting warning had been the true purpose of their meeting.

A week later, Adam was gone. He changed trains in Paris, aware that this was as far south as he had ever travelled in his life. On Professor Leonard's advice, he slipped some francs to the guard and was allotted a spare sleeping compartment to himself.

He didn't sleep. He tossed in the darkness, France rattling by beneath him, and he thought (far more than he would have liked) of Gloria and of the look on her face when she had said to him, 'I don't know why. I think maybe it's because you're a touch boring.'

He might have been less stung if they hadn't just made love. Twice.

'Boring?'

'No, not boring, that's unfair. Bland.'

'Bland?'

'No.'

'What, then?'

'I don't know. I can't put my finger on it. I can't think of a word.'

Great. He was a category unto himself – a unique category indefinable by words but falling somewhere between 'boring' and 'bland'.

He had lost his temper, hurling a pillow across the room and swearing at her. He could still recall every moment of the long walk back to his own college, creeping down the staircase from her rooms, stepping through the pale dawn of Trinity Great Court, the bittersweet taste of self-pity rendering him immune to the daggered look from the porter on duty in the lodge.

Pathetic, really, when looked at from a distance, from the darkened sleeping compartment of a train hurtling through the French night, for example. He tried to stem the flow of his thoughts, or at least divert their course.

16

When he failed, he turned on the light and worked on his Italian grammar.

Dawn rose, bringing with it the barely discernible mass of a steep Alpine valley. A few hours later, they were free of the mountains.

All he saw of Milan was the Fascist splendour of the Stazione Centrale as he hurried between platforms to make his connecting train. He was aware of the heat and the smell of unfamiliar tobacco, but not much else. He briefly glimpsed Shelley's 'waveless plain of Lombardy' before nodding off.

A deep and dreamless sleep carried him all the way to Florence, where he was woken brusquely by the guard, who talked at him in a language quite unlike the Italian he'd learned at school and recently brushed up on. Ejected on to the platform, it certainly wasn't the kind of reception he'd been led to believe he might receive in Italy.

He found a pensione on Piazza Santa Maria Novella, a short walk from the station. The owner informed him that he was in luck; a room had just fallen vacant. It was easy to see why. Adam made a speculative survey of the dismal little box in the roof and told himself it was only for one night.

He stripped off his shirt and lay on the sagging mattress, smoking a cigarette, unaccustomed to the humidity pressing down on the city. Was this normal? If so, why had no one thought to mention it? Or the mosquitoes, for that matter. They speckled the ceiling, waiting for night to fall and the feast to begin.

He squeezed himself into the shower room at the end of the corridor and allowed the trickle of water to cool him off. It was a temporary measure. His fresh shirt was lacquered to his chest by the time he'd descended four flights of stairs to the lobby.

The storm broke as he stepped from the building, the sharp crack of thunder echoing around the piazza, the deluge following moments later as the amethyst clouds deposited their load. He stood beneath the awning, watching the rain drops dancing on the road. Water sheeted down from overflowing gutters; drain holes were lost to sight beneath spreading pools of water. And still the rain came, constant, unvarying in its strength. When it ceased, it ceased suddenly and completely.

A church bell struck half past the hour, and immediately people began to appear from the shelter of doorways around the piazza – almost as if the two events were connected, the bell alerting the inhabitants of the quarter to the passing of danger, as it had always done. The sun burst from behind the departing slab of cloud. It hit hard, flashing off the steaming flagstones.

Scuttling figures skipped over puddles, hurrying to make up for lost time. Adam joined their ranks, map in hand, heading south out of the piazza. In Via dei Fossi rainwater still streamed from jutting eaves high overhead, driving pedestrians off the pavements into the road, forcing them to do battle with squadrons of scooters and cars. The narrow street filled with the sound of horns and curses, the cacophony played out with leaps and bounds and wild gesticulations, the distant rumble of the departing storm like a low kettle-drum roll underscoring the deranged opera.

A twinge of anxiety stiffened his stride, though not at the chaos unfolding around him. He knew the city intimately, but only from books. What if he was disappointed? What if Florence's 'unique cultural and artistic heritage', which he'd detailed in his essays with such hollow authority, left him cold? As if on cue, he found himself on a bridge spanning the River Arno – no lively, sparkling torrent, but a strip of brown and turbid water, a river fit for a factory district.

Five minutes later he reached his destination, and his apprehension melted away. The Brancacci Chapel in the church of Santa Maria del Carmine was deserted when he entered it, and it remained so for the next quarter of an hour. Michelangelo and Raphael had both come here to study, to copy, to learn from the young man who had changed the face of European painting: Tommaso Guidi, nicknamed Masaccio by his friends, the scruffy boy-wonder, dead at twenty-seven. Others had contributed to the same cycle of frescoes – Masolino, Fra Lippo Lippi, names to be reckoned with – but their work was flat, lifeless, when set alongside that of Masaccio.

His figures demanded to be heard, to be believed in; some even threatened to step out of the walls and shake the doubters into credence. Real men, not ciphers. And real women. His depiction of Adam and Eve's expulsion from the Garden of Eden required no context in order to be appreciated. More than five hundred years on, it still struck home: the fallen couple, with their bare, rough-hewn limbs, granite hard from toil, cast out like country labourers by some unforgiving landlord. Adam's face was buried in his hands, a broken man. Eve covered her nakedness in shame, but her face was raised, crying out to the heavens. All the anger, frustration and incomprehension in the world seemed contained within that gaping, shapeless hole Masaccio had given her for a mouth.

The more Adam stared at the image, the more he saw,

and the less he understood. A definition of true art? He was still cringing at his own pomposity when a couple entered the chapel.

They were French. His thick dark hair was oiled back into two symmetrical wings that protruded a short distance from the forehead. She was extremely slender, quite unlike Masaccio's Eve, or maybe as Eve would have looked some years after her banishment from the bounty of Eden – pinched and emaciated.

'Good afternoon,' said the Frenchman in accented English, looking up from his guidebook.

It rankled that he was so readily identifiable, not just as a fellow tourist but an Englishman.

'American?' asked the Frenchman.

'English.'

The word came out wrong – barked, indignant – a parody of Anglo-Saxon self-importance. The couple exchanged the faintest of amused glances, which only annoyed him more.

He looked at the man's perfectly coiffed hair and wondered just how distressing that flash downpour must have been for him. Or maybe the oil helped; maybe it assisted run-off.

He only realized he was staring when the Frenchman shifted nervously and said, 'Yes . . .?'

Adam gestured to the frescoes. '*Las pinturas son muy hermosas,*' he said in his best Spanish.

As he left the chapel, abandoning the couple to Masaccio's genius, he wondered whether his antagonism towards them owed itself to their interruption of his experience, or whether the work itself had somehow unleashed it in him.

3

❧ ⚜ ❧

Has the Englishman arrived yet?

No, Signora.

When?

Tomorrow.

Tomorrow?

That's what he said in his letter. The twelfth.

I wish to see him as soon as he gets here.

You've already said, Signora.

You won't forget?

Why would I forget? Move a little to the side, please.

Gently. Don't push.

I'm sorry. Turn over, please.

You don't have to do this, Maria.

I know.

I'm happy to hire someone else.

You really expect me to cook and clean for someone else?

You're a good woman.

Thank you, Signora.

Just as your father was a good man.

He had the highest respect for you too, Signora.

There's really no need to be quite so formal, not when you're giving me a bed-bath.

He had the highest respect for you too.

You know, Maria, I believe you're in danger of developing a sense of humour in your old age.

Turn over, please.

4

※ ※

They left Florence through the Porta Romana, heading south to Galluzzo, where they wound their way up into the hills past a sprawling Carthusian monastery.

The climbing road was flanked by olive groves, neat rows of trees laid out in terraces, their foliage flashing silver in the sunlight. Vineyards and stands of umbrella pines studded the hillside. Every so often, an avenue of dark cypresses indicated a track leading to some isolated farmhouse, which invariably was also guarded by a small cohort of the tall, tapering conifers. Apart from the tarmac road along which they were travelling, there was little to suggest the passing centuries had wrought any meaningful change on the tapestried landscape.

Adam lounged in his seat, taking in the view, the cooling breeze from the open window washing over him, ruffling his hair. The taxi driver was still talking nineteen to the dozen despite Adam's earlier confession that most of the words were lost on him. Every now and then Adam would catch the man's eye in the rear-view mirror and grunt and nod his assent – an arrangement that seemed to work to the complete satisfaction of both parties.

When the road levelled out he turned and peered through the rear window, searching for a glimpse of Florence. The city was lost to view behind the tumble of hills rolling in from the south. Somehow it seemed appropriate; she was hiding herself, even now.

All morning he had walked her streets, the stone chasms hacked into her, grid-like. Her buildings were no more welcoming – the palaces of rusticated stone, modelled on fortresses (or so it seemed); the churches with their unadorned exteriors, many sheathed in black-and-white marble; the museums housed in all manner of forbidding structures. And yet, behind those austere façades lay any number of riches.

Adam had chosen carefully, almost mathematically, limited as he was by the short time at his disposal. There had been disappointments, acclaimed works which had left him feeling strangely indifferent. But as the taxi worked its way higher into the hills, he consoled himself with the knowledge that it had been a first foray, a swift reconnaissance. There would be plenty of opportunities to return.

San Casciano sat huddled on a high hill, dominating the surrounding countryside. Its commanding position had largely determined the course of its history, apparently, although the entry in Adam's guidebook made no mention of the last siege the town had been forced to endure. Even as the taxi approached, it was evident that the ancient walls girdling the town had not been constructed to withstand an assault by the kind of weaponry available to the Allies and the Germans.

These weren't the first scars of war Adam had witnessed. Even Florence, declared an 'open city' by both sides out of respect for her architectural significance, had suffered. As the Allies swept up from the south, the Germans had dug in, blowing all but one of the city's historic bridges. They may have spared the Ponte Vecchio, but this consideration came at a price. The buildings flanking the river in the vicinity of the bridge were mined, medieval towers and Renaissance palaces reduced to rubble, the field cleared for the forthcoming battle. As it was, the Allied troops had simply crossed the Arno elsewhere on makeshift Bailey bridges and swiftly liberated the town.

Years on, the wound inflicted right in the heart of the old city remained raw and open. If efforts had been made to restore those lost streets to their former glory, it was not evident. Modern structures with smooth faces and clean sharp lines stood out along the river's southern frontage, like teenagers in a queue of pensioners. The very best you could say was that the space had been filled.

In San Casciano that work was still going on. The town was pockmarked with the ruins of bomb-damaged buildings left to lie where they'd fallen. Impressively, Nature had reclaimed what she could in these plots. Young trees sprouted defiantly; shrubs had somehow detected enough moisture in piles of old stones to put down roots and prosper; weeds and ferns sprang from crevices in crumbling walls. The bland new concrete edifices that studded the historic centre were further evidence of the severe pounding the town had taken.

The Pensione Amorini had been spared. One part of the ancient vine clinging to its scaling stucco façade had been trained over a pergola, which shaded a terrace out front, overflow for the bar and trattoria occupying the ground floor. Signora Fanelli was expecting him – he had phoned ahead from Florence – and she summoned her teenage son from a back room to help with Adam's bags.

'*Oofa*,' said Iacopo as he tested the weight of both suitcases. He left the heaviest – the one containing the books – for Adam to lug upstairs.

The room was far more than he had hoped for. Large and light, it had a floor of polished deep-red tiles, a beamed ceiling and two windows giving on to a leafy garden out back. It was furnished with the bare essentials: a wrought-iron bed, a chest of drawers and a wardrobe. As requested, there was also a desk, though no chair, which brought a sharp rebuke from Signora Fanelli.

Iacopo skulked off in search of one, his parting glance holding Adam to blame for this public humiliation. He returned with the chair and disappeared again while Signora Fanelli was still demonstrating the idiosyncrasies of the bathroom plumbing to Adam.

Adam declared the room to be '*perfetto*'.

'*Perfetta*,' she corrected him. '*Una camera perfetta*.'

She relieved him of his passport, flashed him a smile and left. Only her perfume remained – a faint scent of roses hanging lightly in the air.

He hefted his suitcase on to the worm-eaten chest at the end of the bed and began to unpack. She must have had the boy young – seventeen, eighteen – though you'd have said even younger judging by her looks. For some reason he'd pictured an elderly woman, small in stature and of no mean girth. Instead, he was being housed by a stringier version of Gina Lollobrigida in *Trapeze*.

It was a pleasing thought.

Another image from the same film barged its way into his head unbidden – Burt Lancaster's over-muscled physique squeezed into a leotard – and the moment passed.

The road to Villa Docci proved to be a dusty white track following the crest of a high spur to the north of town. It rose and fell past ochre-washed farmhouses, hay meadows giving way to olive groves and vineyards tucked behind high hedgerows ablaze with honeysuckle, mallow and blood-red poppies. His mother would have been thrilled, stopping every so often to call his attention to some plant or flower. That was her way. But all Adam was aware of was the mocking chant of the cicadas pulsing in time to the pitiless heat.

He was about to turn back, convinced that he'd made a mistake, when he saw two weathered stone gateposts up ahead. Beyond them an avenue of ancient cypresses climbed sharply towards a large villa, the trunks of the trees powdered white with dust thrown up from the driveway. There was no sign beside the gateposts, but a quick glance at the hand-drawn map Signora Docci had sent him confirmed that he had at last arrived.

Nearing the top of the driveway he stopped, uncertain, sensing something. He turned, glancing back down the gradient, the plunging perspective of the flanking cypresses.

Something not right. But what? He couldn't say. And he was too hot to ponder it further.

The cypresses gave way to a gravel turning area in front of the villa. There were some farm buildings away to his left, down the slope, beyond a stand of holm oaks, but his attention was focused on the main structure.

How had Professor Leonard described the architecture of the villa? Pedestrian?

Admittedly, his own knowledge on the subject was drawn almost exclusively from a battered copy of Edith Wharton's book on Italian villas, but there seemed to be nothing whatsoever run-of-the-mill about the building in front of him. Though not as large or obviously grand as some, its symmetry and proportions lent it an air of discreet nobility, majesty even.

Set around three sides of a flagstone courtyard, it climbed three floors to a shallow, tiled roof with projecting eaves. Arcaded loggias occupied the middle and upper storeys of the front façade, while the wings consisted of blind arcades with pedimented and consoled windows. There was not much more to it than that, but every detail of it worked.

The building felt no need to proclaim its pedigree; rather, it exuded it like a well-cut suit. You were left in little doubt that the hand of some master lay behind its conception – long-dead, unrecognized, forgotten. For if one of the more illustrious architects of the period had been responsible for bringing it into being, that fact would have been preserved in the historical record. As it was, he had found almost no references to Villa Docci during his preliminary research.

He skirted the well-head in the middle of the courtyard and mounted the front steps. There was a stone escutcheon set in the wall above the entrance door, a rampant boar

28

the centrepiece of the Docci coat of arms. He tugged on the iron bell-pull.

She must have been observing him from inside, waiting for him to make his approach, for the door swung open almost immediately. She was short and stout, and she was wearing a white blouse tucked into a black skirt. Her dark eyes reached for his and held them, vice-like.

'Good morning,' he said in Italian.

'Good afternoon.'

'I'm Adam Strickland.'

'You're late.'

'Yes. I'm sorry.'

She stepped aside, allowing him to enter, appraising him with a purposeful eye as if he were a horse she was thinking of betting on (and leaving him with the distinct impression that she wouldn't be reaching for her purse any time soon).

'Signora Docci wishes to see you.'

At either end of the long entrance hall was a stone stairway leading to the upper floors. When she made for the one on the left, Adam fell in beside her.

'May I have a glass of water, please?'

'Water? Yes, of course.' She changed tack, heading for a corridor beside the staircase. 'Wait here,' she said.

He didn't mind. It allowed him to cast an eye around the interior. Any suspicions that the quiet elegance of the villa's exterior owed itself to little more than chance vanished immediately. You sensed the same poised hand at work in the proportions of the vast drawing room that occupied the central section of the ground floor, giving on to a balustraded terrace out back. The flanking rooms were connected by a run of doorways, perfectly aligned, which generated a telescopic sense of perspective and permitted an uninterrupted view from one end of the villa to the other.

Adam retreated at the sound of approaching footsteps, not wishing to be caught snooping by the maid, or the housekeeper, or whatever she was.

Signora Docci lay propped up on a bank of pillows in a four-poster bed of dark wood, reading. She inclined her head towards the door as they entered, peering over the top of her spectacles.

'Adam,' she said, smiling broadly.

'Hello.'

'Thank you, Maria.'

Maria acknowledged the dismissal with a nod, pulling the door closed behind her as she left.

Signora Docci gestured for Adam to approach the bed. 'Please, it's not contagious, just old age.' She laid her book aside and smiled again. 'Well, maybe it *is* contagious.'

Her hair hung loose, tumbling like a silver wave around her shoulders. It seemed too long, too thick, for a woman of her advanced years. A tracery of fine lines lay like a veil across her face, but the flesh was firm, shored up by the prominent bones beneath. Her eyes were dark and wide-spaced.

He extended his hand. 'Pleased to meet you.'

They shook, her grip firm and bony.

'Please.' She indicated a high-backed chair near the bed. 'I'm glad you're finally here. Maria has been fussing around for days, tidying and cleaning.'

It was hard to picture: stern, monosyllabic Maria preparing for his arrival.

'She is a good person. She will let you see that when she's ready to.'

He was slightly unnerved that she'd read the thought in his face.

'So, how was your trip?'

'Good. Long.'

'Did you stop in Paris?'

'No.'

'Milan?'

'Just Florence. And only for a night.'

'One night in Florence,' she mused. 'It sounds like the title of a song.'

'Not a very good one.'

Signora Docci gave a short, sharp laugh. 'No,' she conceded.

Adam took a letter from the inside pocket of his jacket and handed it to her. 'From Professor Leonard.'

She laid the letter beside her on the bed. He noted that her hand remained resting on it.

'And how is Crispin?' she asked.

'He's in France at the moment, looking at some cave paintings.'

'Cave paintings?'

'They're very old – lots of bison and deer.'

'A cave is no place for a man his age. It'll be the death of him.'

Adam smiled.

'I'm serious,' she said.

'I know, it's just . . . your English.'

'What?'

'It's very good. Very correct.'

'Nannies. Nannies and governesses. My father is to blame. He loved England.' She shifted in the bed, removing her spectacles and placing them on the bedside table. 'So tell me, how is the Pensione Amorini?'

'Perfect. Thanks for arranging it.'

'How much is she charging you?'

'Two thousand five hundred lire a day.'

'It's too much.'

'It's half what I paid in Florence.'

'Then you were had.'

'Oh.'

'You should pay no more than two thousand lire for half-board.'

'The room's large, clean.'

'Signora Fanelli knows the power of her looks, I'm afraid. She always has, even as a young girl. And now that she's a widow, well . . .'

'What?'

'Oh, nothing,' she shrugged. 'Men are as men are. Why should they change?'

Adam's instinct was to defend his sex against the charge, but the news about Signora Fanelli's marital status was really quite agreeable. He chose silence and a grave nod of the head.

'How long will you be with us?'

'Two weeks.'

'Is it enough time?'

'I don't know. I've never studied a garden before.'

'You'll find it's a little neglected, I'm afraid. Gaetano left last year. It was his responsibility. The other gardeners do what they can.' She pointed to some French windows, which were open, although the louvred shutters remained closed. 'There's a view behind those. You can't see the memorial garden from here, but I can point you in the right direction.'

Adam pushed open the shutters, squinting against the sunlight flooding past him into the room. He found himself in an arcaded loggia. As his eyes adjusted to the light, he made out the commanding view. Patchwork hills spilled away to the west, their folds cast by the lowering sun into varying grades of shade. There was a timeless, almost mythical quality to the panorama – like a Poussin landscape.

'It's special, isn't it?' said Signora Docci.

'If you like that kind of thing.'

This brought a laugh from her. Adam peered down on to the gardens at the rear of the villa, the formal arrangements of gravel walks and clipped hedges.

'There are some umbrella pines at the edge of the lower terrace, on the left. If you walk through those and follow the path down, you'll come to it.'

Just beyond the knot of pines the land dropped away sharply into a wooded valley.

'Yes, I see.'

He pulled the shutters closed behind him as he re-entered the room.

'Why put it down there? In the valley, I mean.'

'Water. There's a spring. Or there was. It's dry now, like everything. We need rain, we need lots of rain. The grapes and olives are suffering.' She reached for a slender file on the bedside table. 'Here. My father put it together. It's not much, but it's everything we know about the garden.'

Adam was to come and go at his leisure, she went on.

33

He was more than welcome to work out of the study if he wanted to, and of course the library was at his disposal. In fact, he was to have free run of the villa, everything except the top floor, which, for reasons she didn't explain, was off limits. Maria would prepare him something for lunch if he wanted it.

'We don't stand on ceremony around here. If you need something, you just have to ask.'

'Thank you,' he said. 'Thank you for everything.'

'*Non c'è di che*,' replied Signora Docci with a mock-formal tilt of the head. 'Come back and see me when you've walked round the garden.'

Adam was leaving the room when she added, 'Oh, and if you see a young woman down there, it is probably my granddaughter.' A smile flickered at the corners of her mouth. 'Don't worry, she's quite harmless.'

He passed through the drawing room and out on to the flagstone terrace at the back. From here a flight of stone steps, bowed with centuries of wear, led down to a formal parterre – an expanse of gravel laid out with low, clipped box hedges arranged in geometric patterns. Lemon trees in giant terracotta pots were dotted around. He had read enough to know that the climbing roses and wisteria trellised to the retaining wall were a later addition in the 'English style' which had swept the country the previous century, consigning so many ancient gardens to the rubbish heap of history. Parterres had been ripped up to make way for bowling-green lawns, which soon burned to a crisp under the fierce Italian sun. Borders had been dug to house herbaceous plants suited to far gentler climes, and all manner

34

of vines and creepers had been let loose, scaling walls and scrabbling up trees like unruly children. In many cases, the prevailing winds of fashion had wrought wholesale destruction, but it seemed that here at Villa Docci the original Renaissance terraces had survived almost entirely unscathed.

This was confirmed when he descended to the lowest level. A circular fountain held centre-stage, set about with tall screens of tight-clipped yew, dividing the terrace into 'rooms'. The formal gardens stopped here at a high retaining wall which plunged twenty feet to an olive-clad slope occupying the sunny lap of the hill. There were stone benches set at intervals along the balustrade, embracing the view. At the north end of the terrace was a small chapel pressed tight against a low sandstone cliff, its entrance flanked by two towering cypresses, like dark obelisks. At the other end lay the grove of umbrella pines which Signora Docci had drawn his attention to from the loggia.

He settled himself down in the resin-scented shade of the pines and lit a cigarette. He looked up at the villa standing proud and grave on its knoll, like some captain on his poop-deck. All of the upper windows were shuttered, suggesting that the top floor was not only out of bounds but also out of use. He smiled at the thought of a deranged relative, some mad Mrs Rochester, closeted away up there.

Viewed from this angle, there was an air of austerity about the building, a robust, fortress-like quality. And yet somehow this seemed in keeping with both its setting and function. It was not a pleasure palace; it was the centre-piece of a working estate. The farm buildings, just visible from where he was sitting, were arranged around a yard below the villa. There was no shame in the association, and the villa declared as much with the artless candour of the face it chose to present to the valley. Again, he was left with a palpable sense of the mind behind the design.

In almost no time he had fallen under Villa Docci's spell, and the idea that he might have to devote his time to the study of a small part of its garden, one component stuck way down in the valley, was already a building frustration.

The answer came to him suddenly and clearly. He would change the subject of his thesis. Who could protest? Professor Leonard? On what grounds? Their remit as students was broad to the point of being all-embracing. If Roland Gibbs had settled on a mouldering Romanesque church in Suffolk as a subject for his thesis, how did an Italian Renaissance villa-estate compare? He would have to play the Marxist historical card – that angle was increasingly popular within the faculty – not art and architecture for their own sakes, but as manifestations of the socioeconomic undercurrents of the time.

His heart already going out of the matter, he opened the file Signora Docci had given him and began to read. The language was rich, formal, turn-of-the-century.

Flora Bonfadio was only twenty-five years old when she died in 1548 – the year after she and her husband Federico Docci, some two decades her senior, took possession of the new villa they had built near San Casciano. Not much was known of Flora's history. Some had speculated that she was related to the poet and humanist Jacopo Bonfadio, but there was no hard evidence to this effect. As for the Doccis, they were a family of Florentine bankers who, like the Medicis, originated from the Mugello, a mountainous region just north of the city. Although they had never risen

36

to the Medicis' level of prominence – who had? – by the sixteenth century they were nonetheless established as successful financiers. They had to have been for Federico Docci to afford the luxury of carving out a country estate for himself and his young wife.

Villa Docci instantly became a port of call for artists and writers, and was renowned, apparently, for the extravagant parties thrown by its generous host. This was not an unusual development. To create a cultural watering hole in the hills was the goal of many wealthy Florentines, almost a necessary stage in their development; a chance to share some of their ill-gotten gains with the more needy while rubbing shoulders with the greatest talents of the age. High finance and high art coming together as they have always done. A simple trade in an age driven by patronage.

Adam recognized only two names on the list of those reputed to have attended Federico's gatherings at Villa Docci. The first was Bronzino, the well-known court painter. The second was Tullia d'Aragona, the not-so-much-well-known-as-notorious courtesan and poetess. Her inclusion lent an appealing whiff of scandal to the list, hinting at dark and dangerous goings-on at Villa Docci. Whether or not this was true, Federico's dream of a rural *salon* was abruptly shattered after a year with the death of his wife. There were no records as to the cause of Flora's untimely demise. Federico must have been devastated, though, because he never remarried, the villa and the estate passing to another branch of the Docci clan on his death.

Amongst all this historical fog, one thing was clear: in 1577 Federico had laid out, according to his own design, a small garden to Flora's memory.

Adam turned the page to be presented with a hand-drawn map of the garden. He instinctively closed the file. Better to approach the place blind and untutored the first time, as Professor Leonard had suggested.

The pathway meandered lazily down into the valley, a thread of packed earth, untended and overgrown. The trees on either side grew denser, darker, as he descended, deciduous giving way to evergreen: pine, yew, juniper and bay. He heard birds, but their song was muffled, diffuse, hard to locate. And then the path gave out. Or at least it appeared to. Closer inspection revealed a narrow fissure set at an angle in the tall yew hedge barring his way.

He paused for a moment then edged through the crack.

Beyond the hedge, the path was gravelled, with trees pressing in tightly, their interlocking branches forming a gloomy vault overhead. After a hundred yards or so, the trees fell away abruptly on both sides and he found himself in a clearing near the head of a broad cleft in the hillside. This was evidently the heart of the garden, the central axis along which it unfolded.

To his right, set near the top of a tiered and stone-trimmed amphitheatre, stood a pedestal bearing a marble statue of a naked woman. Her exaggerated *contrapposto* stance thrust her right hip out, twisting her torso to the left, while her head was turned back to the right, peering over her shoulder. Her right arm was folded across her front, modestly covering her breasts; her hair was wreathed with blossoms; and at her feet flowers spilled from an overturned vase, like water from an urn.

Unless he was mistaken, Federico Docci had cast his wife in the image of Flora, goddess of flowers. This was not so surprising, but the conceit still brought a smile to his lips.

If there was any doubt as to the identity of the statue, on the crest above, a triumphal arch stood out proud against a screen of dark ilex trees. On the heavy lintel borne up by fluted columns, and set between two decorative lozenges, was incised the word:

$$\boxed{\text{N}\;\boxed{\text{FIORE}}\;\text{N}}$$

The Italian for flower: 'Flora' in Latin. There was something telling, tender, about Federico's decision to employ the Italian form of his wife's Christian name – an indication, perhaps, of a pet name or some other private intimacy lost to history.

Two steep stone runnels bordered the amphitheatre, descending to a long trough sunk into the ground. Leaves and other debris had collected in the base of the trough, and a dead bird lay on this rotting mattress, pale bones showing through decaying plumage. A weather-fretted stone bench was set before the trough, facing the amphitheatre. It bore an inscription in Latin, eroded by the elements, but just possible to make out:

ANIMA FIT SEDENDO ET
QUIESCENDO PRUDENTIOR

The Soul in Repose Grows Wiser. Or something like that. An appropriate message for a spot intended for contemplation.

The presence of an overflow outlet just below the rim of the trough steered his gaze down the slope to a high mound bristling with laurel and fringed with cypresses. From here two paths branched off into the dark woods flanking the overgrown pasture that ran to the foot of the valley, and at the far end of which some kind of stone building lurked in the trees.

A flight of shallow steps led down to the mound. Adam skirted the artificial hillock, wondering just what it represented. It didn't represent anything, he discovered; it existed to house a deep, stygian grotto.

The irregular entrance, designed to look like the mouth of some mountain cave, was encrusted with cut rock and stalactites. The angle of the sun was such that he couldn't make out what lay inside.

He hesitated for a moment, shook off a mild foreboding, then stepped into the yawning darkness.

5

Did you see him before he left?
  Briefly. I told him you were resting.
  I wanted to see him. Wake me up next time.
  Of course, Signora.
  Did he say anything?
  About what?
  The garden, of course.
  No.
  Nothing?
  He was very silent.
  Silent?
  Distracted.
  He's handsome, don't you think? Tall and dark and
slightly dangerous.
  He's too pallid.
  It's not his fault, Maria, he's English.
  And he's too thin.
  A bit, I agree.
  He needs fattening up.

41

That will come with time. He hasn't grown into his body yet.

I think he's strange.

Really?

When he left, I saw him walking back and forth between the cypresses at the top of the driveway. Big long steps.

Interesting.

Worrying. It must be the heat.

No, it means he's worked it out.

Signora?

The cypresses taper towards the top of the driveway.

Taper?

The two rows narrow as you approach the villa – to increase the sense of perspective.

I didn't know.

That's because I don't tell anyone.

Why not?

To see if they notice. Only two people have ever noticed. Three now.

And the other two?

Both dead.

Let's hope for the Englishman's sake there's no connection.

You know, Maria, you really can be quite amusing when you want to be.

6

Adam was awakened by a dull but persistent pressure in his right buttock. His fingers searched out the offending object but couldn't make sense of it. He opened his eyes and peered at an unopened bottle of mineral water. Overhead, the blades of the ceiling fan struggled to generate a downdraught. He was flat on his back on the bed, fully clothed still, and the wall lights were ablaze, unbearably bright.

He swung his legs off the bed and made unsteadily for the switch beside the door. The beat in his temples informed him that he'd drunk too much the night before. And then he remembered why.

He searched the tangle of memories for irredeemable behaviour.

Nothing. No. He was in the clear.

He pushed open the shutters, allowing the soft dawn light to wash into the room.

Unscrewing the cap of the mineral water bottle, he downed half the tepid contents without drawing breath.

He hadn't registered it before, but there was a tinted print on the wall above the bed – a garish depiction of Christ in some rocky landscape, two fingers raised in benediction. Presumably the artist had gone for a beatific expression, but the Son of God was glancing down with what appeared to be the weary look of someone who has seen it all before – as if nothing that unfolded on the mattress below could ever surprise him. He might even have been a judge scoring a lacklustre performance: two out of five for effort.

Harry, thought Adam. Why Harry? Why now? And why hadn't he, Adam, said no?

The only consolation was that when Signora Fanelli had come to his room just before dinner with the news that 'Arry was on the telephone, he had assumed the worst, that their mother or father had suffered some terrible fate. As it turned out, the news was only marginally less calamitous. Harry was coming to visit.

Reason had quickly stemmed the trickle of loneliness that welcomed the idea.

'Why, Harry?' Adam had demanded.

'Because you're my baby brother.'

'You mean you couldn't make my farewell dinner in Purley, but Italy's not a problem?'

'I don't do farewell dinners in Purley, not when I'm in Sheffield.'

'What were you doing in Sheffield?'

'None of your business. Anyway, what's the fuss – I phoned, didn't I?'

'No, as it happens.'

'Well I meant to.'

Of course, Harry couldn't say when he'd be arriving or

leaving – 'For God's sake, Adam, what am I, a fucking train timetable?' – only that he had things to do in Italy and that he'd fit Adam in along the way.

Fortunately, this time he'd be on his own, unlike his last impromptu visit. Harry had shown up in Cambridge earlier in the year with a fellow sculptor from Corsham in tow, a garrulous Scotsman with child-bearing hips and a face like a bag of spanners. Finn Duggan had taken an instant and very vocal dislike to the university and all associated with it. Leaping to his feet in the Baron of Beef on the first evening, he had challenged all the 'snotty wee shites' present to drink him under the table. A mousey astrophysicist from Trinity Hall had duly obliged, plunging Finn Duggan into a deep and dangerous gloom for the remainder of the weekend. Violence had only narrowly been avoided following Harry's mischievous speculation that the loser's beers had been spiked with some chemical cooked up in one of the university labs.

No Finn Duggan this time, thankfully, but Harry required maintenance, supervision even. And Adam had enough on his mind already.

For a brief while it had all seemed so clear: switching the subject of his thesis from the memorial garden to Villa Docci itself. But that was before he'd stepped through the breach in the yew hedge.

Even now he couldn't say just why the place had affected him so much. All he could point to was a vague sensation of having been momentarily transported somewhere else, a parallel world, unquestionably beautiful but also disquieting.

No doubt the unassuming entrance was intended to

produce the effect of stumbling upon a lost Arcadia, but there was something illicit in the act of pushing your way through a hedge that smacked of trespass, each subsequent step in some way forbidden. This sense of intruding was reinforced by the personal nature of what lay beyond the hedge: the touching tribute of a grieving husband to his deceased wife. The other Renaissance gardens Adam had studied in preparation for his trip were far grander stages on which the most high-blown ideas of the age were played out – Man and Nature in uneasy coexistence; Man imposing himself on Nature, moulding Her to his own ends, yet constantly fighting Her hold over him, struggling to rise above his baser instincts to the role ordained for him by God.

Not that God or any other Christian imagery figured in the elaborate cycles set out by wealthy Romans and Florentines in the grounds of their country estates. The language of the garden was purely pagan, its world a mythical earthly paradise populated with marble gods and demigods and other outlandish creatures from Greek and Roman legend, where water gushed from Mount Parnassus, pouring along channels, tumbling over waterfalls, spraying from fountains and trickling down the rough-hewn walls of woodland grottoes.

The memorial garden at Villa Docci sat firmly within this tradition, and although it couldn't match its eminent counterparts at Villa di Castello, Villa Gamberaia and Villa Campi for sheer size and grandiosity, it stood out for its human dimension, its purity of purpose, the haunting message of love and loss enshrined in its buildings, inscriptions, and groupings of statues buried away in the woods.

The hour or so Adam had spent strolling the circuit had intrigued him, unsettled him, whereas the villa itself had simply awed him with its serene perfection. The choice was no longer clear to him. Which of the two should he spend his time on?

This was the dilemma he'd been struggling with over dinner at the pensione when a bottle of red wine had landed on his table with a thud.

It was attached by a lean brown arm to a man whom Adam had noticed drinking alone at the bar. He was dark, rangy, handsome in a dishevelled kind of way. He pushed his lank hair out of his eyes.

'Can I?' he asked, in Italian, not waiting for a reply but dumping himself in the chair opposite. He glanced at the open file beside Adam's plate. 'It's not good,' he said.

'What?'

'Reading and eating at the same time. The stomach needs blood for digestion. When you read, the brain steals the blood.'

'Really?'

'It's what my father used to say, but he was an idiot, so who knows? I'm Fausto.'

Adam shook the strong hand offered him. 'Adam.'

'Can I?' Fausto helped himself from Adam's pack, tearing off the filter before lighting the cigarette. 'You're English?'

'Yes.'

'I like the English,' declared Fausto, sitting back in his chair and plucking a stray shred of tobacco from his tongue. 'London Liverpool Manchester A-stings.'

'A-stings?'

'The battle of A-stings.'

'Oh, Hastings.'

'A-stings. Exactly,' said Fausto, not altogether happy about being corrected, although it didn't stop him filling Adam's glass from the bottle of red wine he'd arrived with.

Adam took a sip.

'What do you think?'

Adam knew the word for 'drinkable' in Italian. So presumably 'undrinkable' was *non potabile*.

'Excellent,' he replied.

Fausto smiled. 'That's why I like you English. You're so fucking polite.'

Fausto, it turned out, had done his homework. He knew from Signora Fanelli the purpose of Adam's visit, and even its intended duration. Not that that was saying much – everyone did – tourists being something of a rarity in San Casciano. Apparently, the last foreign visitors of any note had been a bunch of New Zealanders – the ones who'd liberated the town from the Germans back in 1944. Fausto described in elaborate detail, much of it lost on Adam, the fierce siege that had laid waste to his birthplace – a sad inevitability, given San Casciano's pivotal role in the main German line of defence south of Florence.

Despite this, Fausto seemed to harbour a grudging respect for the German military machine which had so success- fully slowed the Allied advance northwards, mining bridges and roads, its troops fighting a relentless rearguard action against overwhelming odds, taking severe casualties but never losing their discipline or their fighting spirit, forever melting away, withholding their fire until you were right on them, and always ceasing fire at the first sign of the Red Cross.

Fausto was speaking from first-hand experience. He'd been a member of a partisan group who'd assisted the Allies in their push on Florence, fighting alongside the British when they entered the city; men from 'London Liverpool Manchester'.

And Hastings?

No, that was something else, Fausto explained – an interest in historic battles.

He was lying. He knew more about the battle of Hastings than was healthy for any man to know. They were well into the third bottle of wine before Harold even got the arrow in the eye.

Fausto was enacting this event with a slender breadstick when Signora Fanelli appeared at the table.

'Fausto, leave him alone, look at him, he's half-dead.'

Fausto peered at Adam.

'Leave the poor boy alone. Go home. It's late,' Signora Fanelli insisted, before returning to the bar.

'A beautiful woman,' mused Fausto, helping himself to yet another of Adam's cigarettes.

'What happened to her husband?'

'The war. It was a bad thing.'

'What?'

Fausto's dark eyes narrowed, as if judging Adam worthy of a response.

'We were fighting for our country. Our country. Against the Germans, yes, but also against each other – Communists, Socialists, Monarchists, Fascists. For the future. There was . . . confusion. Things happened. War permits it. It demands it.' He drew on the cigarette and exhaled. 'Giovanni Gentile. Do you know the name?'

'No.'

'He was a philosopher. A thinker. Of the right. A Fascist. He had a house in Florence. They went to his door carrying books like students, carrying books to fool him. And then they shot him.' He took a sip of wine. 'When they start killing the men of ideas you can be sure the Devil is laughing.'

'Did you know them?' asked Adam.

'Who?'

'The ones who did it?'

'You ask a lot of questions.'

'It's the first chance I've had.'

Fausto cracked a smile and he laughed. 'I talk too much, it's true.'

'What?' called Signora Fanelli from across the room. 'I don't see you for months and now I can't get rid of you?'

'I'm going, I'm going,' said Fausto, holding up his hands in capitulation. Turning back to Adam, he leaned close. 'Things can make sense at the time, but as you get older those consolations no longer help you sleep. It's the only thing I've learned. We all think we know the answer, and we're all wrong. Shit, I'm not sure we even know what the question is.'

Adam drew his own consolation from the words: that Fausto was even more drunk than he was.

Fausto drained his glass and rose to his feet. 'It's been a pleasure. You be careful up there at Villa Docci.'

'Why do you say that?'

'It's a bad place.'

'A bad place?'

'It always has been. People have a tendency to die there.'

Adam couldn't help smiling at the melodramatic statement.

'You think I'm joking?'

'No . . . I'm sorry. You mean Signora Docci's son?'

'You heard about Emilio?'

'Not much. Only that he was killed by the Germans during the war.'

Fausto crushed his cigarette in the ashtray. 'So the story goes.'

There was no time for Adam to pick him up on this last comment.

'Out!' trumpeted Signora Fanelli, advancing towards them wielding a broom.

Fausto turned to meet his attacker. 'Letizia, you are a beautiful woman. If I were a richer man I would try to make you my wife.'

'Ahhhh,' she cooed sweetly. 'Well, you're about to become even poorer. Three bottles of wine.'

'I'll pay,' said Adam.

'He'll pay,' said Fausto.

'No he won't,' said Signora Fanelli.

Fausto delved into his pocket, pulled out some crumpled notes and dropped them on the table. 'Goodnight everybody,' he said with the slightest of bows, 'Fausto is no more.'

He left via the terrace, the life somehow draining out of the room along with him.

Signora Fanelli set about stacking chairs on the tables. 'Fausto, Fausto,' she sighed wearily. 'You mustn't take him too seriously, he's a bit depressed at the moment.'

'Why?'

'The Communists did not do well at the election in May . . . only twenty-two per cent, the poor things,' she added with a distinct note of false sympathy.

Twenty-two per cent sounded like a not inconsiderable slice of the electorate.

'You're not a Communist?' Adam asked.

'Communism is for young people with empty stomachs. Look at me.'

He had been, quite closely, and he would happily have paid her the compliment she was fishing for if the Italian words hadn't eluded him.

'Fausto isn't so young,' he said.

'Fausto was born an idealist. It's not his fault.'

He had wanted to sit there, chatting idly, observing the play of her slender hips beneath her dress as she worked the broom around the tables. But she had dispatched him upstairs with a bottle of mineral water and firm instructions to drink the lot before bed.

This he had failed to do.

Instead, he had flopped on to the mattress and set about constructing a gratifying little scenario in his head. His last memory before drifting into drunken slumber had been of Harry barging into the room just as Signora Fanelli was peeling off an emerald green chenille bathrobe.

canines, jutting cheekbones, and a bony crest rising across the skull from ear to ear, met at its apex by two ridges running from the sides of the eye sockets.

Adam reached out and ran his hand over the skull, his fingers tracing the cranial ridges.

That's when he heard the footsteps.

He turned to see Maria enter the study from the terrace. The reproachful cast of her eye would have driven him from the library steps if he hadn't already been descending.

'Very interesting,' he said pathetically, nodding behind him.

'Would you like some coffee?'

'Yes, thank you.'

Maria stopped and turned at the door to the library. '*Orangotanghi*,' she said, her eyes flicking to the skulls.

'Oh,' he replied in English. 'Right.'

The moment she was gone, he reached for the dictionary.

He hadn't misunderstood her.

Despite her offer of coffee, Maria barely concealed her relief at not having to feed him at lunchtime. Towards three o'clock, she appeared in the study with a summons from the lady of the house.

He found Signora Docci sitting in her bed, patting at her face and neck with a wet flannel. A typewriter sat beside her on the bed, an unfinished letter in its jaws.

'I've asked Foscolo to prepare a bicycle for you,' she said. 'To spare you the walk every day.'

'Thank you, that's very kind.'

'I don't want your death on my conscience, what with this heat.'

7

The walk to Villa Docci failed to clear his head; all it did was shunt the pain from the front of his skull to the back of it, where, he knew from hard experience, it would remain lodged for the rest of the day. The heat was building fast under a cloudless sky, and his shirt was clinging to him by the time he arrived.

He had anticipated having to force a decision on himself. In the end, it came naturally, when he was not even halfway through his brisk tramp around the memorial garden.

There was something not quite right about the place, and this was where its appeal lay. There were no great questions clamouring for answers; they were more like restless whispers at the back of his mind.

According to the records, Flora had died in 1548, the year after Villa Docci's completion, so why had her husband waited almost thirty years – till the very end of his own life – to lay out a garden to her memory? Then there were the small anomalies within the garden itself, not exactly discordant elements, but somehow out of keeping with the mood and tone of the whole. Why, for example, the triumphal arch on which Flora's name was carved in its Italian form? It was such a pompous piece of architecture, crowning the crest above her like some advertising hoarding. At no other point in the itinerary did the garden look to declare its purpose. Rather, it encrypted it in symbols and metaphors and allegory.

He was honest enough to know that a more pragmatic consideration was also pushing him towards a study of the garden over the villa: the file prepared by Signora Docci's father. It offered a model from which to work, a template for his own thesis, a document easily massaged, expanded, made his own with the minimum of effort. It was short, and a tad dry, but thorough in its scholarship. There were numerous references in both the text and the footnotes, most of them relating to books or original documents to be found in the library. It would take a few days, but all of these would have to be checked out first, their suitability as potential padding material carefully assessed.

Retreating to the cool of the villa, he found Maria prowling around, marshalling a couple of browbeaten cleaning ladies and handing out chores to Foscolo, the saturnine handyman.

Adam set up shop in the study. Light and lofty, it occupied the northwest corner of the building just beyond the library, with French windows giving on to the back terrace. Unlike the other rooms of the villa, which were plainly and sparsely furnished, the study was crowded with furniture, paintings, objects and books – as if all the incidental clutter conspicuously absent from the rest of the villa had somehow gathered here.

On the wall beside the fireplace was the smal[l] panel of Federico Docci which Signora D[occi] mentioned to him the previous day. It showed some man of middle years whose sharp featu[res] only just beginning to blunt with age. He wa[s repre]sented in half length, seated in a high-backed c[hair,] hands resting lightly on a book; through a win[dow in] the wall behind him, hills could be seen rolling [to a] distant ocean. Painted in three-quarter face, the[re was] something fiercely imperious in the tilt of his he[ad,] the set glare of his dark, slanting eyes. And yet the [suspi]cion of a smile played about his wide and generous [lips] – a contradiction which seemed almost self-mo[cking,] attractively so.

A vast glazed mahogany cabinet filled the wall b[ehind] the desk. Its lower shelves were given over to book[s, the] majority of them relating to the Etruscans. A large se[ction] was devoted to anthropological texts. These were [in a] variety of languages – Italian, French, English and [German] – and were decades old. The upper shelves of the ca[binet] were home to all manner of strange objects, mostly [of an] archaeological nature: clay figurines, bronze implem[ents,] bits of pottery, fragments of stone sculpture, and the [like.] On the very top shelf were two skulls, their hollow [eye] sockets deep pools of shadow behind the glass.

Adam opened the cabinet door and, with the aid of [some] steps from the library, found himself face to face wit[h the] macabre display. They weren't human skulls, but [they] weren't far off – primates of some kind. Although si[milar] in size, there were distinct differences. The skull on th[e left] was narrower and less angular. Its partner had l[ong]

7

The walk to Villa Docci failed to clear his head; all it did was shunt the pain from the front of his skull to the back of it, where, he knew from hard experience, it would remain lodged for the rest of the day. The heat was building fast under a cloudless sky, and his shirt was clinging to him by the time he arrived.

He had anticipated having to force a decision on himself. In the end, it came naturally, when he was not even halfway through his brisk tramp around the memorial garden.

There was something not quite right about the place, and this was where its appeal lay. There were no great questions clamouring for answers; they were more like restless whispers at the back of his mind.

According to the records, Flora had died in 1548, the year after Villa Docci's completion, so why had her husband waited almost thirty years – till the very end of his own life – to lay out a garden to her memory? Then there were the small anomalies within the garden itself, not exactly discordant elements, but somehow out of keeping with the mood and tone of the whole. Why, for example, the triumphal arch on which Flora's name was carved in its Italian form? It was such a pompous piece of architecture, crowning the crest above her like some advertising hoarding. At no other point in the itinerary did the garden look to declare its purpose. Rather, it encrypted it in symbols and metaphors and allegory.

He was honest enough to know that a more pragmatic consideration was also pushing him towards a study of the garden over the villa: the file prepared by Signora Docci's father. It offered a model from which to work, a template for his own thesis, a document easily massaged, expanded, made his own with the minimum of effort. It was short, and a tad dry, but thorough in its scholarship. There were numerous references in both the text and the footnotes, most of them relating to books or original documents to be found in the library. It would take a few days, but all of these would have to be checked out first, their suitability as potential padding material carefully assessed.

Retreating to the cool of the villa, he found Maria prowling around, marshalling a couple of browbeaten cleaning ladies and handing out chores to Foscolo, the saturnine handyman.

Adam set up shop in the study. Light and lofty, it occupied the northwest corner of the building just beyond the library, with French windows giving on to the back terrace. Unlike the other rooms of the villa, which were plainly and sparsely furnished, the study was crowded with furniture, paintings, objects and books – as if all the incidental clutter conspicuously absent from the rest of the villa had somehow gathered here.

54

On the wall beside the fireplace was the small portrait panel of Federico Docci which Signora Docci had mentioned to him the previous day. It showed a handsome man of middle years whose sharp features were only just beginning to blunt with age. He was represented in half length, seated in a high-backed chair, his hands resting lightly on a book; through a window in the wall behind him, hills could be seen rolling off to a distant ocean. Painted in three-quarter face, there was something fiercely imperious in the tilt of his head and the set glare of his dark, slanting eyes. And yet the suspicion of a smile played about his wide and generous mouth – a contradiction which seemed almost self-mocking, attractively so.

A vast glazed mahogany cabinet filled the wall behind the desk. Its lower shelves were given over to books, the majority of them relating to the Etruscans. A large section was devoted to anthropological texts. These were in a variety of languages – Italian, French, English and Dutch – and were decades old. The upper shelves of the cabinet were home to all manner of strange objects, mostly of an archaeological nature: clay figurines, bronze implements, bits of pottery, fragments of stone sculpture, and the like. On the very top shelf were two skulls, their hollow eye sockets deep pools of shadow behind the glass.

Adam opened the cabinet door and, with the aid of some steps from the library, found himself face to face with the macabre display. They weren't human skulls, but they weren't far off – primates of some kind. Although similar in size, there were distinct differences. The skull on the left was narrower and less angular. Its partner had longer canines, jutting cheekbones, and a bony crest rising across the skull from ear to ear, met at its apex by two ridges running from the sides of the eye sockets.

Adam reached out and ran his hand over the skull, his fingers tracing the cranial ridges.

That's when he heard the footsteps.

He turned to see Maria enter the study from the terrace. The reproachful cast of her eye would have driven him from the library steps if he hadn't already been descending.

'Very interesting,' he said pathetically, nodding behind him.

'Would you like some coffee?'

'Yes, thank you.'

Maria stopped and turned at the door to the library. '*Orangotanghi*,' she said, her eyes flicking to the skulls.

'Oh,' he replied in English. 'Right.'

The moment she was gone, he reached for the dictionary.

He hadn't misunderstood her.

Despite her offer of coffee, Maria barely concealed her relief at not having to feed him at lunchtime. Towards three o'clock, she appeared in the study with a summons from the lady of the house.

He found Signora Docci sitting in her bed, patting at her face and neck with a wet flannel. A typewriter sat beside her on the bed, an unfinished letter in its jaws.

'I've asked Foscolo to prepare a bicycle for you,' she said. 'To spare you the walk every day.'

'Thank you, that's very kind.'

'I don't want your death on my conscience, what with this heat.'

She asked him how his work was going, and he came clean about his dilemma, now resolved.

'You like the house?'

'I do. A lot.'

She looked on approvingly as he spelled out why exactly. He asked her who the architect had been.

'No one really knows. There is a reference somewhere to a young man, a Fulvio Montalto. My father looked into it, but he could find no records. It is as if he just disappeared. If it was him, he never built another villa. A sadness, no? A great talent.'

'Yes.'

'I'm glad you think so. The house does not speak to everybody. Crispin never felt much for it.'

Adam hesitated, still not accustomed to hearing Professor Leonard referred to as Crispin.

'No,' he said, 'he hardly mentioned it.'

'What *did* he mention?'

'Well, the memorial garden, of course.'

He could see from her expression that this wasn't what she'd intended by her question.

'He said you were old friends.'

'Yes, old friends.'

'He also said your husband died some years back. And your eldest son was killed during the war.'

'Emilio, yes. Did he say how exactly?'

'Only that the Germans who took over the villa were responsible.'

'They shot him. In cold blood. Up there. Above us.' Her voice tailed off.

He wanted to ask her why and how and if that was the

reason the top floor was off limits. The pain in her drawn eyes prevented him from doing so.

'You don't have to say.'

'No, you might as well hear it from me.'

She spoke in a flat, detached monotone which clashed with the sheer bloody drama of her story. She told him how the Germans had occupied the villa, installing their command post on the top floor because of the views it afforded them over the surrounding countryside. She and her husband Benedetto were obliged to move in with Emilio and his young wife Isabella, who lived in the big house on the slope beyond the farm buildings.

Relations with the new tenants were strained at times, but generally civil. The Germans were respectful right from the first, giving them fair warning to vacate the villa, suggesting that all works of art be stored out of harm's way, and even assisting in this exercise. At no point were the stores stripped, the cattle slaughtered, the wine cellar pillaged. The estate was allowed to function as normal, just so long as it provided the occupiers with what little they required for themselves.

On the day in question – an unbearably hot July day – the inexorable Allied advance rolling up from the south finally reached San Casciano, and the Germans began moving out of the villa. All day, lorries came and went to the sounds of the fierce battle raging just up the road. Her younger son Maurizio arrived from Florence to be with his family for yet another awkward handover to yet another occupying force. At nightfall, though, San Casciano was still firmly under German control. That's why the family was surprised when, just as they were finishing dinner, they heard the sound of gunfire coming from up at the villa.

It was Emilio who insisted on going to investigate, more out of curiosity than anything, because the gunfire was accompanied by the unmistakable sounds of music and laughter. Maurizio agreed to go with him, along with a third man, Gaetano the gardener, who had also heard the ruckus.

Approaching the villa from the rear, they saw furniture being tossed from the top-floor windows, splintering on the terrace below. Incensed, Emilio stormed inside and upstairs, Maurizio and Gaetano hot on his heels. Most of the Germans were gone. Only two remained, left behind to burn documents and destroy equipment so that it wouldn't fall into Allied hands. Fuelled by drink, they had overstepped their orders, using the frescoes for target practice and hurling furniture out of the windows – pathetic acts of destruction that enraged Emilio.

A fierce argument ensued. If Emilio hadn't pulled out his pistol and fired a warning shot, it might have ended there, with heated words. But it didn't. The Germans opened fire, killing Emilio before fleeing.

'That's terrible.'

'Yes, it was. Just a few more hours and we would have come through the war untouched.'

There were questions Adam wanted to ask, but Signora Docci steered the conversation back to Professor Leonard, saying that he had shown himself to be a very good friend in the aftermath of the tragedy.

'How did you meet him?'

'Through my father. They worked together on an archaeological excavation. Well, not together exactly. It was an

Etruscan site near Siena. My father was in charge; Crispin was one of the young people who did all the work – a student, like you, in Italy for the summer. It was the year your Queen Victoria died. 1901. We were very aware of it here. She often came to Florence. Papa even had the honour of meeting her once.' She paused. 'Anyway, he brought Crispin home one day, out of pity, I think, as you would a stray dog. He was so poor and so thin and so very intelligent. He stayed with us for a month that first summer.'

She smiled, remembering.

'My sisters were very excited about him being here. Not me, though. I was very distant with him, very . . . haughty. And he completely ignored me. As you can imagine, this was very annoying. I thought he was just like my father, lost in his books and his artefacts, blind to the living world. Later I discovered he knew exactly what he was doing.'

'What *was* he doing?'

'Playing. The dance, he called it.'

'The dance?'

'Courting, of course.'

'Really? I always thought –' He broke off.

'What?'

He hesitated. 'I don't know, that he was, you know . . .'

'Yes . . .?'

'Well, a homosexual.'

An incredulous expulsion of air gave way to helpless laughter. The application of the flannel to her mouth muffled the sound.

When she eventually collected herself, Adam said, 'I'll take that as a "no".'

'No,' she said emphatically. 'No.'

'He was never married, though, was he?'

'There were lots of opportunities. He was very handsome.'

Adam couldn't picture it, but that didn't mean anything.

'He has high praise for you,' said Signora Docci.

'Me?'

'You sound surprised.'

'I am.'

'You're here, aren't you? Doesn't that tell you something?'

'Should it?'

'It's many years since I first suggested the garden to Crispin – as a subject for one of his students, I mean. He said he would wait for the right person.'

This didn't fit with what the professor had told him: that the offer of the garden had only recently come from her. He wondered which of them was lying. And why?

'Apparently, you have a good mind, an enquiring mind.' She must have seen him squirm. 'You're not comfortable with flattery?'

'No.'

'He also said you were extremely lazy.'

'That's more like it.'

This brought a laugh from Signora Docci.

He was able to put in a couple more productive hours in the library, despite the distraction.

Why had Professor Leonard not even hinted at the true nature of his relationship with Signora Docci? Unless he had completely misunderstood her, everything pointed to

61

some kind of love affair between the couple. Maybe love affair was overstating it. In 1901 that probably meant little more than an unchaperoned stroll through the gardens, or a charged look across a crowded room, although somehow he doubted it. Signora Docci's few words on the subject had shown the strain of many more left unspoken. And she had almost choked herself laughing when he'd cast aspersions on Professor Leonard's sexuality.

He found himself speculating on what had happened to keep them apart. It was probably doomed from the start – a penniless student and a young heiress. Much would have been expected of any potential spouse of Signora Docci. He would have been well vetted, the future of the villa and the estate a prime consideration. And a young foreigner with an interest in Etruscan archaeology would hardly have offered much comfort in that department.

These were, of course, wild imaginings, but he let his mind roam the possibilities until it was time to leave.

Foscolo the rock-ribbed handyman insisted on being present when Adam took possession of the bicycle. He had a big square head planted on a small square body, and his iron-grey hair was clipped to a brush. There wasn't much to say on the subject – it was an old black bicycle with a wicker basket – so Adam shook Foscolo's knuckled hand and thanked him. This wasn't good enough for Foscolo, who wanted confirmation that all was in working order. Adam dutifully cycled around the courtyard a few times for his audience of one and declared the brakes to be 'eccellente'. Foscolo grunted sceptically and raised the saddle an inch or two.

Pedalling back to San Casciano, Adam deviated from

the main track, exploring. The dusty trail petered out in an olive grove. It wasn't a totally wasted detour. He found himself presented with an impressive view of Villa Docci. From afar, the shuttered, silent rooms of the top floor seemed even more striking, more ominous.

His thoughts turned to Signora Docci's account of her eldest son's death at the hands of the Germans. They also turned to Fausto's curious, half-mumbled comment on the same subject just the evening before: '*Così dicono.*'

So the story goes.

8

❧❧❧

Either he was so distracted that he didn't hear her foot-
falls, or she deliberately set out to creep up on him. Probably
a bit of both.

He was standing at the head of the valley, on the brow
above the amphitheatre, staring up at the triumphal arch.
A warm light from the lowering sun was bleeding through
the trees, flushing the garden amber. Even the dense wood
of dark ilex beyond the arch seemed somehow less forbidding.

It was here, just inside the tree-line, that the spring was
located – a low artificial grotto housing a trough of rusticated stone. Under normal circumstances, water would
have filled the trough before overflowing into a channel
that ran beneath the arch to the top of the amphitheatre,
where it divided.

He was standing astride this channel, staring up at the
arch, when he heard her voice.

'Hello.'

She was off to his left, beneath the boughs of a tree. Her

long black hair was tied back off her face in a ponytail and she was wearing a sleeveless cotton dress cinched at the waist with a belt.

'You haven't moved since I first saw you,' she said in accented English, stepping towards him.

He thought at first it was the dappled shade playing tricks with the light, but as she drew closer he could see that her smooth, high forehead was indeed marked with scars. One was short and sat just beneath the hairline in the centre. From here, another cleaved a diagonal path all the way to her left eyebrow.

'I thought maybe the garden had a new statue,' she said.

Adam returned her smile. 'I'm sorry, I was thinking.'

He held her dark, almond eyes, conscious of not allowing his gaze to stray to her forehead. Not that she would have cared, he suspected. If she'd wanted to conceal the disfigurement she could quite easily have worn her hair differently, rather than drawing it straight back off her face.

'You must be Adam.'

'Yes.'

'I'm Antonella.'

'The granddaughter, right?'

'She told you about me?'

'Only that you were harmless.'

'Ah,' she replied, a crooked gleam in her eye, 'that's because she thinks she knows me.'

She craned her long neck, looking up at the inscription on the lintel of the arch.

N FIORE N

'What were you thinking?' she asked.

'It's not symmetrical.'

'No?'

'The decorative panels at the side – look – the diagonals run the same way.'

It was hard to make out – the stone was weathered and stained with lichen – but there was no mistaking the anomaly.

'I never noticed before,' she said quietly. 'What does it mean?'

'I don't know. Probably nothing.' He glanced over at her. 'It's a bit overblown, don't you think?'

'Overblown?'

'The arch. For the setting, I mean.'

'I don't know the word.'

'Overblown. It means . . . pretentious.'

'*Pretenzioso*? Maybe. A bit,' she said. 'You don't like it?'

'No, I do. It's just –'

He broke off, aware that he was in danger of sounding a bit, well, overblown himself.

'No, tell me,' she insisted. 'I think I know what you mean.'

The triumphal arch was a classical architectural form that had been revived during the Renaissance, he explained, but so far he'd found no precedent for this one in any of the other gardens he'd researched. Moreover, its inclusion seemed at odds with the discreet symbolism and subtle statements of the rest of the cycle.

Maybe Antonella was being polite, but she asked if he had any other insights he was willing to share with her.

He should have confessed it was early days still, but the prospect of a leisurely stroll in her company overrode these thoughts.

The amphitheatre that fell away down the slope behind them was not exclusive to Villa Docci, he explained, although it was narrower and more precipitous than the one in the Sacro Bosco, the Sacred Wood, at Bomarzo near Rome. Interestingly, Pier Francesco Orsini had also dedicated that garden to his deceased wife, Giulia Farnese, although the parallels stopped there. The memorial garden at Villa Docci was an exercise in restraint compared to the riotous imagination on display in the Sacro Bosco, with its mausolea, nymphaea, loggias and temples, and its stupefying array of bizarre creatures carved from solid rock: sirens, sphinxes, dragons, lions, a giant turtle, even an African war elephant holding a dead soldier in its trunk.

The more temperate approach at Villa Docci was exemplified by the statue of Flora on the plinth near the top of the amphitheatre. The corkscrew pose, with the left leg bent and resting on a perch, was a traditional stance, typical of the mid to late sixteenth century – a form that had found its highest expression in the sculptures of Giambologna and Ammannati. In fact, as the file pointed out, the statue of Flora was closely modelled on Giambologna's marble Venus in the Boboli Gardens in Florence, although like many of the imitations spawned by that masterpiece, it lacked the original's grace and vitality.

'I don't know about the others,' said Antonella as they circled beneath Flora, 'but for me she is alive.'

Her look challenged him to contest the assertion. When he didn't, she added, 'Touch her leg.'

He wished she hadn't said it. He also wished she hadn't reached out and run her hand up the back of the marble calf from the heel to the crook of the knee, because it left him no choice but to follow suit.

He tried to experience something – he *wanted* to experience something – and he did.

'What do you feel?' asked Antonella.

'I feel,' he replied, 'like a sweaty Englishman molesting a naked statue in the presence of a complete stranger.'

Antonella gave a sudden loud laugh, her hand shooting to her mouth.

'I'm sorry,' she said. 'Maybe you will see her differently with time.'

'Maybe.'

'Go on, please.'

'Really?'

'I come here every day if I can.'

It wasn't surprising, he continued, that the statue of Flora had been modelled on Venus, given the close link between the two goddesses. Both were associated with fertility and the season of spring. Indeed, it was quite possible that the goddess of love and the goddess of flowers appeared alongside each other in two of the most celebrated paintings to come out of the Renaissance: Sandro Botticelli's *Primavera* and his *Birth of Venus*.

'Really?'

'It's a new theory, very new.'

'Ah,' said Antonella sceptically.

'You're right, it's probably nothing,' he shrugged, knowing full well that it wasn't, not for her, not if she visited the garden as often as she claimed to.

68

'Tell me anyway.'

There was no need to explain Flora's story; it was in the file, which she had surely read. Her great-grandfather had even included the Latin lines from Ovid's *Fasti* detailing how the nymph Chloris was pursued by Zephyrus, the west wind, who then violated her, atoning for this act by making her his wife and transforming her into Flora, mistress of all the flowers.

No one disputed that Zephyrus and Chloris figured in Botticelli's *Primavera*, but until now scholars had always read the figure standing to the left of them as the hora – the spirit – of springtime, scattering flowers. Hence the name of the painting.

'But what if she's really Flora?' he asked.

'After her transformation?'

'Exactly.'

'I don't know. What if it is her?'

The painting could then be read as an allegory for the nature of love. By pairing Flora – a product of lust, of Zephyrus' passion – with the chaste figure of Venus, then maybe Botticelli was saying that true love is the union of both: passion tempered with chastity.

It was possible to read the same buried message in the *Birth of Venus*. Zephyrus and Chloris were again present, suggesting that the female figure standing on the shore, holding out the cloak for Venus, might well be Flora.

'And Venus again represents Chastity?'

'Exactly. Venus pudica.'

She smiled when he adopted the well-known pose of Venus in her shell, modestly covering her nakedness.

'It's a good theory,' she said.

'You think?'

'Yes. Because if it's right then Flora is a symbol for the erotic, the sexual.'

'Yes, I suppose she is.'

Antonella turned her gaze on Flora. 'Do you see it now?'

He looked up at the statue.

'See the way she stands – her hips are turned away, but they are also . . . open, inviting. Her arm covers her breasts, but only just, like she doesn't care too much. And her face, the eyes, the mouth. She is not *un'innocente*.'

He could see what Antonella was driving at. Maybe he was wrong to have attributed the slight slackness of the pose to the inferior hand of a secondary sculptor. Maybe that sculptor hadn't been striving for delicacy and poise, but for something looser, more sensual. No, that was wrong. He had somehow managed to achieve both – a demure quality coupled with an erotic charge.

'So I'm not wrong?'

'Huh?' he said distractedly.

'I'm not alone. You see it too.'

'It's possible.'

'Possible? It is there or it isn't,' came the indignant reply.

'You're not wrong.'

'Everyone else thinks I am. My grandmother thinks I imagine it, and this says very much about me.'

'What does she think it says about you?'

Even as the words left his mouth he realized it was an impertinent question, far too personal.

'It doesn't matter now,' she replied, 'because we are right and she is wrong.'

He found himself smiling at the ease with which she'd

deflected his enquiry, sparing him further embarrassment. His mind, though, was leaping ahead, questions already coalescing. Was it done knowingly? And if so, why? Why would a grieving husband allow his wife to be personified as some prudish yet pouting goddess, some virgin-whore?

The questions stayed with him as they moved on down the slope to the grotto buried in its mound of shaggy laurel. They entered silently, allowing their eyes to adjust to the gloom.

The marble figures stood out pale and ghostly against the dark, encrusted rock of the back wall. In the centre, facing left, was Daphne at the moment of her transformation into a laurel tree, her toes turning to roots, bark already girding her thighs, branches and leaves beginning to sprout from the splayed fingers of her left hand, which was raised heavenwards in desperation, supplication. To her right was Apollo, the sun god, from whom she was fleeing – youthful, muscular, identifiable by the lyre in his hand and the bow slung across his broad back. Below them, an elderly bearded gentleman reclined along the rim of a great basin of purple and white variegated marble. This was Peneus, the river god, father to Daphne.

The story was straight from Ovid's *Metamorphoses*: the nymph Daphne, fleeing the unwelcome advances of a love-struck Apollo, begged her father to turn her into a laurel tree, which he duly did. It was an appropriate myth for a garden setting – Art and Nature combining in the figure of Daphne. As the file pointed out, there was a relief panel depicting the same scene in the Grotto of Diana at the Villa d'Este in Tivoli. But here in the memorial garden the myth had an added resonance, mirroring the story of Flora – a nymph who also underwent a metamorphosis following her pursuit by an amorous god.

This last observation was Antonella's. It wasn't in the file, nor had it occurred to Adam, which was mildly annoying, although this wouldn't prevent him, he suspected, from claiming it as his own for the purposes of his thesis.

Antonella explained how the water poured from the urn held by Peneus, filling the marble basin. A lowered lip at the front then allowed it to overflow into a shallow, circular pool set in the stone floor. This was carved with rippling water, and at its centre was a female face in relief, staring heavenwards, the gaping mouth acting as a sink hole. The hair of this disembodied visage was bedecked with flowers, identifying it as that of Flora: the goddess of flowers drawing sustenance for her creations from the life-giving spring water.

It was an exquisite arrangement, faultless both in its beauty and in its pertinence to the overarching programme of the garden. The only false note was the broken-off horn of the unicorn crouched at Apollo's feet, its head bowed towards the marble basin. This was a common motif in gardens of the period. A unicorn dipping its horn into the water signified the purity of the source feeding the garden; it announced that you could happily scoop up a handful and down a draught without fear for your life. At some time since that era, though, the unicorn had lost the greater part of its horn.

Adam fingered the truncated stump. 'It's a pity.'

'Yes. What is a unicorn without its horn?'

'A white horse?'

Antonella smiled. 'A very unhappy white horse.'

They headed west from the grotto on a looping circuit,

the pathway trailing off into the evergreen woods blanketing the sides of the valley. They sauntered through the shade, chatting idly as they went. Antonella lived across the valley in a farmhouse she rented from her grandmother. The old building was delightfully cool in summer but bitterly cold in winter, and she had a rule that whenever the well water froze she would decamp to her brother's apartment in Florence. She and Edoardo were the children of Signora Docci's only daughter Caterina, a woman whom Professor Leonard had referred to as 'dissolute', something Adam found hard to square with the self-possessed creature stepping out beside him.

Her parents were divorced, she explained. Her mother lived in Rome, her father in Milan, where he was given to business ventures of a distinctly dubious nature, which promised (and invariably failed to deliver) untold wealth. She said this with a note of mild amusement in her voice.

By now they had passed through the first glade, with its triad of free-standing sculptures representing the death of Hyacinth, and were nearing the small temple at the foot of the garden.

'And what do you do?' Adam asked.

'Me? Oh, I design clothes. Can't you tell?' She spread her hands in reference to her simple cotton shift dress.

'I . . . Yes –'

Her smile stopped him dead. 'My dresses have more colour. Although they're not really mine. There is someone else's name on everything I do.'

'How come?'

'I work at a fashion house in Florence. There can only be one name.'

'Doesn't that bother you?'

'What a serious question.'

'I'm a serious chap.'

'Oh really?'

'Can't you tell?' he said, spreading his hands. 'All my friends are on a beach. Me, I'm here studying.'

'Only because you have to, and only for two weeks. From what I hear, you will probably see a beach before the end of the summer.'

This meant one thing: the news from Professor Leonard of Adam's indolence had not stopped with Signora Docci.

'I dispute that.'

'What?'

'Whatever you've heard.'

'The good things too?' Her eyes sparkled with mischief. 'My grandmother likes you, I think.'

Maybe it was something to do with the way she bared her teeth when she smiled, but at that moment it struck him that the long diagonal scar on her forehead exactly mirrored the cranial ridge on the orang-utan skull in the study.

Antonella turned away – feeling the weight of his lingering look? – and glanced down at the supine figure at their feet.

Narcissus lay sprawled along the rim of the octagonal pool, gazing admiringly at what should have been his reflection. Instead, he appeared to be searching for something he had lost, some trinket he'd mislaid in the debris of twigs and leaves which carpeted the bottom of the pool.

'I'm sorry you cannot see it when the water is here.'

'Will it ever come back?'

'Who knows? But it is not the same without the water. The water gives it life. It makes them breathe.'

She had removed her leather sandals a while before – they now hung lazily from the fingers of her right hand – and looking at her there in her simple cotton dress he saw her as the child she must once have been, wandering the garden, gazing wide-eyed on the coterie of petrified gods, goddesses and nymphs playing out their troubled stories on this leafy stage.

When she made for the temple, he followed unquestioningly. It was a small structure – octagonal, like the pool – and crowned by a low cupola just visible behind the pedimented portico. The floor was of polished stone, the walls of white stucco, as was the dome. The building was dedicated to Echo, the unfortunate nymph who fell hard for Narcissus. He, too preoccupied with his own beauty, spurned her attentions, whereupon Echo, heartbroken, faded away until only her voice remained.

'I love this place.'

Her words resounded off the clean, hard surfaces, the acoustic effect no doubt intentional. Simple painted wooden benches ran around the walls, and there was a lengthy Latin inscription carved into the architrave beneath the dome. According to the file it was a line from Socrates: *The hour of departure has arrived, and we go our separate ways, I to die, and you to live. Which of these two is better only God knows.*

He approached the cast-iron grille in the centre of the floor. This had puzzled him on his previous visits. There was no reference to it in the file, and all his efforts to dislodge it and discover what lay beneath had failed.

'The water falls into a small well then carries on to the pool outside. The sound in here . . . it is not easy to describe.' She thought on it for a moment. '*Sussurri.*'

'Whispers.'

'Yes. Like whispers.'

They covered the rest of the circuit in near silence, stopping briefly in the last of the glades, with its statue of Venus stooped over a dead Adonis – the final element in the itinerary, its message of grief and loss almost overwhelming after the other stories they had witnessed.

Any more would have been too much. The garden transported you just far enough. As soon as you felt the grip of its undertow, it released you.

Even without the sculptural programme the place would have exerted an unsettling pull. There was something mysterious and otherworldly about a wooded vale. Maybe it was the sense of enclosure, of containment, coupled with the presence of water, but it somehow reeked of ancient gatherings and happenings. You sensed that you weren't the first to have been drawn here, that naked savages had also stumbled upon it and thought the place bewitched.

Federico Docci would have been hard pressed to find a better spot for his memorial garden than one already haunted by flickering figures from some spectral past. And he had cleverly turned the location to his own ends, planting large numbers of evergreen trees to screen off views, to guide the eye, to tease and disorientate, whatever the season. He had punched holes in this sombre vegetation, shaping glades that smacked of sacred groves, connecting them with curling pathways that widened and narrowed as they went, the loose geometry almost musical – a pleasing rhythm of space and enclosure, of light and shade.

Having laid out this new kingdom, Federico had then dedicated it to Flora, goddess of flowers, and populated it with the characters from ancient mythology over whom she held sway: Hyacinth, Narcissus and Adonis. All had died tragically, and all lived on in the flowers that burst from the earth where their blood had spilled – the same flowers that still enamelled the ground in their respective areas of the garden every spring.

Their stories cast a melancholy pall over the garden. They were tales of desire, unrequited love, jealousy, vanity and untimely death. But they also spoke of hope. For just as the gods had interceded to immortalize the fallen youths, so Federico had ensured that the memory of his wife, snatched from him at a tender age, would live on.

These were the thoughts swirling through Adam's head as he and Antonella wended their way back up the hill to the villa. It was the first time he had fully grasped the beauty of the scheme – its logic, subtlety, and cohesion – and he wondered whether Antonella's company had somehow contributed to this epiphany.

He glanced over at her, walking beside him with her loose springless stride, shoulders back like a dancer. She seemed quite at ease with the silence hanging between them.

She caught his look and a smile stole over her features. 'It's like waking up, isn't it?'

'Hmmm?'

'Leaving the garden. It takes time to come back to the real world.'

He felt a sudden and foolish urge to tell her how beautiful

77

she was. And why. Because she wore her beauty carelessly, without vanity – the same way she wore the wounds on her face.

He checked himself just in time.

She cocked her head at him. 'What were you going to say?'

'Something I would have regretted.'

'Yes,' she said quietly, 'it can do that too.'

It was Antonella's idea that they stop on the lower terrace and settle themselves down on one of the benches over-looking the olive grove. She asked for a cigarette, which she smoked furtively, glancing up at the villa every so often to check she wasn't being observed.

'My grandmother doesn't approve,' she explained.

'I think you're safe. I mean, she's bedridden, right?'

Antonella shrugged. 'Maybe. She likes to create dramas.' She paused. 'That's not fair. She was very ill this winter . . . *una bronchite*, how do you say?'

'Bronchitis.'

'The doctor was worried. We all were. She has stayed in her bed since then.'

'Have you tried to get her up?'

'Have we tried?' She sounded exasperated.

'You think she's pretending?'

'I think she does not care any more. She is leaving soon, before the end of the year.'

'Where's she going?'

Antonella turned and pointed, smoke curling from the cigarette between her fingers. 'There.'

On a rise just beyond the farm buildings, a large house

rose foursquare, its stuccoed walls washed orange by the sun and streaked with the shadows of the surrounding cypresses. Too grand for a labourer, but maybe not grand enough for the lady of the manor.

'Why's she moving?'

'It was her decision. She wants Maurizio – my uncle – to have the villa.'

'Maybe she's changed her mind.'

'She would say.'

'Maybe she's saying it the only way she knows how.'

'You don't know my grandmother. She *would* say.'

Strolling back to the villa, they passed close to the small chapel pressed up against the sandstone cliff. She asked him if he'd seen inside. He had tried, he said, but the door was always locked.

The key was conveniently located for all would-be thieves beneath a large stone right beside the front step – a fact on which he remarked. 'You never know when someone might need it,' said Antonella simply.

The lock gnashed at the key then conceded defeat. The interior was aglow, a ruddy sunlight slanting through the windows. Aside from a handful of old wooden pews the interior was almost completely devoid of furnishings. The thieves wouldn't have been disappointed, though. The simple stone altar bore a painted triptych of the Adoration of the Magi. As they approached – silently, reverently – Adam tried to place it.

The colliding perspectives, the elongated figures and the warmth of the tones suggested a painter from the Sienese school. The date was another matter. To his semi-trained eye, it could have been anything from the mid fourteenth to the mid fifteenth century, later even. It wasn't a masterpiece, but it was distinctive, an unsettling blend of innocence and intensity – like the gaze of a child staring at you from the rear window of the car in front.

'I must go there,' said Adam.

'Where?'

'Siena.'

'I'm impressed.'

'Don't be. I couldn't tell you anything else about it.'

'No one can.'

'I'm sure someone could.'

'I hope they don't. Then there would be no more mystery.'

They made a quick tour of the chapel, stopping at a small plaque set in the wall beneath one of the windows. There was a name and a date etched into the stone:

EMILIO DOCCI

27. 7. 1944

'My uncle,' said Antonella.

'Your grandmother told me what happened. It's a terrible story.'

'He's buried there.' She pointed at the unmarked flag-stones at her feet. 'I never really knew him. We were living in Milan, and I was only ten or eleven when it happened.'

Which would make her what . . .?

'Twenty-four,' she said, reading his mind. 'And you?'

'Twenty-two next month.'

The words had a ring of desperation about them, as if he was trying to narrow the gap on her, and he quickly moved the conversation on.

'Why did he keep his mother's surname?'

'To keep the Docci name alive. So did Maurizio. Not my mother – she's a Ballerini.'

'And you?'

'I'm a Voli. Antonella Voli.'

He returned her bow. 'Adam Strickland.'

'Strickland,' she repeated. It wasn't designed to roll off an Italian tongue.

Adam glanced back at the plaque. 'Is Emilio the reason the top floor of the villa isn't used?'

'Yes.'

It had been her grandfather's idea, apparently. The day after Emilio's murder, the Allies had liberated San Casciano. Soldiers arrived. They searched the villa for intelligence left by the Germans before moving on. Her grandfather then had all the broken furniture from the terrace carried back upstairs. When this was done, he closed and locked the doors at the head of the staircase, sealing off the top floor. The rooms had remained that way ever since – undisturbed – on her grandfather's insistence. When he died some years later, people assumed that Signora Docci would have them opened up, aired, repaired, re-used. But she had left them just as they were, just as they had always been.

Adam lingered a moment when they left the chapel, casting a last look around the interior. Unless the information in the file was incorrect, then somewhere beneath the stone floor also lay the bones of Flora Bonfadio, dead some four hundred years.

They found Maria spreading the table on the terrace with a coarse white linen cloth. When Antonella stooped to kiss her on both cheeks, there was no mistaking the unguarded look of warmth in the older woman's eyes. It visibly dimmed when she took in Adam hovering at a distance.

'You must stay and meet my uncle and aunt. They'll be here soon. Also my cousins.'

'I should be going.'

Maria's expression suggested that this wasn't such a bad idea. It also suggested that her grasp of the English language was far better than she liked to let on.

'I insist,' said Antonella.

He stayed for only half an hour, but it was time enough to be won over by Maurizio's easy-going charm and his wife's mischievous wit. They made an attractive couple. He was dark and trim and distinguished looking, with a dusting of grey at the temples; Chiara Docci was a blonde and sharp-featured beauty whose husky laugh betrayed her passion for cigarettes, which she smoked relentlessly, to the evident disapproval of her two children, Rodolfo and Laura.

'Mama, please,' said Laura at one point.

'I'm nervous, *cara*. How often does one meet a hand-some young man who also has a brain?'

Adam fielded her look and felt his cheeks flush.

'Is it true?' Maurizio asked. 'Does he also have a brain?'

'I've only just met him,' Antonella replied, playfully noncommittal.

Chiara blew a plume of smoke into the air. 'That's all it takes, my dear. The moment I met your uncle I knew I would have to search for mental stimulation elsewhere.'

It was an odd sight for Adam, watching children openly laughing at a parent's joke. And so wholeheartedly that he wondered for a moment if there wasn't just a small grain of truth in Chiara's quip. Somehow he doubted it, though. Maurizio was laughing along like a man who knows quite the reverse is true. His teeth were improbably white, Adam noted.

'Your brain, my looks, wasn't that the deal?' retorted Maurizio, well aware that his wife left him standing in the looks department.

'So what went wrong?' said Antonella, nodding at her cousins, the offspring.

More laughter. And more wine. Then a discussion about a forthcoming party at the villa, which Adam would be a fool to miss. Adam, though, wasn't really listening. He was observing them, with their lively banter and their air of easy affluence, their coal-black hair and their honeyed complexions. A breed apart.

He felt a sudden urge to be gone. Maria spared him having to make an excuse, materializing from the villa with the news that Signora Docci was ready to receive her family.

Antonella accompanied Adam to the courtyard, where the bicycle stood propped against the well-head.

'My grandfather's,' she said, her long fingers sliding over the leather saddle. 'He used to put us in the basket when we were young and make us shout *Ay Caramba!*'

She kissed him on both cheeks, her hand lightly touching his arm as she did so.

Negotiating the turn at the bottom of the driveway, he could still feel the delicate pressure of her fingers at his elbow.

9

Have they gone yet?

Didn't you hear the car leave?

Are you angry, Maria?

Angry?

You always answer a question with a question when you're angry.

Do I, Signora?

Or sad.

They were talking about the party like it is theirs already . . . all the friends they're inviting.

We need their friends. So many of mine are gone.

But it's your party, Signora, it always has been.

I thought you hated the party.

I do. But that's not the point.

And what about Antonella? How did she seem to you?

Antonella?

Do you think she likes him?

Who?

Who do you think? Adam, of course.

I've hardly seen them together. How can I say?
Because you know her better than any of us.
Yes, I think she likes him.
A lot?
Maybe.
Oh dear.
Signora?
Sit down, Maria. The chair there. Pull it up to the bed.
Closer. Good, now give me your hand. That's right.
Signora . . .?
There's something I need to talk to you about, Maria,
something we should have talked about long ago.

10

Adam lowered the camera. 'Damn,' he muttered, not for the first time.

The light was perfect, clear and limpid after three days of flat summer haze, but now he found he was unable to photograph the glade in its entirety. The three statues distributed around the clearing resolutely refused to fall within the frame at the same time.

Waist-deep in the laurel at the southern edge, he was able to capture both Zephyrus – the west wind, his cheeks puffed out, blowing with all his might – and Hyacinth, supine on his pedestal, dead, the discus lying beside him. But Apollo was out of shot.

In fact, wherever Adam placed himself, the 50mm lens on his father's old Leica ('Don't bother coming home if you lose it') was unable to accommodate more than two of the three figures at any one time.

The story they enacted was simple enough, which only increased his frustration at not being able to trap it in a single shot: Zephyrus, jealous of Apollo's love for Hyacinth, a beautiful Spartan prince, decided to take action. While Apollo was teaching the youth to throw a discus, Zephyrus whipped up a wind which sent the discus crashing into Hyacinth's skull, killing him instantly. The hyacinth flower then sprouted from the ground where his blood fell.

At the northern fringe of the grove stood Apollo, with his grief-stricken face and his arms outstretched towards the fallen boy. He was perched on a conical, rough-carved mountain peak. Maybe it was intended to signify Mount Parnassus, the home he shared with the Muses, but its inclusion seemed gratuitous. Mount Parnassus didn't figure in the story as handed down by Ovid and, besides, Apollo was already identifiable from his bow and his lyre.

The statue of Hyacinth only raised further questions. Why place him face down in the dirt, his long hair sprawled across his features so that only a small section of his delicate mouth was showing? And why clad a young man renowned for his athletic prowess in a loose, long-sleeved robe, rather than baring his physique?

The file offered no insights. Nor, for that matter, did the copious notes amassed by Signora Docci's father while preparing the document, although these *had* yielded some lines from Keats' *Endymion* about Zephyr's role in the death of Hyacinth. It was a nice fat chunk of poetry which would help flesh out his thesis, but like the other little discoveries he'd accumulated over the past few days, it left him feeling strangely indifferent.

He was safe now – he knew he already had enough to shape a convincing paper – and he should have been celebrating. He couldn't, though, not with so many questions tugging at his thoughts. They had proliferated ever since his tour of the garden with Antonella, when for a brief moment it had all seemed so clear, so straightforward.

The steep rise housing the amphitheatre was evidently an artificial construct, but why had Federico Docci gone to the effort and expense of shifting so many tons of earth for the sake of one feature? Such a vast undertaking was hardly in keeping with the discretion he'd shown elsewhere in the garden. And as for the amphitheatre itself, why nine levels instead of the seven on display in the amphitheatre at Bomarzo?

Like false notes in an otherwise flawless piece of music, these questions jarred, they refused to be ignored. He had tried to dismiss them, but each time he breached the yew hedge at the entrance to the garden, he knew they'd still be there. Even now, while engaged in the purely practical exercise of photographing the garden, two more had just presented themselves to him in the form of the Apollo and Hyacinth statues.

He fired off one last shot of Hyacinth then made his way back through the woods towards the grotto. It occurred to him that he was developing an unhealthy fixation on the garden. This was hardly surprising. Since his arrival he had barely thought about anything else. When he wasn't walking around it, he was invariably reading about it, shipping books and papers back to the pensione every evening in the bike basket so that he could continue studying through dinner and on into the early hours.

There had been no one in the trattoria to chide him for reading and eating at the same time. Disappointingly, Fausto hadn't shown his face since that first evening, and was unlikely to do so any time soon according to Signora Fanelli.

Apparently it was the first time in a long while that he'd stopped by her place. Adam might have been imagining it, but he'd detected a whiff of disappointment on her part, too.

No Fausto. And no Antonella, not for three days.

'She is working very hard,' Signora Docci had revealed to him during one of his regular audiences in her bedroom. 'Apparently, there are important clients in town, buyers from big American department stores.'

She had made little effort to conceal the note of mild mockery in her voice.

'You don't approve of what she does?'

'It's the job of old people to disapprove of everything young people do.'

'Oh, is that right?'

'If we don't disapprove, then the young have nothing to fight against and the world will never change. It cannot move on.'

'I'd never thought of it that way.'

'I should hope not; you have better things to think about.'

'Such as?'

'Oh, I don't know' – she waved her hand vaguely about in the air – 'Elvis Presley.'

'I'm impressed.'

'Antonella keeps me informed of these things.'

'And you dutifully disapprove.'

'Elvis Presley is clearly a young man of questionable morals.'

'Based on your knowledge of his music.'

'And his films.'

'Which you've seen?'

'Of course not. You don't understand. The old people are allowed to argue their case from a position of complete ignorance. In fact, it's essential.'

Adam laughed, as he often found himself doing when in her company. 'Maybe she likes what she does,' he said. 'Maybe she's good at it.'

'My friends who know about such things tell me she has great talent. But I always saw her as more than just a seam-stress.'

'I'm sure there's a lot more to it than just sewing.'

Signora Docci gave a low sigh. 'You're right, of course. Ignore me. I think I am still a little angry.'

'Angry?'

'You should have seen her before, before this –' Her fingertips moved to her forehead. 'She was so beautiful. Now she hides herself away in a back room and works with her hands. *La poverina.*'

Her words riled him, especially the last two, replete with pity: the poor thing.

'I disagree,' said Adam. 'I can't see her hiding herself.'

'No?' Her tone was flat, sceptical.

'I know I've only met her once, but it's what struck me most – that she's not ashamed, not embarrassed. The way she wears her hair, the way she carries herself. She's not hiding.'

'You think she doesn't look in the mirror every morning and wish it was different?'

'Maybe. I don't know. But she's more beautiful because of it, because of the way she is with it.'

'You really believe that?'

'I do. Yes.'

At first he took her look for one of weary sufferance, and he suddenly felt very young, he suddenly felt like a person in the presence of someone who has spent considerably more time on the planet. But there was something else in her eyes, something he couldn't quite place. He only realized what it was when a slow and slightly wicked smile spread across her face.

'You're playing with me.'

'It's nice to see you defending her. And you're right – she is more beautiful because of it.'

'How did it happen?'

'It was near Portofino, at night. Her mother was driving. She was also lucky. She only broke two ribs.'

Signora Docci had not elaborated. In fact, she had terminated the conversation then and there on some doubtful pretext, banishing him back downstairs to his books.

Maybe that's what the problem was, mused Adam, strolling back past the grotto: the routine, the rigmarole, long periods of study broken by conversations with a bed-bound septuagenarian. Toss the pitiless heat into the pot, and it was little wonder he was losing his grip.

He climbed the steps sunk into the slope behind the grotto, resolving as he did so to break the pattern, to introduce some variety into his life, maybe eat out one night, cycle off somewhere for half a day, or even hitch a lift into Florence – anything to add some variety, jolt him out of his folly.

He stopped at the base of the amphitheatre and stared up at Flora on her pedestal near the top. He would never be able to see her as he had that first time. Antonella's words had irrevocably coloured his judgement. When he looked on the goddess twisting one way then the other he no longer saw the classic pose borrowed from Giambologna, he saw a woman contorted with some other emotion, he saw the provocative thrust of her right hip.

Why put her there, near the top but not at the top? In fact, why put her there at all, in a nine-tiered amphitheatre? And why nine instead of seven tiers? Or five for that matter? What was so special about nine? The nine lives of a cat? A stitch in time . . .? The nine planets of the solar system? No, they hadn't known about Pluto back then. Shakespeare, maybe – *Macbeth* – the witches repeating their spells nine times. Not possible. Shakespeare couldn't have been more than a boy when the garden was laid out. Close, though. And the occult connection was interesting. How had the witches put it?

> *Thrice to thine, and thrice to mine,*
> *And thrice again to make up nine.*

The trinity to the power of three – a powerful number – thrice sacred, like the Holiest of Holies, composed of the three trinities. And something else, some other dark association with the number nine. But what?

He pulled himself up short, the resolution fresh in his mind yet already ignored. He lit a cigarette, dropped the match in the trough at the foot of the amphitheatre and made off up the pathway.

He was a few yards shy of the yew hedge barring his exit from the garden when the answer came to him.

The nine circles of Hell in Dante's *Inferno*.

It was several moments before he turned and hurried back down the path to the amphitheatre.

It wasn't that the statue of Flora was placed on the second tier from the top – he couldn't remember just which category of human sin or depravity had been enshrined by Dante in the second circle of his *Inferno* – it was the inscription on the triumphal arch standing proud on the crest above that settled it:

FIORE

It took him ten minutes to locate a copy of the book in the library, just time enough to recover his breath. He dropped into a leather chair and examined the tome: *La Divina Commedia* by Dante Alighieri, an Italian edition dating from the late nineteenth century.

His dictionary was back at the pensione, but with any luck he wouldn't need it, not immediately. Even his rudimentary Italian should be up to establishing which class of sinner inhabited the second circle of Dante's Hell, his *Inferno*.

He had never actually read *The Divine Comedy* right through. He had skimmed it, filleted a couple of commentaries, done just enough to satisfy an examiner that he was well acquainted with the text. He could have put forward a convincing argument for the timeless appeal of Dante's epic poem, the crowning glory of his life, twelve years in the writing, completed just before his death in 1321. He could also have listed a number of great writers and poets who openly and willingly acknowledged their debt to the work – William Blake, T.S. Eliot, Samuel Beckett and James Joyce. He could even have come up with some specifics, lines in *The Waste Land* that Eliot had lifted straight from *The Divine Comedy*.

Never having read *The Waste Land* – or any works by Beckett and Joyce, for that matter – he would have been hard pressed to say what exactly these modern men of letters had seen to inspire them in a medieval poem about a lost soul's journey through Hell, Purgatory and Paradise.

It didn't matter, though. He could recall enough of *The Divine Comedy* to know that there was some kind of connection with the memorial garden.

Finding himself lost in a dark wood, Dante is approached by the spirit of the poet Virgil, who guides him down through the nine circles of Hell and on into Purgatory. The spirit of Beatrice – the love of Dante's life, long since dead – takes over as guide for the last leg, escorting Dante up through Paradise towards a final meeting with God.

Adam's interest lay in the opening of the story: Virgil leading Dante from the dark wood and through the gates of Hell. Was it by chance that a dense wood of dark ilex trees bristled menacingly at the head of the memorial garden? Or that the triumphal arch stood so close by? Or that if you read the two curiously unsymmetrical decorative motifs flanking FIORE as the letter N, then you had an anagram of INFERNO, of Hell? Was it possible that Federico Docci had moved, if not Heaven, then earth, and lots of it, to shape a steep slope for a simple amphitheatre? Or had he done so in order to recreate the plunging layers of Hell so vividly detailed by Dante in the first part of his poem?

These were some of the questions that had carried Adam up the hill from the garden at a run, and that now had him furiously flipping through the old book.

He found what he was looking for in the fifth Canto of *Inferno*: *Così discesi del cerchio primaio giù nel secondo . . .*

So I descended from the first circle down to the second . . .

His eyes roamed over the text: a dark place . . . the cries and curses of the sinners as they're whirled around in a vicious wind that never stops . . . *i peccator carnali.*

He read on a little to confirm that he hadn't misunderstood. He hadn't.

If the ilex trees stood for the dark wood where Dante lost his way, and the triumphal arch represented the gates of Hell, then Federico Docci had chosen to place the statue of his dead wife in the circle of Hell that housed the carnal sinners, the adulterers.

He was still trying to take this on board when Maria entered the library from the drawing room.

'Maria.'

'Sir.' Why had she taken to calling him Sir? 'Signora Docci wishes to see you.'

'Thank you.'

He didn't move.

'Is everything all right, sir?'

'Yes.'

His mind was still reeling from the discovery, yes, but

his sweat-soaked shirt was also glued to the back of the leather chair, and he worried what sound it would make if he got to his feet in her presence.

He was right to have waited till she left. It was a ripping sound, a bit like Velcro.

Signora Docci wasn't in her bed, which threw him at first. She had only ever been in her bed. But now it was empty, neatly made, the white cotton counterpane smoothed flat as ice.

'Out here,' came her voice from the loggia.

She was wearing a navy-blue skirt and a white cotton blouse, and was seated in a rattan chair. Her feet were bare and resting on a footstool. Her hair, which she had always worn loose, was drawn back in a ponytail; and in the sunlight flooding the loggia, her face had lost some of its pallor. She looked like a passenger lounging on the deck of an ocean liner – the first-class deck.

'I thought we'd have tea alfresco today,' she said matter-of-factly. Unable to keep up the pretence, a slow smile broke across her face. 'You should see your expression.'

'I'm surprised.'

'It's hardly the Raising of Lazarus. Anyway, it's your fault.'

'My fault?'

'Well, not directly. It's the shame of talking to you every day from my bed. It's not dignified.'

'You don't have to feel dignified on my account.'

'Oh, I don't – it's entirely on my own account.' She turned her face into the sun. 'It is a long time since I felt the sun on my face.' She gestured towards the tea service laid out on the low table. 'Do you mind?'

Adam poured the tea, as he always did. She was very particular – milk first, then the tea, then half a spoon of sugar.

'You were running,' she said.

'Running?'

'Well, trying to. I saw you from there.' She pointed towards the low wall of the loggia.

Instinct told him to keep the discovery to himself. If indeed that's what it was. Maybe he had imposed Dante on the garden, or the garden on Dante. He needed to be sure. And that would take time.

'I thought I was on to something. I was wrong.'

She wasn't going to let him get away with it that easily. 'What?'

'Zephyr,' he replied, still formulating his response.

'Zephyr?'

'The west wind.'

'Yes, I know.'

'Well, in the myth he's Flora's husband; in life Federico was her husband. I suddenly thought, I don't know, that maybe the statue of Zephyr had been modelled on Federico. I wanted to see if there was a resemblance with the portrait in the study.'

'Interesting.'

'Except there's no likeness,' he shrugged.

If she sensed his evasion, she didn't say anything. What she *did* say surprised him.

'There's a bedroom in the north wing, big, with its own bathroom. It's yours if you want it.'

He wasn't sure if he'd heard right.

'It's an invitation.'

'To stay?'

'Not for ever,' she said with a small smile. 'Think on it. You don't have to decide now. And I won't be offended if you say no.'

'Thank you.'

'It will save you money.'

'It's not my money, it's the faculty's.'

'That doesn't mean you can't spend it on something else. Crispin doesn't need to know. And if he did, he'd hardly ask for it back. Am I wrong?'

'No.'

'So?'

It wasn't the money. Something else altogether accounted for his hesitation.

'My brother's coming to stay.'

'You never mentioned you had a brother.'

'I try not to think about it too much.'

Signora Docci smiled. 'When is he arriving?'

'That's not the kind of question you ask Harry.'

'And what does Harry do?'

'He's a sculptor.'

'A sculptor?' She sounded intrigued.

'Of sorts. He's very modern – lots of welded steel dragged off scrapheaps.'

'Is he presentable?'

'That's not a word I've ever associated with him.'

Signora Docci laughed. 'Well, there's another room for Harry if he wants it. You decide. It doesn't matter to me either way.'

But it did, he could see that; he could see an elderly woman about to be displaced from her home and extending an invitation of hospitality, possibly her last. What settled

98

it for him, though, was the chance it offered to see more of Antonella. If their paths hadn't crossed in the past few days, it was only because he was always long gone, back at the pensione in San Casciano, by the time she showed up to visit her grandmother in the evening.

11

Signora Fanelli was a bit put out to hear that Adam would be leaving, less so when he offered to cover the cost of the room for a full week.

'When will you go?'

'Not tomorrow, but the day after that day.' He made a mental note to look up the Italian for the day after tomorrow.

Signora Fanelli was busying herself in the trattoria, polishing glasses in readiness for the evening trade. The front of her dress was cut lower than usual, and a gold cross dangled alluringly at her cleavage. He hadn't registered it before, but there was something of Flora in her high collarbones.

'The Signora really invited you to stay?'

'Yes.'

'Strange.'

'Why?'

'She's very private.'

'She doesn't seem very private.'

'She wasn't. Before. She was very . . . vivacious.'

'What happened?'

She looked up with her large dark eyes. 'The murder, of course.'

'You mean Emilio?'

'A bad thing.' She crossed herself with the barest of movements, drawing his eyes once more to her low neckline.

The family had never really recovered from the death of Emilio, she went on, although Signora Docci's husband, Benedetto, had taken it worse than she had. He faded from view. He was rarely seen out and about, not even at harvest time when the grapes and the olives were picked and pressed. Then suddenly he was dead, of a heart attack. In her opinion, those Germans might just as well have shot him too, because he was dying from the moment they killed his eldest boy.

'What happened to them – the Germans?'

'Killed, both of them, in the battle of Florence.'

'Justice.'

'You think so? Two lives for one? Ten, maybe . . . fifty . . . a hundred of their lives. To kill him like that, a man who had welcomed them into his own home.'

The memory still angered her. It was a physical thing, shocking to an English eye.

She swept a stray strand of hair out of her face. 'They changed this place. It's not the same. Everyone knows what happened here, and we still feel it. What they did in a moment, we live with for ever.'

Later, when he had showered, he read through the letter he'd written to Gloria, relieved that he hadn't got round to posting it. He thought he'd struck just the right note of magnanimity, forgiving her for the brutal termination of their relationship, but there was something pompous and self-pitying tucked away in his words. What did she care what he thought? She had wanted company to see her through to the summer break. He shouldn't be forgiving her; he should be admonishing himself for failing to read the signs earlier.

His mind turned to Signora Fanelli, to the flash of fire in her eyes and the dark passion in her voice when she had spoken about Emilio's murder. He also dwelt on her parting words to him downstairs.

'I'm sorry you're leaving, but I understand.'

It was a simple enough statement, but her gaze had faltered, as if with embarrassment, as if she had revealed too much of herself. Had there been something provocative in that bashful glance? It wasn't impossible. Their relationship had hovered somewhere between easy familiarity and flirtation since their very first exchange, when she had corrected his English with a wry little smile. Over the past days they had joked, he had flattered her, and she had found any number of pretexts on which to playfully chide him. It wasn't exactly a remarkable relationship, but there was no denying a certain alchemy.

When he headed downstairs for dinner, there was nothing in Signora Fanelli's manner to suggest that any of these thoughts had ever occurred to her. She was too busy to show him to his table as she usually did. Instead, she pointed to the terrace and barked, 'Outside.' And when she finally got round to taking his order, there was none of the usual banter while he prevaricated (far more than was ever necessary). She insisted that he start with the *cacciucco*, whatever that was, then hurried off.

Cacciucco proved to be steamed mussels in a spicy red sauce. It was excellent, certainly too good to do anything other than eat, not that the messy operation allowed for a book on the table, let alone three. The moment the debris was cleared away, he opened *The Divine Comedy*. Many of the words didn't even appear in his dictionary, and it soon became depressingly clear that he could spend the rest of his time in Italy toiling through the text and still not reach the end. He persevered, though, the thrill of the breakthrough fresh in his mind.

He had punished the evidence, but everything still pointed to a clear link between the garden and Dante's *Inferno*. Just like Dante, Federico Docci had constructed his own multi-layered Hell, and by placing Flora on the second tier from the top he was sending out a message about his young wife, he was saying that she was an adulterous whore.

It was no longer a question of whether or not Federico Docci had made this damning declaration, but why? Why bother laying out a garden to her memory at all if that's the way he felt about her? It didn't make sense, not unless there was more to the story, more that Federico had buried away in the rest of the cycle.

This called for a close examination of Dante's poem; it demanded a thorough search for any further associations with the garden; it meant ploughing on regardless. Which is precisely what he did – right through the main course of spit-roasted Val d'Arno chicken, a warm and windless night descending on the terrace.

Dante and Virgil had barely breached the gates of Hell

when Signora Fanelli arrived at his table with a compli-
mentary brandy.

'You work too hard.'

'Feeling better?' he asked.

She gave a coy and contrite smile. 'I'm sorry. It's been
a bad night. I'll tell you later.'

She never got a chance to. Some late diners and the usual
diehards at the bar meant she was still working flat out
when he finally headed upstairs to bed.

He was woken by a swathe of light cutting through the
darkness. There was a figure silhouetted in the doorway
of his room.

It was Signora Fanelli.

He closed his eyes, feigning sleep, his mind struggling to
digest this new development. So he hadn't been wrong,
after all.

'Adam,' she whispered, creeping towards him. Her hand
settled gently on his shoulder. 'Adam.'

He did a poor job of pretending to stir.

'Yes . . .?' he croaked weakly.

'It's 'Arry,' she said. 'On the phone.'

Harry went straight in without so much as a 'hello', and
from that moment on Adam was behind in the story, struggling to make up ground.

It had something to do with being in Milan and meeting
a girl at the station and the girl was Swiss and she was
lost and it was late and she had an address of a hotel
nearby and they went there and it was a cheap place with
no porters and Harry had carried her bag upstairs for her

104

while she checked in and when he came down he found that she had checked out. Permanently. With his bag. The one he'd innocently left in her company. The one with all his money in it.

It was not unlike a number of stories Adam had heard from Harry over the years.

'Harry, what time is it?'

'What, late for the fucking opera, are we? Christ, it's late, okay, and I'm stuck in this shitty hotel in Milan with a suitcase full of newspapers belonging to a Swiss girl.'

'I doubt she was Swiss.'

'You doubt she was Swiss!?'

'I doubt it.'

'Well, she didn't have pigtails and a bloody great milch cow on a leash, if that's what you mean!'

'Calm down, Harry.'

'*You* calm down. You're not the one in Milan with the suitcase full of newspapers.'

'Do you have your passport?'

'Of course,' sighed Harry indignantly.

'Any money?'

'Not enough to buy a ticket out of here, or I wouldn't be calling.'

'Where are you phoning from? The hotel?'

'Yes.'

'Do they speak English?'

'They think they do.'

'Okay, listen. This is what I suggest . . .'

As Adam talked, he watched Signora Fanelli going about her business, closing up for the night. She bolted the shutters to the terrace but left the doors open so that the cool night air could circulate. She was wiping down the counter when he finally replaced the receiver on the cradle.

He was suddenly aware of himself standing there barefoot in his pyjama bottoms and the grubby T-shirt he'd pulled on hurriedly.

'Problems?' she asked.

'Do you have a brother?'

'Yes.'

'Is he a disaster?'

She laughed. She laughed some more when he related the story of Harry's plight. She then poured them both a night-cap and apologized for being so short with him earlier in the evening. Lucrezia, one of the cooks, had shown up drunk again. Signora Fanelli sympathized – Lucrezia's husband was a violent brute, he had always been a violent brute, even as a boy – but the drinking was getting out of hand. She didn't know what to do. They talked her quandary to a standstill before making their way upstairs to bed.

Adam's room lay on the corridor leading to her apartment. When they reached his door, he said goodnight to her. She didn't walk on, though, she didn't even reply, not at first. She stared at the floor then looked up at him and said, 'Iacopo's not here tonight. He's staying with a friend.'

He knew what the words meant – her son was away, she was alone – but he didn't know what *she* meant. And he wasn't going to risk making a fool of himself.

He didn't have to. She took him by the hand and drew him into his room, closing the door behind them.

There was nothing urgent in her actions, not at first. She led him through the darkness to the bed then eased his shirt up and over his head, discarding it on the floor. She ran her hands over his skin, her fingers tugging at the desultory thicket that almost qualified as chest hair. When she raised her face towards his, he stooped to kiss her. Her tongue was small, pointed, inquisitive. She must have felt him stirring against her belly, because she placed a hand in the small of his back and drew him closer.

They stood like this, kissing, for quite some while. His hands roamed, enjoying what they felt through the cotton dress, her nipples hardening beneath his touch.

Slowly, she dropped to her knees and drew his pyjama bottoms down over his thighs. He felt her breath against him, and for a moment she seemed to be contemplating what to do next. Then she closed her lips around him.

She did almost nothing; she just let him grow there in the moist warmth of her mouth, the palms of her hands resting gently against his thighs.

Then her mouth was gone and she was standing once more, turning her back to him.

He slid the zipper down and eased the dress from her shoulders until it fell and gathered in a heap at her ankles. She didn't step free of it until he had released the clasp of her bra.

She beat him to the panties, bending to remove them, before turning once more to face him. She was breathing hard now, and she gripped him firmly in her hand as they locked mouths again, her tongue stabbing at his this time.

Without warning, she pushed him back on to the bed and was astride him before he had time to shuffle himself neatly to the middle of the mattress. Her pelvis pressed against his hardness, her hair dense, abrasive, already damp.

She cupped a hand behind his neck and drew his head off the bed, guiding his mouth to her breasts.

She arched low, pressing her lips to his ear. 'This is our secret,' she whispered. 'You understand?'

He grunted.

She removed her nipple from his mouth. 'Do you understand?'

'Yes.'

She forced him back on to the mattress. There was nothing he wanted more than to enter her there and then, but she wasn't having it, not yet.

She edged her way up his body until her purpose was plain. Seizing the iron rail at the head of the bed to steady herself, she straddled his face and lowered herself towards him.

12

To anyone who didn't know, there was nothing in their behaviour to betray what had passed between them. The elderly Roman couple – the only other residents of the pensione still at their breakfast when Adam headed downstairs – smiled at him politely, as they had done for the past few mornings. No evidence there that Signora Fanelli had shared with them the details of her nocturnal romp with the Englishman. In fact, no evidence at all that it had ever occurred.

It was only when she brought him his coffee that he detected something. She stood a fraction closer to him than she usually did when placing the cup and saucer on the table.

He lingered over his breakfast in the hope that a private moment would present itself, an opportunity to at least acknowledge their steamy encounter. Maybe it wouldn't have mattered so much if she hadn't slipped from his bed while he was sleeping. His last memory had been of her astride him, exhorting him with words he didn't understand, the crucifix swinging at her neck, brushing his chest.

That second time had done for him almost immediately. Had he even held her afterwards? He hoped he had.

The Romans finally pottered off, and when Signora Fanelli reappeared from the kitchen she asked breezily, 'Another cappuccino?'

'Thank you.'

The counter-top coffee machine coughed and sputtered and hissed ominously. Adam pushed back his chair and strolled over.

'Did you sleep well?' she asked.

It sounded suspiciously like a dig.

'I'm sorry,' he said.

'Why?'

'I fell asleep.'

She fired a furtive glance at the door to the kitchen. 'That was my intention. I have a business to run here. I also need my sleep.' There was a pleasing edge of irony to her voice.

Steam from a slender nozzle blasted some milk in a battered tin jug.

'Eight years,' she said, under cover of the racket. 'Since I made love.'

'It's a long time.'

She twisted the tap closed and looked up at him. 'It was worth the wait.'

'It was very special. No, incredible.' He hoped she could see from his face that he wasn't being polite. She had taken him to a place he'd never been before.

At that moment Iacopo entered from the terrace, breathless from running. Adam was probably wrong to detect something knowing in the boy's look.

'Well?' asked his mother.

'He's leaving in twenty minutes.'

'Signore Carnesecchi,' she explained, turning to Adam. 'He's going down into Florence.'

She was ahead of him, looking out for him. He'd told her he needed to send money to Harry.

Iacopo passed by them, out of the room.

'No one must ever know,' she said.

'I understand.'

'I live here. You don't. That's why it happened.'

There must have been something injured in his expression, because when she slid the cup of coffee across the counter she gave his hand a brief and stealthy squeeze.

'Well, not the only reason.'

Signore Carnesecchi made a living from fruit and vegetables, which was mildly amusing. His surname translated as 'dried meats'.

His wife and son were travelling with him to the market in Florence. They rode in the cab of the old open-sided truck while Adam squeezed in with the crates stacked in the back.

Tomatoes predominated, with beans running a close second. Judging from the smell, there was also a batch of strawberries buried away somewhere. It was a bumpy but fragrant journey down out of the hills.

Bouncing around on the boards, watching the world receding behind him, Adam caught himself in a flush of pride. Was it trivial that a beautiful woman had wanted him? He suspected it was. Was it immature and vindictive to imagine Gloria getting wind of the encounter? Certainly.

But sitting there in the back of the truck, the sun warming his face, it felt good, he felt alive. And he hadn't felt alive for quite some while, he now realized.

Eight years since she last made love – that's what she had said – which meant that he wasn't the first person she'd given herself to since the death of her husband. Araldo had been killed in 1945, right at the end of the war. Adam knew this because he had asked her while they were lying damp and entwined after their first bout on his bed.

It was a grim tale, which made her willingness to share it with him all the more touching. Araldo had been a victim of the blood-letting that followed the liberation of Italy by the Allies – an uncertain and anarchic time when many were held to account for their actions during the German occupation. If she knew the exact details, she didn't share them with him. She spoke vaguely of an accusation levelled against her husband. The word 'collaboration' wasn't mentioned, but she did hint at an incident which had resulted in the arrest and execution of two local partisans by the Germans.

She was more specific when it came to the details of what subsequently happened. Araldo left the house one morning for Impruneta, where he worked as a stonemason. He never arrived. They dragged him from his car on a quiet country road and put three bullets in his head.

Who 'they' were, she didn't know for sure, although she had her suspicions. A name sprang to Adam's mind, too. Fortunately, it was the wrong name.

Fausto had played no part in Araldo's death, she went on, of that she was fairly sure. He had shown his face at the funeral. A number of his comrades-in-arms hadn't.

'You can't know a man – I mean, you can't *really* know a man – unless you've known him as a child. I've known Fausto all my life, since we were babies in our mothers' arms. If I thought for one moment he'd had anything to do with it, or even that he knew it was going to happen and did nothing . . . well, I think I would have killed him by now.'

Sitting there in the back of the truck, this was a shocking and sobering statement to recall. At the time, however, it had exerted a strangely aphrodisiacal effect.

The warehouse was a low steel-and-concrete structure in the San Lorenzo district of Florence. The streets around it were thronging with people. They parted like a bow wave before a boat, closing in again behind the truck. Most ignored him sitting there among the crates; some waved. A knot of grubby children made obscene gestures. When he returned them, he was pelted with stones snatched from the gutter.

He helped unload the crates then turned down Signore Carnesecchi's offer of a ride back to San Casciano in an hour's time. He said he'd make his own way back.

The city was in the grip of a stifling heat, and he baked himself for a while on the terrace of a café in Piazza della Signoria, the tourists pouring past him in weary droves. He dropped off two rolls of film at a photographic shop on Piazza Repubblica and parted with some of the money in his pocket for a crude straw hat and a pair of sunglasses – purchases which might have felt extravagant if the cash hadn't been destined for Harry. God only knew what he would spend it on.

There was no queue worth speaking of at the American Express office. The counter clerk relieved him of his bundle of notes and, when questioned, pointed him in the direction of a reputable bookshop.

They didn't have an English language edition of *The Divine Comedy*, but a long walk and four hundred lire later he was the proud owner of a battered translation by Dorothy L. Sayers.

He toyed with the idea of settling down with it in some shady corner of the Boboli Gardens, or of visiting one of the many museums, galleries and churches on his list. They were idle thoughts, though. He knew where he was really headed.

He had logged and stored away the name of the fashion house, as well as the district in which it was located. More than that, Antonella hadn't revealed to him. It proved to be enough. A newspaper vendor in Piazza Santa Croce directed him to the street and the building.

It was a large crumbling palazzo. Adam stepped through a small door set in towering wooden gates and found himself in a generous courtyard open to the heavens. It was a world apart, sealed off, immune to the amplified din of the cars and scooters in the narrow street outside. You could even hear the soft fall of water in the fountain. There were other sounds, too, snatches of activity drifting through the open windows around the courtyard: the staccato beat of a typewriter, someone answering a phone, the scrape of a chair against a stone floor. If the brass plaques attached to the wall outside were anything to go by, the building was home to a number of businesses.

The fashion house where Antonella worked occupied the

entire north wing of the palazzo, although you wouldn't have known it from the ground-floor reception area. Cool and cavernous, it was also completely anonymous – no company name in sight, no products on show. A handful of modern leather chairs served as a small seating area, and there was an ornate rococo desk which dwarfed the already petite receptionist behind it.

The rubber soles of his shoes squeaked painfully on the tiled floor as he made his way over. She only looked up from her magazine when the noise ceased at her desk. She studied him with some interest, but seemed to find little to repay her curiosity. When he asked to see Antonella, her manner grew more obliging. She straightened in her chair, requested his name and reached for the phone.

Adam cast an eye around him while he waited. The décor was a self-conscious blend of old and new. The chrome chandelier hanging from the high, beamed ceiling was positively futuristic, and there was an abstract metal sculpture bolted to the wall behind the receptionist's desk – a large circular monstrosity, some five or six feet in diameter, consisting of shards of steel welded together haphazardly. It would have had Harry in raptures.

'Adam . . .'

Antonella appeared at the foot of the stone staircase. She was wearing a navy-blue linen dress that hugged her slender figure. Approaching, she kissed him on both cheeks.

'Nice hat.'

'All the rage this season, or didn't you know?'

She smiled. 'I'm surprised.'

'Me too. I wasn't sure I had the right place.'

She glanced around her. 'Umberto thinks it's good for

business. He says it's – how do you say? – enigmatic. The rest is not like this. Come, I'll show you. Do you have time?'

'I'm not disturbing you?'

She dismissed the question with a wag of the hand.

Adam thanked the receptionist as he passed by. 'Don't mention it, sir,' she replied sweetly, keen to win favour with Antonella.

She wasn't the only one.

The cutters and seamstresses toiling in the run of rooms upstairs all greeted her warmly. It didn't surprise him that she was liked, but she seemed to command a respect way beyond her years. The reason became clear when she pushed open yet another door.

'And this is where I work,' she announced. 'It's very messy.'

Two windows, half-shuttered against the sunlight, over-looked the courtyard. There was a desk, some low book-cases, as well as a large workbench that filled the centre of the room. She was right; every available surface was loaded with clutter: piles of sketches, samples of cloth and leather, pots of pens and brushes, empty cups and over-flowing ashtrays.

'I want to say it's not normally like this.'

The only remotely clear area was an architect's drawing-board against the wall, and maybe only then because it offered an angled surface. There was a half-finished drawing taped to it, a colour sketch of a leather handbag. It was quite unlike any other handbag Adam had ever seen.

'It's our new thing. Umberto wants us to do accessories – bags, belts, scarves, maybe even shoes.'

The walls were papered with more sketches, dresses mostly. They had loose flowing lines, and all were cut from the distinctive cloths which were clearly the hallmark of the company: bold geometric designs in vivid colours. They were the same dresses Adam had witnessed taking life next door.

'Does Umberto do anything around here?' he asked.

'Umberto is a genius. I am only his hands.' There was no trace of false modesty in her words. 'I would introduce you, but he's not here now.'

'Out with the Americans?'

'Ah, you've spoken to my grandmother. Then you will know that she does not approve of what I do.'

'Has she seen it for herself?'

Antonella seemed amused by the idea. 'She thinks all fashion is trivial, which of course it is. But she doesn't understand that it can also bring pleasure.' She picked up some material from the workbench. 'Here.'

Only when he took it from her did he realize it was a piece of suede, as soft as silk.

'Imagine that against your skin,' she said. 'Imagine a skirt made of it.'

'That might be asking a bit too much.'

She laughed and took the suede from him. 'When are you moving in – to the villa, I mean?'

'She told you?'

'Of course.'

'Tomorrow.'

'You don't have to.'

He hesitated. 'You think it's a bad idea?'

'I think I haven't seen my grandmother so alive for a

long time. But it doesn't mean you have to, just because she asked. She can be very . . . *prepotente*.'

'Overbearing?'

'I don't know the word, but it sounds right.'

'I want to,' said Adam. 'It's good for work, I'm near the garden, the library's right there . . .'

'And is this work?'

She reached for his copy of *The Divine Comedy*, which he'd abandoned on the workbench.

'No,' he lied, 'just never read it before.'

It was her idea that they sneak off for lunch. Beneath the trees in a small piazza around the corner, they shared a carafe of Chianti and a thick slab of *bistecca fiorentina* done with a light hand. The restaurant owner fussed around Antonella as if she were a long-lost daughter.

Adam filled her in on Harry's predicament, which had brought him down into town at short notice.

'When does he arrive?'

'God knows. Maybe never. As soon as he gets his hands on the money anything could happen.'

'But you want him to come or you would have told him not to.'

'I suppose,' he said, surprised that it was so apparent to her.

Her own brother Edoardo sounded like an altogether different character – level-headed, responsible and reliable. 'I don't know where he gets it, but he is proof that two negatives can make a positive.'

'And you?' asked Adam.

'Me? Oh, I'm not easy.'

'What's your worst characteristic?' asked the Chianti.

She thought on it. 'My temper.'

'Really? I don't see it.'

'Pray you never do.'

Adam laughed.

'So?' she asked.

'What?'

'Quid pro quo – your worst characteristic.'

'An uncompromising sense of justice. It gets me into all kinds of scrapes.'

'Very funny.'

'Jealousy.'

'Jealousy?'

'Yes.'

'Of what?'

'I don't know. Everything. Other people's success. My girlfriend's old boyfriends. It's very mean-spirited of me, I know.'

'You have a girlfriend?'

There was a satisfying note of forced indifference in the question. It suggested that the answer mattered to her. He was glad to be able to say, 'Not any more.'

'What happened?'

'I'm not quite sure.'

He tried his best to explain, though, raking over the dead embers of his relationship with Gloria.

When he was done, Antonella said, 'I don't like the sound of her.'

'I should hope not. I've painted the blackest picture I can.'

The couple at the next table turned and stared when she laughed.

13

❧ ❧

Have you finished?

Yes.

So, Doctor, your prognosis?

Your reactions seem fine. Your leg muscles are still very weak, though, from lack of use. You really shouldn't move around unassisted. There's a danger you'll fall.

And the pain?

The tablets I gave you before should help.

They did.

You've finished them already?

Something a bit stronger might be better.

I'm not sure that's . . . advisable.

My son is coming to dinner this evening, to finalize the details of the party. You did get an invitation, didn't you?

Yes, Signora, and my wife replied promptly. We are always honoured to be invited.

Call me a foolish old woman, Doctor, but I wish to be on my feet when I greet Maurizio at the door this evening.

And, as I say, the pain can be really quite unbearable at times.

I understand.

It shall be our secret. I wouldn't want to worry anyone.

I'll return this afternoon with something a little more . . . appropriate.

Cheer up, Doctor. At Christmas your patient was at death's door, and now she's on her feet.

14

It was Antonella's idea that Adam kick his heels for a couple of hours after their lunch. What with it being a Friday, she could break early from work and run him back to San Casciano. Piazzale Michelangelo was the designated pick-up point because it lay on her route out of town. The large, sweeping terrace sat on the hillside south of the river, offering a panoramic view over Florence, the terracotta roofscape breaking like a muddy sea around the towers, domes and spires.

He headed straight there, the prospect of trudging the streets of the city centre on a bellyful of raw meat and red wine not a particularly appealing one. Better to flee the heat and make for the higher ground, the tree-clad slopes. Besides, the Romanesque church of San Miniato al Monte was perched just above the piazzale, and it was one of the few places Professor Leonard had insisted he visit.

It didn't disappoint. It was a small building, beautifully proportioned and elaborately decorated, with an unusual elevated choir. The interior was gloomy and pleasantly cool. He hovered close to a tour group of Americans, hitching a free ride. At a certain point, he allowed them to wander ahead. Something had caught his eye: a large zodiac set in the stone floor, like a giant clock face, the astrological signs of the twelve constellations made of inlaid white marble.

He patrolled the circumference, wondering just what on earth it was doing here, this pagan symbolism in a Christian church. Did anyone know the answer? Had the guide passed over it because there *was* no explanation? The guide did mention the zodiac before leading her party from the church, but offered no real illumination. Its presence there was open to speculation, she said. Adam found this strangely comforting. If its exact significance had gone missing over the centuries, then why shouldn't the same hold true for the memorial garden? Maybe he really was on to something. Maybe the book in his hand really did hold the key to some lost interpretation.

He had found nothing new in Dante's words to suggest this was the case by the time Antonella showed up at the wheel of an extremely small car. She called it her 'blue frog' and she said she loved it. This didn't square with the way she treated the little Fiat 600, hurling it around the corners, wrenching it up through the gears until it was screaming in protest.

Crammed into the passenger seat, hurtling down a precipitous cobbled street, Adam found himself wishing he had opted to thumb a lift back to San Casciano. The city ceased abruptly, cobbles giving way to dirt and dust, stone walls to high, banked hedgerows.

It was a narrow country lane. Very narrow. Must be one-way. Had to be, given the speed they were travelling at.

It wasn't. But it was nice to know the brakes worked.

He asked Antonella to drop him off on the outskirts of San Casciano. It wasn't that he feared for the lives of the residents – although the thought had crossed his mind – he was more concerned that Antonella might sense something of what had gone on the night before if allowed to come face to face with Signora Fanelli. He was only delaying the inevitable. When Antonella suggested coming by the pensione in the morning and transporting his bags to Villa Docci, he could hardly refuse the offer.

He found Signora Fanelli on her hands and knees, scrubbing the floor of the trattoria. It was a position he recognized. She got to her feet, wiping the sweat from her brow with the back of her hand, which didn't help.

It was lust, he realized, pure and simple, unassailable. He was no different to Paolo and Francesca in the second circle of Dante's Hell, blown about for all of time by fierce winds, doomed by their – how had Dante put it? – *dubbiosi disiri*. Their dubious desires.

'Is everything okay?'

'Yes,' he replied absently, thinking that he'd already reached the fifth circle of Hell in Dorothy L. Sayers' translation and he'd yet to come across a sin he hadn't been guilty of at one time or another.

'The money for Harry?'

'Yes. No problem.'

How much further would he have to descend into Dante's

ordered underworld before he could finally declare himself innocent of the transgression on show?

'How did you get back?'

He told her.

'She's a beautiful girl, isn't she?'

'Is she?'

'You don't think so?'

'No. Yes. I suppose.'

'She's wild, that one. Well, not any more. But she used to be.'

'Wild?'

'Like her mother. But it's different now. They say she's changed.'

'Changed?'

'That's what they say.'

He headed for the bar in Piazza Cavour before dinner, as he did every evening, aware that this was the last time he would watch the ragged boys playing football, scampering to and fro between the goalposts chalked on to the walls, stopping to splash their faces with water from the old stone trough whenever one of them scored. The piazza started to fill – slow but steady trickles of humanity from the side streets – and the young footballers grudgingly relinquished their pitch to their elders.

You could go a whole day in San Casciano barely seeing a soul, but come early evening, the entire town (or so it seemed) took to the streets, making for Piazza Cavour. Couples, families, black-shawled widows bent with the weight of years; they all gathered, sauntering around.

Signora Fanelli had painted a picture of a fractured community, yet here they all were, congregating, carrying

125

on as normal. He wondered what their stories were, and whether thirteen years was really time enough to forgive and forget.

He worked during dinner, although at a certain point it ceased to be work, Dante's wild imagination and spectacular imagery carrying him effortlessly along. On reaching the seventh circle of Hell, he was pleased to finally encounter a sin he hadn't committed: murder. Strangely, Dante rated this as a less grievous offence than both hypocrisy and flattery, which he had placed in the eighth circle. Here, a group of souls was walking endlessly around in a circle, a devil slicing them open from top to toe each time they passed him, only for the wounds to re-heal. These were the Sowers of Discord and Schism, the prophet Muhammad chief among them. True to form, Dante had devised a punishment appropriate to the sin, splitting each of them apart for all eternity, as they had sought to divide others during their lifetimes.

But amongst all the unfortunates being eviscerated by devils, boiling in rivers of blood and choking on human excrement, there was still no sign of any of the characters from the garden. Frustrated, he started to skip ahead, skimming the pages for their names: Flora, Zephyr, Daphne, Apollo, Hyacinth, Echo, Narcissus. This is what he was doing when a figure appeared at his shoulder.

'Hi.'

Adam turned and looked up at Fausto. He appeared more presentable than before. His chin was still blackened with stubble, but he'd run a comb through his long lank hair, and he was wearing a clean shirt, buttoned up to the neck – small concessions to smartness which didn't quite mask a congenital disregard for externals.

'Can I?' he asked, dropping into the chair opposite.

Adam pointedly checked the number of cigarettes in his packet. 'Sure.'

Fausto smiled. 'Don't worry, I brought my own this time.'

'How are you?'

'Good. Tired. Working too hard.'

'I don't even know what you do.'

'The minimum,' grinned Fausto. 'I have a small place on the hillside there. There's always something to do. Right now I'm building a shed for a pig.'

'You have a pig?'

'Not yet. But it'll be the happiest pig alive when I do.' He glanced at Adam's book. 'Dante, eh? "*Lasciate ogni speranza, voi ch'entrate*".'

It was a well-known line from the poem, the inscription on the gates of Hell: Abandon all hope, ye who enter.

'You know it?'

'Do I know it? Do you know Shakespeare? Do you know Milton? Dante is a son of Tuscany.' Fausto laid his hand on the book. 'This is the reason the Tuscan language is the language of Italy, did you know that?'

'Yes.'

When writing *The Divine Comedy*, Dante had shunned Latin in favour of his Tuscan vernacular, a clear break from tradition, and one which had enshrined the dialect as the national language.

'A great man – like Machiavelli, another Tuscan.'

'I know.'

'But I bet you don't know that Machiavelli wrote *The Prince* just down the road from here.'

'Really?'

'Sant'Andrea in Percussina, not even three kilometres away. He was forced to leave Florence, like Dante. Two great works written in exile. Coincidence? I don't think so.'

Fausto wasn't lying; he knew a lot about *The Divine Comedy*, right down to the names of the Popes Dante had consigned to his Hell. In fact, Fausto seemed to know a lot about pretty much everything, which wasn't altogether surprising – he had been a student at the university in Florence when war broke out.

A member of the Partito Socialista at the time, he said he was involved in the struggle against the Fascists' creeping grip on the university. Then, when the Armistice was signed and the Italians suddenly found themselves under occupation by the Germans, their former allies, he became caught up in the fight for national liberation. At first, he helped distribute underground newspapers with punchy titles like *Avanti!* and *Avanguardia*. Then he picked up a gun and began to fight, heading for the hills and joining a partisan group. Many had, men of all kinds, all classes. Signora Docci's younger son, Maurizio, had done the same thing. A radical, a member of the Comitato Interparti di Firenze at the time, he had abandoned politics for the gun.

'I never fought with him, but he was known as a good leader, a good fighter . . .' Fausto paused. 'You see, in the end words don't count for much. You have to hurt your enemy. The Americans understood that – you English, too. You have to kick him hard enough till he leaves you alone.'

Fausto couldn't have been much more than Adam's age at the time, and Adam found himself reaching for equivalents in his own life. The best he could come up with was an unremarkable stint of National Service, and adding his name to a petition censuring Anthony Eden for his handling of the Suez Crisis.

The liberation of Italy didn't bring happier times, Fausto went on. The socialist and communist factions, united under the banner of a common cause, fragmented once more. The Americans were damned if they were going to allow the country to go to that dog Stalin, and promptly set about showering the Christian Democrat Party with dollars in a bid to buy the soul of the country. Years on, they still were.

'Really?'

'Millions of dollars every year. But a rich, Anglo-Saxon, Protestant country can't impose its values on a poor, Latin, Catholic one. We're poor. We earn a quarter of what you do in England – one sixth of what the Americans do.'

'The country's getting richer, I heard.'

Fausto exhaled, fixing Adam with a stare. 'True. And if it continues, maybe the Americans will win in the end.'

'Ah, the Americans, the Americans,' sighed Signora Fanelli, approaching their table. 'What have they done now, Fausto?'

'You want to know what the Americans have done?'

'Not really.'

She flashed a wicked smile and replaced their empty carafe of wine with a full one. 'On the house – a leaving present.'

'What a woman,' said Fausto with a strange mix of

indignation and desire, watching her walk away. He topped up their glasses. 'You're leaving?'

'Not Italy. I'm going to stay at Villa Docci.'

Fausto nodded a couple of times. 'I thought I told you to be careful.'

'You said it was a bad place.'

'And it is.'

Fausto's evidence was pretty compelling. When he was done presenting it, it occurred to Adam that if you mined the history of any family you might unearth a grim catalogue of intrigues, deceits and unusual deaths; but somehow you couldn't help thinking that the Doccis had suffered more than their fair share of misadventure over the centuries.

As their fortunes had fluctuated, the estate had fallen in and out of the family's possession. Somehow it had always returned, though. Something – a marriage of convenience, a betrayal or a bribe – always ensured that the family and the property were never separated for too long.

The times they were together, it was rarely a happy union. People died in fires, fell from their horses, smothered their loved ones, or had their throats slit in the night. Presumably, many had led quite happy and uneventful lives at Villa Docci, but Fausto's point was this: the house attracted ill-luck to itself, like a flame draws moths, and he selected his stories to bear out his argument.

'And Emilio?' asked Adam.

'What about him?'

'You think what happened is all part of the same thing?'

'Who knows what really happened?' shrugged Fausto.

'I do. Signora Docci told me.'

'What did she say?'

Adam spelled out the bare bones of the story as recounted to him. When he was finished, Fausto sat in silence for a moment.

'Well, most of it's correct.'

'And the rest?'

Fausto lit a cigarette. 'Emilio was a Fascist, a party member, did you know that?'

'No.'

'It's because of him the Germans were so respectful when they took over the villa. It's also the reason he was so angry when he saw the damage they were doing that night. It wasn't part of the agreement, the understanding. He lost his temper, I can see that. But I still can't see him pulling out his gun.'

'But he did. There were witnesses – Maurizio and the gardener . . .' He couldn't remember the name.

'Ah, Gaetano,' sighed Fausto. 'Who knows what Gaetano saw, or what he heard. He didn't seem too sure himself at the time. That came later.'

'I don't understand.'

Fausto leaned close across the table. 'He changed his story.'

'Why?'

Fausto shrugged. 'I never asked him.'

'Why not?'

'You know the story of Pandora?'

'Yes.'

'Well, sometimes it's best to ignore the whispers inside the box.'

15

Antonella appeared punctually at the pensione at ten o'clock the following morning. The encounter between her and Signora Fanelli passed off quite painlessly, the two women exchanging easy pleasantries. The suitcases were loaded into the Fiat and Antonella sped off to Villa Docci. Adam followed on the bicycle. He was dispatched with a kiss on both cheeks from Signora Fanelli. Iacopo offered a limp and clammy hand by way of farewell, but only when prompted by his mother.

Arriving at the villa, he was surprised to find Maurizio unloading his suitcases from Antonella's car. There had been a family gathering the evening before to finalize the arrangements for the party, and Maurizio had stayed on overnight in order to make the rounds of the estate workers.

'They always have complaints, but this year is worse than normal.'

'Because of the drought?'

'Exactly.'

They carried the cases upstairs together. Adam already

knew the bedroom assigned to him, but the dark, musty space he had briefly looked in on was almost unrecognizable now that the tall windows were thrown open, allowing light and air to flood it to its corners. Vases of sweet-smelling flowers were distributed around the room.

Even Maurizio was impressed. 'Maria has been busy. I don't think it has ever looked so good.'

Maurizio headed off on his duties, and Adam joined Signora Docci and Antonella on the terrace for coffee. Antonella had errands to run; she only stayed long enough to invite Adam to Sunday lunch at her farmhouse the following day. It was a chance to meet her brother Edoardo and some of their other friends. When she rose to leave, Adam too made his excuses, saying he had to work.

'But it's the weekend.'

'He's not here for your amusement, *Nonna*.' Antonella turned to Adam. 'Don't let her tell you what to do. If you want to work, you work.'

'He has the whole afternoon to work. I won't be here to distract him. I'm going into Florence.'

'*Nonna?*'

'What?'

'Are you ready for Florence?'

'The question, my dear, is whether Florence is ready for me.'

She left just before lunch in a navy-blue Lancia saloon, dragged from a barn and dusted down. She gave a mock-regal wave from the back seat as the vehicle pulled away. It might have been the wave, or maybe it was the sight of Foscolo at the wheel in a chauffeur's cap, but it was the first time Adam had seen Maria smile. The smile suited her face, although the moment she sensed his eyes on her, it was gone.

He unpacked his suitcases then made for a shaded corner of the terrace with *The Divine Comedy*. He tried to progress, but his eyes kept sliding over the text. In the end, he closed the book, conceding defeat to the source of his distraction.

The top floor was reached by a lone stone staircase, centrally placed, in keeping with the perfect symmetry of the villa. Wooden double-doors barred his passage at the head of the stairs. He wasn't surprised to find them locked. He *was* surprised, however, when a voice echoed in the stairwell.

'The Signora has the key.'

He spun, startled. Maria was standing at the foot of the steps. He felt the weight of her flat, inscrutable gaze as he descended towards her.

'Can I prepare you something for lunch?'

'A sandwich, thanks.'

'You should eat more. You're too thin.'

'I eat a lot at dinner.'

'I'll remember that,' she said.

There was a levity in this last remark which gave him the courage to ask, 'Maria, why is it locked?'

'It was the Signore's wish. The Signora chooses to respect it.'

'Don't you think it's a bit . . .' he searched for the word '. . . macabre?'

'A bit? It sits over this house like a curse. Not for much longer, though. Signore Maurizio has plans.'

'Plans?'

'I don't know the details. The usual?'

'Excuse me?'

'Ham and cheese?'

'Yes, thank you.'

He took the sandwich with him to the memorial garden. He ate it on the stone bench at the base of the amphitheatre, looking up at Flora on her plinth. She seemed to be taunting him. So did the inscription carved into the bench – The Soul in Repose Grows Wiser – a quotation from Aristotle, he now knew.

He was anything but 'in repose', his thoughts turning once again to his conversation with Fausto the evening before. It had robbed him of sleep; it had hovered over him like a cloud all day.

If Fausto was to be believed, then Gaetano the gardener had changed his account of what happened the night of Emilio's murder. Why would he do that? More importantly, how could he get away with it? The truth was, he couldn't, not without the collusion of Maurizio. Their stories had to tally. This suggested some kind of compact between the two men, arrived at subsequent to Emilio's death. From here it was a short step to the unthinkable – too short not to take, even if you didn't want to.

No, it was an absurd notion. He was drawing wild conclusions based on a couple of exchanges with an unkempt Italian communist he'd met in a bar.

He reached for his cigarettes and lit one. As he did so, he caught sight of Maurizio strolling down the path towards him.

Adam got to his feet as nonchalantly as he could. 'Hi.'

'Hello.'

Maurizio looked up at the statue of Flora, then down, past the grotto to the Temple of Echo nestling among the trees at the bottom of the pasture.

'I haven't been here for a long time.'

'You don't like it?'

Maurizio appeared intrigued by the question. 'I haven't thought about it. But no, I don't think I do. I find it a bit . . . *sombro*.'

'Sombre.'

'Yes.'

'Death is, I suppose.'

'I suppose,' parroted Maurizio. 'We came here a lot when we were children. This was our world.' He glanced down at the trough sunk into the ground at the foot of the amphitheatre. 'The water was cold, even in the summer. Very cold.' He looked up, smiling. 'One minute and eighteen seconds – Emilio's record, for holding his breath. I was never close. Not even a minute.'

The idea of Emilio prostrate in the narrow trough gave rise to another image, dark and unsettling: of Emilio stretched out in his coffin beneath the flagstone floor of the chapel. Adam shook off the fleeting thought.

'And your sister?' he asked, unable to recall the name of Antonella's mother.

'Caterina? Oh, she held the watch.'

'What is she like?'

Maurizio gave a thin smile. 'Difficult. You will meet her at the party.'

'She's coming?'

'It is the only time she comes – for the party.' He paused. 'You will still be here, I hope.'

'Yes. I mean, if that's okay.'

'Of course it is. You must be there . . . after everything you've done for my mother.'

It was a weighted compliment, and for a moment it seemed Maurizio was about to steer the conversation this way. He didn't, though; he asked if Adam would accompany him on a quick tour of the garden.

They had just passed through the glade of Hyacinth when Maurizio said, 'Can I ask you to do something for me? A favour.'

'Of course.'

'It's about my mother. You have had a very good effect on her.'

'I doubt that.'

'It's true. She says so herself. Anyway, it shows. We can all see it.' He paused. 'But something worries me, something Maria has told me. She takes pills for the pain. Not Maria, my mother, I mean . . . although I'm sure there are times when Maria could use them too.'

Adam smiled politely at the joke.

'Recently she has taken a lot. The doctor was here yesterday. Twice. He came back with more pills. Maria found them. She thinks they are even stronger than before.'

His gaze lingered meaningfully on Adam.

'I'm not sure I understand.'

'My mother is a proud woman. She has always pushed herself. Maybe she is pushing herself too much. Maybe even to impress you.'

'Me?'

'It's possible. Her new companion . . .'

His tone was tinged with mockery, and it rankled.

'What's the favour?' Adam asked, just shy of unfriendly.

'That you keep an eye on her. That you don't encourage her . . . to push herself too much.'

'Of course.'

'She is still weak.'

'I understand.'

They were able to put this moment of mild antagonism behind them for the remainder of the circuit. Adam even laughed when Maurizio described how his sister had once dressed the statue of Venus in one of their mother's old party gowns.

Returning to the foot of the amphitheatre, Adam recovered his copy of *The Divine Comedy* from the bench.

'A masterpiece,' observed Maurizio.

'Absolutely.'

'Where have you got to?'

'The ninth circle of Hell.'

Maurizio searched his memory. 'The ninth circle . . .?'

'Caina. Those who've committed crimes against their own flesh and blood. Dante named it after Cain, who killed his brother Abel.'

Later that night, lying in the big old bed, staring into the darkness, he tried to make sense of his reply to Maurizio's innocent enquiry.

The words had issued from his mouth, and in that respect they had been his. But even now he felt no ownership of them, no responsibility for them. He had not intended to speak them. They had tumbled from his lips unbidden. This might have been less troubling if there had been more truth to them.

138

He had, in fact, progressed well beyond the ninth circle of Hell – with its icy lake and its host of sinners frozen up to their necks – and on into Purgatory.

The most worrying thing, though, was the change his words had wrought in Maurizio. The mention of Cain and Abel had, for the briefest of moments, cast his features in stone and turned his eyes cold and crystal-hard.

16

He woke late after a fitful night's sleep. The new day brought a new clarity with it. He had allowed his mind to run away with him; he had imagined things that weren't there – or, at the very least, misinterpreted those that were. This realization gave him comfort, and he forced himself to think only of things that wouldn't jeopardize that.

His resolve faltered somewhat when he headed downstairs to the study. He couldn't be sure, but he had the distinct impression that someone had been through his papers on the desk. There was something not quite right about the topography of the various piles. Some sat too close together, others were too neatly ordered. The first thing he did was delve through them and pull out all of his scribblings relating to Emilio's death. These he burned in the grate.

He made his way to the cavernous, brick-vaulted kitchen in the south wing, Maria's spotless domain. She was nowhere to be found, although the air was thick with the caustic odour of bleach liberally and recently applied. It was Sunday; maybe she was at church.

The room gave little away about its tenant aside from a whisper of brisk and efficient orderliness. The surfaces were clear, the fresh fruit and vegetables neatly piled in their terracotta bowls, the copper pans back on the long shelf, arranged from left to right in ascending order of size. There was certainly no visible record of the small feast Maria had prepared for him and Signora Docci the evening before.

The dinner had been a subdued affair at first. Visibly depleted by her foray into Florence, Signora Docci had nevertheless reported the trip in some detail, describing a visit she had paid to an old friend – 'Her husband is a homosexual, but after all these years she still cannot see it.' She went on to list the numerous purchases she had made, everything from a fennel-flavoured salami to an antique ebony walking stick, which she had handed to him across the candlelight of their table on the back terrace.

It had a whalebone pommel in the form of a human skull. Adam stared at the pale, carved death's-head.

'It's appropriate,' said Signora Docci. 'I shall be clutching it until the end. I don't mind being reminded of that fact.'

Fearful that he was being drawn out of his conversational depth, Adam headed for shore. He asked her about the skulls in the study, the ones high up in the cabinet behind the desk – orang-utan skulls, if he had understood Maria correctly.

'My father was a naturalist, a botanist. This was before he became an archaeologist. He was many other things, too. He was a . . . disorientated man, I can see that now. At the time it was, well, exciting.'

They were indeed orang-utan skulls, keepsakes from a

trip the family had made to the Dutch East Indies in the last century. Signora Docci said she couldn't remember if her mother had put up a fight when her father first proposed that the whole family travel with him. In fact, there was much she couldn't recall about that period in her life, being only six years old in 1884, the year they steamed out of Livorno.

'Your Mr Darwin was to blame, with his theories of evolution and natural selection. My father was a scientist, but he was also a religious man, a strict Catholic; it was not easy for him to accept the new ideas. He fought them for twenty years with words, then he went in search of the evidence his arguments lacked. That's why he dragged us halfway round the world.'

Her memories of the East might have been patchy, but they were somehow no less vivid for it. She could recall the grandeur of her parents' state-room on the boat over. She remembered the latitude starting to tell on familiar constellations, the Great Bear's tail dipping below the horizon as they slipped southwards on the Suez Canal. This phenomenon was pointed out to her by a Scotsman many years her senior with whom she developed a close relationship (but only, she now realized, because her nanny had been so eager to spend time in the company of Walter F. Peploe – The F stands for foolish, Nanny had said).

Walter F. Peploe claimed to be an expert on all matters pertaining to the weather, and he certainly had the equipment to prove it. The captain allowed him to lash a louvred cabinet fitted with thermometers and other paraphernalia to a spar in the after-part of the ship. His pride and joy, though, was what he called his 'Richard' barograph – a free-swinging contraption that he'd rigged in his cabin, which gave accurate atmospheric readings irrespective of the ship's roll. He was adamant that all vessels should be fitted with such a device if they were to avoid the perils of a sudden tempest. His stated aim in life was to persuade the Dutch authorities in Java to adopt the barograph on all government vessels plying the treacherous waters of the East Indies, and thereby make his fortune.

He was a little disappointed when their own ship's passage of the Indian Ocean unfolded without incident, even if the clement weather was borne out by the readings on his barograph. Denied the opportunity of forewarning the captain of some impending climatic disaster, he devoted his time to investigating the idiosyncrasies of the ocean currents. This involved dropping numerous messages over the side of the ship, and to this end he regularly dispatched the young Signora Docci to loot empty beer-bottles from the ship's pantry – considerably more bottles, it seemed to her, than the actual number of messages he spent so much of his time dictating to Nanny back in his cabin.

Maybe some of those bottles were cast up on foreign shores, their notes returned, as requested, to his home address in Glasgow. If they were, he never got to know of it. Within six months of their arrival in Java, a Dutch postal packet went down with all hands in a typhoon off the island of Celebes. Walter F. Peploe was among those listed missing presumed dead. 'The silly fool,' Nanny had said. 'I can just see him at the end with his stupid barograph, oh so pleased with himself, shouting "See, I told you so!"'

News of the meteorologist's untimely end only reached the Doccis just before they boarded the boat home, after a trying year in the tropics. Most of their time had been spent on Borneo, with a brief interlude in northern Sumatra, because that island was also home to orang-utans – the great apes that had lured her father halfway round the world.

Again, her memories were patchy yet precise. She could recall the Dutch gentlemen, kind and courtly, dressing for dinner in heavy black tail-coats despite the enervating heat and humidity. They were forever smoking cigars and drinking gin and bitters. She also remembered the black teeth of the natives (considered a mark of beauty), the milky white water of the coral reefs, and the smoke of the volcanoes rising in misty clouds against the clear blue sky. Then there was the virgin forest which clad almost everything and called no one master. This was where they spent the greater part of their time, beneath the dense green canopy, where only the odd stray sunbeam penetrated to the mulchy forest floor. There were no views in the forest, no horizons, just the trees closing in behind you as you travelled through it. And then there was the eternal imminence of death.

She had a strong recollection of the natives on Sumatra huddling in the tree-tops whenever the tigers came, which was often. There were no tigers on Borneo, but the *banteng* – the wild buffalo – was just as feared. It attacked for no apparent reason, and with lightning speed. One time a rhinoceros broke from a bamboo thicket, sundering their rank of bearers, leaving a path as broad as a cart track behind it in the matted undergrowth. And of course there were the snakes, the stuff of childhood nightmares. The King Cobra had been known to pursue men for many miles, although if you had the presence of mind to shed one of your garments, it would halt to attack that, buying you precious moments to escape.

She described how they had emerged one morning from their hut to find a giant python coiled in a wooden cage, unable to escape, having swallowed whole the former occupant of the cage, a goat they kept for its milk.

Her most vivid memories, though, and the most disturbing, were of her father, of his physical and then his mental deterioration. When he wasn't hunting orang-utans, he was preparing their skins and skeletons. He would emerge from his makeshift charnel house exhausted, reeking of putrefaction, his hands cut and red raw from the arsenical soap he'd applied to the bones to deter insects. The feet of the trestle table he worked on were placed in bowls of water – a barrier to the ever-present ants – but somehow they always found a way on to his specimens. When he began to take this as a personal affront, her mother started to worry. When he threatened to shoot one of the bearers for sneaking sips of the arrack in which he preserved his pelts, it was time to talk of calling a halt to the venture.

He resisted the suggestion, insisting that the skins and skeletons were a lucrative source of income – which they were, zoological museums paid handsomely for both – and rejecting the counter-argument that he had not travelled to the tropics in the name of Mammon but of Science.

With hindsight, Signora Docci went on, it was clear that the expedition was doomed from the first. It was the final stab of a desperate man intent on debunking Darwin. To her father's credit, his position had shifted since *The Origin*

145

of Species was first published, moving from one of knee-jerk ridicule to a more tempered assessment of the scientific facts. The third phase of his own private evolution had taken the form of a pre-emptive strike: there was nothing wrong with Darwin's theories of natural selection because the most esteemed Christian thinkers, including Saint Augustine and Saint Thomas Aquinas, had already sanctioned a kind of 'derivative creation', the argument being that when God declared 'Let the waters produce . . .' and 'Let the earth produce . . .' he was conferring forces on the elements that enabled them, in accordance with his laws of Nature, to produce various species of organic beings. Her father's efforts to harmonize the new science with Catholic orthodoxy soon foundered, though, as he struggled to bend the words of the venerable theologians to his own ends.

Instead, he reached for another theory – his last, and the one that had carried him and his family to the East Indies. This conceded to Darwin the development of new species by natural selection, Man included, while allowing for a divine, overarching plan. Put simply, her father argued that, after innumerable generations of influence, natural selection had run its course, spent its load. All life on earth had now entered an era of 'conservative heredity' in which the power of adaptation in organisms had slowed to the point of being almost non-existent. This theory permitted a return to the old idea of the absolute fixity of living species, with Man at the top of the pyramid, as intended by God.

Where better to search for proof of this than among the anthropoids – the order of great apes whose existence now haunted man like some ancestral ghost? It was a matter of reliable record that two types of orang-utan inhabited Borneo, living side by side, even nesting in the same trees. The *Mayas Tjaping* (as it was called by the locals) was a larger animal, with a square head flanked by fatty cheek pads. The *Mayas Kassa* was slighter, its face narrower, more delicately featured.

From the presence of orang-utans on the neighbouring island of Sumatra – the only other place on the planet where they were to be found – one could safely conclude that all orang-utans shared a common heritage reaching back to a distant epoch when a land connection existed between the two islands. The big question – and one which her father believed answered itself – was this: given the separation of the Bornean and Sumatran orang-utans hundreds of thousands, if not millions, of years previously, why had the two populations not evolved independently of each other according to the Darwinian model? By all accounts, they were the same, right down to the subtle differences of physiognomy between the two types of orang-utan, both of which were also present on Sumatra.

This wasn't to say Darwin was wrong – there was too much evidence in favour of his evolutionary theory – simply that he was no longer right. The power of heredity had evidently increased since the primordial era to the point that living organisms were now fixed and immutable.

The logic was sound, even to her mother's sceptical ears, or she wouldn't have consented to accompany her husband to one of the least hospitable corners of the planet.

There was, however, one problem.

After a few months on Borneo her father had only identified one type of orang-utan – the *Mayas Tjaping*, big and square-headed. Some had fatty cheek-expansions, while others didn't, but this distinction seemed to be no more than a feature of age in the male of the species. It was looking increasingly likely that the sound logic was based on unsound evidence. There was only one way to tell.

It was on their trip to Sumatra that her father almost lost his mind, and on a couple of occasions his life (Dutch authority in the northern province of Aceh extending no further than the range of their guns from a handful of forts). During his time there, he shot, skinned and prepared the skeletons of more than fifteen orang-utans. They, too, were all of one type – a different type, smaller than the *Mayas Tjaping*, with narrower faces and hair of a paler hue than their Bornean cousins. For that was what they clearly were: cousins, and several times removed.

Her father must have recognized the deep irony of his predicament, but he refused to accept it. Only after they had all returned to Borneo, and after another spate of slaughter, was he forced to concede the inevitable: the findings of his fellow naturalists who had visited the Malay archipelago before him were flawed, and by following in their footsteps he had not only failed in his mission to challenge Darwinian thinking, he had actually lent weight to it.

There were indeed two types of orang-utan, but one type inhabited Borneo, the other Sumatra. Geographically divided, the species had adapted itself according to the demands of two different environments. And there was no reason whatsoever to assume that this wasn't an ongoing situation.

His only consolation came from his wife. Signora Docci's

long-suffering mother tried to make him see that he had made an important contribution to the sum of zoological knowledge. He might even have identified a new sub-species of primate. There was certainly a strong case to be made for this. Most in his position would have leapt at the chance of laying claim to a part of the Tree of Life, even if it was just one small bifurcation at the end of a branch.

Not her father.

On their return to Italy, he resigned his post at the univer-sity, destroyed all his papers relating to the expedition and turned his attention to archaeology, immersing himself in the lost culture of the Etruscans. He kept only two memen-toes of his time in the East Indies, but strangely they were the most significant reminders of his failure – the orang-utan skulls in the study cabinet, manifestly different: one Bornean, the other Sumatran.

Adam had barely spoken a word during Signora Docci's account of her childhood adventure, more than content to be carried along by her colourful tales and the soft, meas-ured tones of her voice. When she, too, fell silent, his power of speech did not return.

Signora Docci gave an apologetic smile. 'I'm sorry. I have bored you.'

'No. You haven't. It's interesting.'

'The reminiscences of an old lady? I doubt it.'

'Really. It must have been a fascinating time, Man strug-gling to come to terms with who he really was . . . is.'

'Oh, I doubt we ever will.' She took a sip of wine. 'Men like my father went in search of Eden, but they found a far more savage garden.'

Adam hesitated, uncertain about raising the subject. 'The scar on Antonella's forehead . . .'

Signora Docci smiled. 'I should have known you'd see it. The crest on the skull from Borneo . . .'

'Yes.'

'Who knows? I'm not superstitious, but maybe it is punishment for what he did to those poor creatures. It was a massacre. And after they were dead he desecrated their bodies.' She glanced off into the night, then up at the pale sickle blade of a moon. 'Or maybe it was *my* punishment – for failing to stop him.'

'You were too young.'

'Don't underestimate the power of a daughter over her father.' She paused, pensive. 'I knew some of them – quite well, in fact, and I stood by and watched. There was one . . . near Marop . . . a female, a mother. I called her Sabinetta. She used to break off branches and throw them at us every time we went near. When they finally shot her, she wedged herself in the fork of a durian tree and men had to go up to bring her down.' She gave a small smile. 'They didn't go, not at the first, they thought she was pretending. They do, you know. And they're strong, very strong. There are lots of stories, stories with pythons, crocodiles . . .'

She leaned forward, her eyes gleaming in the candlelight, and Adam caught a brief glimpse of her as a young girl bent forward over a campfire, hanging on every word of the stories as they'd been told to her.

'Nothing in the forest is as strong, that's what the Dayaks say. Maybe they are right, I don't know. But I have seen an orang snap off a branch as thick as your arm like that –'

She twisted her clenched fist in the air. Bony fingers unfolded from the fist, reaching for the bottle of red wine. Adam beat her to it. He was filling her glass when Maria appeared silently from the gloom beyond the candlelight.

She said something to Signora Docci. The words came too fast for Adam to understand, but it sounded like a reprimand. She shot him a withering look as she retired with their plates.

'She's right,' said Signora Docci. 'It is late and I have had a long day.'

Adam rose to help her from her chair.

'Thank you,' she said, leaning on her new cane with its death's-head pommel. 'It is strange that you asked about the skulls.'

'Why?'

'Because I went to see her today – Sabinetta. She is in the Zoological Museum in Florence.'

Adam offered to accompany her upstairs to her room. 'Stay,' she insisted, 'finish the wine. Maybe Maria will make you a coffee if you ask her nicely . . . although somehow I doubt it,' she added with a smile. 'Goodnight, Adam.'

'Goodnight.'

She took his hand and squeezed it. 'It's a pleasure to have you here.'

He watched her make her way uncertainly across the terrace. She stopped and turned before entering the drawing room.

'I said my father destroyed all his papers. He thought he had. When I realized what he was going to do, I hid an album of photographs. If you're interested, it's in the cabinet under the shelves in the library, the ones near the study. The key is behind a copy of your Mr Milton's *Paradise Lost*.'

Which is exactly where Adam found it twelve hours later, after his solitary Sunday morning breakfast on the terrace.

There were several photograph albums in the cabinet, but it stood out for its superior age, its tooled leather binding scuffed and cracked. The photos inside also betrayed their age, moments in time trapped in washed-out sepia tones. Many were blurred, the faces shrouded in ghostly veils where the subjects had moved. This was almost always the case with Signora Docci's father – a sign perhaps of the impatience she had hinted at over dinner the night before. She, on the other hand – in her pinafore dress, bonnet and lace-up boots, already tall for her tender years – had obviously taken the photographers' instructions to heart. In every shot she stood as rigid as a marionette, her arms hanging limp at her sides. He recognized her immediately from the penetrating gaze of the wide-spaced eyes fixed directly on the camera lens.

The photographs were arranged chronologically, beginning with the boat-trip over. In one, a rangy, fair-headed young man in a dark suit and a high collar was standing proudly on the deck beside a louvred cabinet raised on legs. This could only have been Walter F. Peploe, the Scottish meteorologist destined for a watery grave, and it occurred to Adam that there must be a whole other family out there somewhere who would cherish the photograph far more than the Doccis ever had.

It was hard to imagine Walter F. Peploe reciprocating the interest shown in him by 'Nanny' as she appeared in the photographs – short, solid, and with the suspicion of a moustache – even if Signora Docci had strongly hinted at some kind of tryst between the pair.

One of the few photos with a handwritten caption showed her father gathered with a group of other European gentlemen, all dressed in evening wear and standing beside a billiard table at somewhere called the Harmonie Club in Batavia. He was one of only two men whose hair wasn't close-shorn. His dense, drooping moustache concealed his mouth and lent his face a grave mien, although his eyes suggested he was smiling, unlike his companions.

From the moment they arrived in Borneo, he was only ever to be seen in a white suit, usually worn with a black neck-tie. He was a slight and vaguely comical figure, even when brandishing a rifle over some dead animal. Signora Docci's mother stood a good half-head taller, and her ever-present parasol only accentuated the height difference, making her tower over him. Standing together in front of a surprisingly modern-looking bungalow, they looked more like two parties to a property sale than husband and wife.

There was a run of what appeared to be pointless photos taken from the ground looking up into the tree-tops. Closer inspection revealed spindly figures hanging from branches high above. Brought to earth, the orang-utans were impressive creatures, even in death – far more impressive than Signora Docci's father or any of the grinning, sharp-featured natives invariably gathered around. One giant specimen, shaggy-haired and barrel-chested, had been lashed by its wrists to the rail of a veranda, crucified for the camera. The vast span of its arms exceeded the height of the tallest man present by a good two feet. Its dislocated jaw animated its face. The unfortunate creature seemed to be giving a lop-sided laugh at its own predicament.

Unsettled by the image, Adam skimmed the remaining pages. He closed the album, thought about replacing it, then removed the others and laid them on the floor in front of him. He could permit himself a quick look. There was still no sign of Maria, and Signora Docci was obviously sleeping late after her trying day.

There were four albums in total, each covering a two- or three-year period between the 1890s and the 1920s. All were a testament to the privileged existence enjoyed by the Doccis. There were race meetings and open-topped road-sters and summer holidays at exclusive beachside hotels. There were walks in the Alps, trips in Venetian gondolas, and camel-rides at the pyramids.

Adam flipped through the albums twice. The second time, he arranged them chronologically and studied the photographs more carefully. He watched Signora Docci grow from a gawky teenager into an elegant young woman, a wife, and finally a mother. It was the first time he had seen any photos of Emilio, and they contradicted his private theory that first-born sons were generally shorter than their younger brothers. Emilio was lean and long-limbed from birth. Facially, he drew more from his mother, inheriting her large eyes and her broad, high cheekbones. These features, combined with his long neck, gave him a faintly startled air, which reminded Adam of something – he couldn't say what exactly – some kind of animal or bird. Maurizio was closer to his father in build and looks: broad-shouldered, square-jawed, with neat, even features. Adam searched for signs of Antonella in her girl-mother Caterina.

There were few, apart from the straight, lustrous hair and traces of the same devilish grin.

The very last photo was a studio portrait of the whole family taken in 1921 in Madrid. The women were seated on a sagging divan, the first soft creases of age also evident in Signora Docci's face. Caterina was seated to her left, glowering in sullen rebellion, a function of her thirteen or fourteen years, or maybe thrown into a mood by her bobbed haircut, which didn't flatter her. The men stood behind: Benedetto – the *pater familias*, his hands gripping the back of the divan in a commanding manner – flanked by his two sons. Maurizio's forehead was stippled with adolescent acne. Emilio's hairline had already receded further than his father's.

Adam stared at the photograph for quite a time. Something about it bothered him. It was a vague and impalpable sensation. This was enough, though, to make him remove the photograph from its gilt corner-mounts. He replaced the albums, locked the cabinet door and made for the study.

He was still poring over the image a short while later when Signora Docci showed up. She entered the study from the back terrace, the approaching tap of her new cane buying him enough time to slip the photo beneath the desk blotter and grab a book lying nearby.

'Good morning,' she said.

'Morning.'

'Did you sleep well?'

'Yes,' he lied.

'It must have been the strong sedative.'

Adam smiled. 'I enjoyed your stories. Really.'

She was wearing walking shoes, dusty from use, and there was a wine bottle in her free hand.

'You've been out?' he asked.

'A walk. A good walk. It's nice to see.'

'What?'

'They can't quite believe it – me, on my feet again. Maybe they're pretending, but they seem to be happy.'

'I'm sure they're not.'

'Pretending or happy?'

He smiled.

She placed the bottle of wine on the desk. 'For your lunch with Antonella. You haven't forgotten, I hope.'

'No.'

'It's from the cellar – good wine, not our own, don't worry.'

He shed the tie as he entered the garden through the yew hedge. The jacket followed when he reached the base of the amphitheatre. He opened the notebook and pulled out the photograph of the Doccis, gazing up at Flora on her pedestal, calling on her to help him.

He felt foolish appealing to a lump of stone, but he had brought the photograph with him for a reason. Why deny it? There was something about the garden that made him view the world differently, even act differently. He could feel it now, some kind of energy within him – not anger, not defiance, but something close, something else. Whatever it was, it had been responsible for him blurting out the stuff about fratricide to Maurizio, he knew that, just as he knew that what he'd seen in Maurizio's eyes was the cold clutch of fear, of guilt.

Ten minutes later there were two cigarette stubs on the stone bench, and the photograph was still mocking him. He left abruptly, frustrated, making for the bottom of the garden, opting for the pathway that ran through the woods via the glade of Adonis.

A light breeze rustled the leaves high overhead, the first hint of wind in almost a week. The grateful shade fell away as he entered the clearing, the high noonday sun beating down on the circular patch of pasture. He made for the statue at its centre.

Venus was frozen in the act of stooping towards her dead love, reaching for him with her left hand. Adonis lay sprawled on his back, limbs splayed, eyes closed, his mouth agape, as if some dreadful cry had died on his lips with his last breath. He was still clutching his bow, the weapon which had failed to protect him against the wild boar while out hunting. The file compiled by Signora Docci's father only made mention of a wild animal. Ovid himself had been more specific: Adonis was gored to death by a wild boar.

He was pleased he'd gone to the source. Maybe there was some kind of symbolic association with the Docci family. A boar figured prominently in their coat of arms.

A noise drew his gaze from the statue. The tree-tops ringing the glade were being swept by a hurrying little breeze. It rose quickly to become a wind, firm and steady. The tree-tops swayed like drunken lovers on a dance floor. Then they dipped their heads in unison before a sustained gust, and a few moments later the wind fell to earth, patting down the parched grass and tousling Adam's hair with its warm hand.

He felt a sudden sense of unease, strong enough to drive him from the glade. Regaining the pathway at the tree-line, he glanced over his shoulder, half-expecting to see someone keeping Venus and Adonis company. But they were alone.

Antonella had given him directions. A track ran close to the bottom of the memorial garden, and if he followed it to the south, it would eventually climb through olive groves and past her farmhouse.

He found the track without difficulty, but something impelled him to double back to the Temple of Echo and take one last look up the garden. The pasture climbed gently towards the grotto with its bodyguard of cypresses. From here the ground rose sharply to the amphitheatre – Flora pearl-white in her concave shell, the triumphal arch looming above her on the crest.

The wind had swelled and was now sweeping straight down the valley towards him, pouring in a constant flow, like invisible liquid. He stood stock-still, staring into it, letting it wash past him into the trees. His eyes started to water. He blinked a few times.

That's when it came to him.

Gregor Mendel.

A name from his school days. Biology classes. Mendelian genetics.

He pulled the photograph of the Doccis from the note-book. His eyes darted across it – father to mother then each of the children in turn.

Emilio, Maurizio and Caterina all shared their parents' obsidian eyes; but even if they hadn't, even if one of them had been born with blue eyes, that would have been okay by Mendel. It would simply mean that both parents carried a recessive gene for blue eyes, which, if combined, would make for a blue-eyed child. They were more likely to have dark-eyed offspring, but it was possible. It was impossible, on the other hand, for two blue-eyed parents – each carrying a double-dose of the recessive gene – to produce a dark-eyed child.

If Adam was right, then the same rule held for another physical trait: the earlobes. Unattached earlobes, where there was an indentation between the bottom of the ear and the side of the face, symbolized the dominant gene. Which meant, therefore, that two 'recessive' people with earlobes directly attached to the side of the face could not have a child with unattached earlobes. It seemed ridiculous, but it was true.

He checked the photo one more time.

There was no mistake. Emilio Docci was the only one in the family whose earlobes hung free. Not dramatically so. But it strongly suggested that he was not his parent's son.

No, it was possible to be more precise.

The clear physical resemblance between Emilio and Signora Docci placed her maternity beyond doubt. It followed, therefore, that Emilio was not his father's son, or rather, that he had not sprung from the loins of the man standing to his left, the man gripping the back of the divan in a parody of patriarchal self-importance.

The unavoidable question had barely formed itself in his head when the answer came to him. Maybe it had always been there. Maybe it was written in his conversations with Signora Docci, but he had failed to read it.

159

The air of mild alarm conferred on Emilio by his large eyes and his long neck had struck a dim note of recognition in Adam, but he was wrong to have ascribed these traits to a passing similarity with some indeterminate creature or bird. He had seen the look before, yes, but it had been in an old framed photograph hanging on the wall of a room in Cambridge: a photograph of the Jesus College rowing crew, eight gangling young men clutching their oars like pikestaffs.

'Don't be too impressed,' Professor Leonard had said to him when he remarked on the photograph. 'I'm not sure we ever won a single race. In fact, I know we didn't.'

17

Adam was late for lunch, not that it mattered. The other guests were considerably later, and Antonella herself was running well behind schedule. In fact, she was foraging around in a sorry-looking vegetable patch beside the farmhouse when he appeared up the track. She was wearing a crumpled T-shirt, shorts and no shoes. She looked magnificent. And angry.

'Someone has been stealing my tomatoes.'

It was hard to imagine anyone wanting to steal her tomatoes; they were so small and pitiful.

'Forgive them. They must really be in need.'

Antonella's affronted scowl softened to a smile and she laughed.

It was a narrow house built around two sides of an open yard paved with bricks. On the third side rose a barn, connected to the house by a high wall with an arched gateway bearing a carved escutcheon of the Docci family with its rampant boar. The stucco on the house had crumbled away in parts to reveal stone walls beneath. An exterior staircase led to the human accommodation on the first floor: 'The animals live downstairs, well, not at the moment.'

The rooms were barely furnished; they didn't require it. The floors, doors, ceilings and walls were all features in their own right, all ancient, all hand-crafted. Her bedroom consisted of little more than a wrought-iron bed, a chest of drawers and a couple of pictures. It was enough. The sight of her discarded nightshirt on the unmade bed was mildly distracting.

A ham was boiling away on the stove in the kitchen, the largest room in the house by some margin. Its beams were browned with age and smoke, and there was a table big enough to plan an invasion on. They weren't going to be eating here, though; they were going to be eating outside. Which is where Adam came in.

His job was to rig up a tarpaulin as a sunshade in the yard. Everything he required was in the barn, including the trestle table and chairs.

Antonella approved of his construction, and once he'd laid the table and folded the napkins and found cushions for some of the chairs, she joined him outside, rewarding him with a glass of the wine he'd brought. She examined the label approvingly before she poured.

'I thought you were a student.'

'Grandmother's best.'

'To Grandmother,' she said, offering her glass to be clinked.

'Grandmother. May she live to be a hundred.'

'Oh, don't worry, she will. Maurizio is convinced of it.'

'Maurizio?'

She smiled enigmatically.

'What?' demanded Adam.

'He is a bit nervous, I think. No one knows what her plans are now that she has . . . come to life again. He has waited a long time for the villa. He thought it would be his when *Nonno* died.'

'I hope he doesn't blame me.'

'You?'

He told her how Maurizio had sought him out in the garden with his concerns about his mother. He told her he had detected a degree of antagonism on Maurizio's part, although he didn't reveal that he had repaid like with like. He also mentioned the pain-killers, reckoning she had a right to know. Antonella seemed more surprised by the fact that Maria had shared the information about the doctor's visit with Maurizio.

'She doesn't like Maurizio.'

'Or maybe she's just genuinely concerned for your grandmother.'

'Maybe.'

'I know I am. She could be running herself into the ground.'

'If she is, nothing will stop her.'

'That's very fatalistic.'

The slight barb wasn't lost on Antonella. Her eyes fastened on to him, dark and hard.

'I love my grandmother, but I also know her well.'

They were rescued by the sound of an approaching vehicle. It blew into the yard in a cloud of white dust: one car, three couples crammed into it. The yard was soon filled with the sounds of laughter.

Two hours later, it was still echoing off the walls. No amount of food or wine – and both kept rolling down the staircase from the house – could dampen it. They even played a game of hoops in between two of the courses. The game was a gift to Antonella from her brother Edoardo, a private joke lost on the rest of the company, and one the siblings refused to share.

Edoardo had his sister's jet-black hair and olive skin. He was a year or so younger than her, big and ebullient, humorous and shrewd. It was hard not to be sucked along in his slipstream. The only person who seemed impervious to its pull was his girlfriend Grazia – a fellow law student. She was also the only person who didn't speak English, not that this stopped her trying to speak it, and at the breakneck speed she spoke her own language. The result was a tumbling Babel of words, most of them French. Whenever Edoardo tried to correct her, she would round on him and say, '*Zitto! Capisce. Non è vero, Adamo?*'

'Shut up. He understands. Don't you, Adam?'

To which Adam would invariably reply, 'Absolutely.'

'Absolutely' became something of a calling cry. It started when Enrico, newly wed to Venetian Claudia with the corn-flower-blue eyes, was offered a top-up of wine. 'Absolutely,' he replied. And it went from there.

Italy is changing fast now that we've joined the Common Market. Absolutely. Domenico Modugno should have won the Eurovision Song Contest with '*Nel Blu Dipinto di Blu*'. Absolutely.

The word only lost its currency when, as the coffee hit the table, someone remarked that the Christian Democrat Party was riddled with former Fascists.

'Be careful what you say,' chipped in the cartoonist who wanted to be a painter, 'their uncle was a Fascist, was he not?'

It was Edoardo who replied. 'Absolutely. And it was Fascists who killed him. So what does that tell you?'

The cartoonist apologized for the comment, was forgiven, and the word didn't rear its head again. The mood remained buoyant, but Adam now found himself struggling to keep up. The banter and the bonhomie had been welcome diversions; they had allowed him to forget about the photograph tucked between the pages of his notebook lying on the sideboard in the kitchen. But now that Emilio had barged his way into the conversation, back into Adam's thoughts, there was no ignoring him.

While the others rattled on around the table, his mind wandered elsewhere – to Gregor Mendel and recessive genes and earlobes and the old photo of the rowing crew on the wall of Professor Leonard's rooms in Jesus College. He tried to prevent them straying further afield, into darker territory, where his conversations with Fausto lurked.

He chipped in from time to time, covering for his distraction, and when the other guests finally left, he was relieved to be forced back to the world around him, pumping hands and kissing cheeks and waving as the car disappeared up the hard white track to San Casciano, carried on a billowing dust-cloud.

He said he'd help tidy up, an offer gratefully accepted by Antonella. They worked hard, methodically, until all that remained was a pile of dripping crockery on the draining board and a red-wine stain on the bricks in the yard, where a glass had been toppled.

They retired to a makeshift wooden bench on a grassy rise beside the barn. It was a calm and peaceful spot, the shifting shadows retouching the landscape as the sun slowly dropped away to the west.

'What a place to live,' said Adam. 'You're very lucky.'

'Oh, I pay for it. The estate needs all the money it can get.'

'Things are bad?'

'Not just here – everywhere.'

She explained that the family that had occupied the house for countless generations had recently moved on, abandoning the countryside for the town, as many were now doing. The moment new tenants were found, she'd be out.

He was surprised to hear that the estate was run on a sharecropping basis – *mezzadria* – an arrangement whereby a family received a house and some land rent-free from the Doccis in exchange for half of the produce generated.

'It sounds almost feudal.'

'That's because it is – from the Middle Ages – but things are changing now. There are politicians in Rome who say *mezzadria* must go. If it does, everything here will change. My grandmother worries a lot. I tell her not to. Maurizio is rich, he will make things work.'

'What does he do?'

'He buys and sells things.'

'What kind of things?'

'The kind that make a profit. He also has two factories in Prato, for clothes. He has made a lot of money since the war.'

Adam hesitated. 'What was Emilio like?'

'Emilio? Why do you ask?'

'Just curious. He was mentioned at lunch.'

She helped herself to another of his cigarettes. 'Well, he *was* a Fascist, it's true. Many people were, my grandparents too, at the beginning. They stopped believing.' She stared off into the distance. 'I was young, but I remember him. He was always reading books. And he made me laugh. He made us all laugh.' She smiled wistfully. 'The funny Fascist.'

'How did they get on, Emilio and Maurizio?'

Her glance said it all: What's it to you?

He was pushing too hard; he needed to tread carefully.

'I mean, their politics were different. Maurizio was a partisan, no?'

Was it motive enough for murder?

'Who told you that?'

'A chap called Fausto, from San Casciano.'

She didn't know him, although the name rang a vague bell.

'It's true, Maurizio was a partisan, and a socialist. He claims he still is a socialist.' There was a note of good-natured cynicism in her voice. 'My grandmother says he fought the Germans because he was always fighting, even when he was a boy. He hates it when she says that.'

But he didn't fight them the night they killed Emilio, did he?

Adam kept this observation to himself, as he did the other questions hammering away in his head. Why had her grandfather sealed off the top floor? As some kind of

167

shrine? Shrines were conceived to be visited; they were places you went to in order to pay your respects. Why close a door and lock it? Why oblige your family to live with the painful memory, rather than allowing it to dissipate over the years? What had Maria said about that deserted floor frozen in time? 'It sits over the house like a curse.'

Dusk was falling when he finally left. Antonella said she'd accompany him back to the villa; she'd hardly seen her grandmother all weekend.

They took a path that wound through the olive grove beneath the farmhouse. It was her path, she said. It hadn't existed a year ago; hers were the only feet to have beaten it into existence. The air grew cooler as they worked their way down through the serried ranks of trees. Fireflies bobbed in the gathering gloom, and the smell of wild herbs came in faint waves: thyme, rosemary and mint. They barely spoke. When Antonella lost her footing on a steep bank, she gripped his arm to steady herself and his hand instinctively went to the gentle curve at the base of her back.

'Thank you,' she said softly as they released each other.

His feeling of contentment faded a touch when they entered the memorial garden. He told her about the unnatural wind that had dropped to earth earlier in the day, rushing through the garden.

'Yes, it happens sometimes in summer. I don't know why.' They walked on a little way. 'The breath of the gods,' she said absently. 'That's what the Greeks called the wind.'

They stopped at the foot of the amphitheatre and looked up at Flora, the fireflies fussing around her like solicitous consorts.

He felt a sudden urge to share her secret, *their* secret. He fought the impulse, but only momentarily.

He told Antonella everything he knew. He told her about the dark wood and the triumphal arch and its anagrammatic inscription of INFERNO. He told her about Dante's nine circles of Hell and the second circle of the adulterers. He told it as it was, without embellishment. And when he was finished he felt as if a great weight had been lifted from his shoulders.

She didn't speak at first. When she did, it was in Italian. '*Incredibile.*'

'Maybe I'm wrong.'

'No,' she said with quiet conviction.

'I can't figure out the rest of the cycle. It doesn't make sense.'

'You will. It will.'

'Something bad happened. I can feel it. I just can't see it.'

She placed her hand on his arm and squeezed. '*Bravo, Adamo.* Really. *Bravo.*'

He wasn't good with compliments, but he knew what to do when he saw her head drawing closer, her neck arching, her lips reaching for his.

They kissed gently. Then again, less gently, their tongues searching each other out. He felt the heat coming off her, and the twin pressure of her breasts against his chest.

When they finally drew apart, she said in a whisper, 'I told myself I wouldn't.'

'That's interesting, I told myself I would.'

He could just make out her smile in the deepening darkness.

They were still holding hands when they left the garden, side-stepping through the yew hedge. They only released each other when, nearing the villa, she stopped to remove a stone from her shoe.

'Why did you tell yourself you wouldn't?'

She slipped her shoe back on and stood upright. 'Because you are going soon.'

'A week.'

'It will only make it worse.'

'But think – what a week.'

He reached for her and she playfully slapped his hand away.

It came at them clear through the still night air – laughter from up at the villa. A devilish cackle. Disturbing if you'd never heard it before. More disturbing if you had.

'Oh Christ.'

'What?' asked Antonella.

'Harry . . .' said Adam, breasting the steps to the back terrace. 'What are you doing here?'

'What does it look like? Having dinner with a beautiful woman.'

Signora Docci smiled indulgently.

'I thought you wouldn't get the money till tomorrow.'

'Arrived the day you sent it.'

Adam tried his best to sound pleased. 'Good.'

'Bad,' said Harry.

'Bad?'

'It's a long story.'

'It is,' said Signora Docci.

Harry turned to her. 'But not uninteresting.'

'No, not uninteresting.'

Oh Christ, thought Adam. 'When did you get here?' he asked, trying to mask the strain in his voice.

'A few hours ago.'

Long enough to have done untold damage.

'Nice lunch?' asked Harry.

'Yes, great – sorry – this is Antonella.'

Harry got to his feet. He was wearing a grubby Aertex shirt, khaki army shorts that reached well below the knee, and his feet were squeezed into black gym plimsolls, one of them worn away at the end so that his big toe poked through. He stooped to kiss Antonella's hand, considerately removing his cigarette before he did so.

'Antonella,' said Harry.

'Harry,' said Antonella.

'Nice dress.'

'Nice shorts.'

'Thank you. Practical in this heat.'

'Absolutely,' said Antonella, for Adam's benefit.

'Please . . .' said Harry, pulling a chair back for her.

'Thank you.'

'Have you eaten?' Signora Docci asked.

Adam held up his hands in surrender. 'Enough for a couple of days.'

'Antonella is an excellent cook.'

'She certainly is,' Adam replied, wondering for a moment if he was trapped in a Jane Austen novel.

Fortunately, at that moment Harry chirped up, bringing them back to some kind of reality, 'So's Maria.'

Maria had just stepped from the villa, carrying a tray. Harry adopted an exaggerated Italian accent. '*Vitello con sugo di* . . .'

'*Pomodoro,*' said Maria.

'*Pomodoro!*' trumpeted Harry. '*Magnifico!*'

Suddenly, the Jane Austen novel didn't seem such a bad prospect. Better that than Harry's impression of Mr Mannucci who used to sell them ice creams from the back of his van when they still lived in Kennington.

Maria produced a rare smile, surprisingly coy. '*Grazie,*' she said, clearing away the empty plates.

'Harry was just telling me a joke,' said Signora Docci.

She looked invigorated, and maybe a little drunk. Or maybe it's the pain-killers, thought Adam.

'You were in the English Channel,' she went on, 'in the seventeenth century.'

'Right, that's right, so anyway . . . the captain of the naval frigate raises the telescope to his eye and he sees five pirate ships on the horizon, bearing down on them. "Bring me my red shirt," he says to his lieutenant. "Your red shirt, sir?" "Just do it, man."

'Anyway, they engage the pirate ships and a fierce battle ensues. The captain's in the thick of it, fighting hand-to-hand, running pirates through all over the place. And against terrible odds they capture all five of the pirate ships. When it's over and everyone's celebrating, the lieutenant asks the captain why he sent for his red shirt. The captain says it's so if he was wounded the men wouldn't see the blood and wouldn't lose heart. Everyone cheers – "What a hero our captain is."'

Harry took a short draw on his cigarette then crushed it in the ashtray.

'So . . .' he went on, a sparkle in his eye, 'a few days later they're still patrolling in the Channel when another shout comes down from the crow's nest. The captain raises the telescope to his eye and this time he sees *twenty* pirate ships on the horizon, bearing down on them fast. The captain lowers his glass and turns to his lieutenant. "Lieutenant," he says. "Yes, Captain?" "Bring me my brown trousers."'

In Harry's defence, he never laughed at his own jokes. But then again, not many other people did, either. This one was different, though, this one wasn't half-bad. Even Adam found himself chuckling, partly from relief that the punch line hadn't been cruder.

Harry turned to Adam. 'That one got them,' he said.

Signora Docci and Antonella were still laughing when Maria appeared with the cheese platter.

The rest of dinner was an ordeal. When Adam looked at Signora Docci, he saw Professor Leonard; when he looked at Antonella, he saw himself kissing her in the garden; and when he looked at Harry, he found himself wondering if one of them had been adopted.

Harry dominated, he seized the steering wheel and told you to sit back and enjoy the ride, because that's what you were going on, whether you liked it or not. Strangely, neither Signora Docci nor Antonella appeared to mind.

Harry announced that he'd come to Italy to visit the Venice Biennale, the international art festival. This was news to Adam, and not unwelcome news – it meant

Harry had somewhere else to go to. British artists were a world force to be reckoned with right now, Harry insisted, especially in the field of sculpture, *his* field. Lynn Chadwick had snatched the sculpture prize from under Giacometti's nose at the last Biennale, and there were many British contemporaries right up there with him, worthy heirs to Henry Moore and Barbara Hepworth: Meadows, Frink, Thornton, Hoskin – mere names until he brought them to life with his vivid descriptions of their work.

These sculptors constituted a new movement, he claimed. Not for them the bald abstraction of their predecessors. Their creations were rooted in a post-war world of broken buildings and broken people. Their language was one of terror and trepidation. They tore into the human form, flaying it, tearing it limb from limb, discarding what they didn't want. And when they were done, they found themselves presenting to the world an army of creatures – part man, part beast, and sometimes part machine. As one of Harry's teachers at Corsham had said to him: 'When you've seen the inside of a Sherman tank after a direct hit, it all becomes the same thing.'

It was a Europe-wide movement – a new geometry of fear – and as long as there were wars or even the prospect of them, it would always have meaning.

Adam had sat through the speech many times before, but it was somehow more persuasive this time, more heartfelt. Antonella and Signora Docci certainly seemed convinced by it, firing off questions that Harry eagerly answered. And as Adam sat and watched, he felt a rare twinge of pride in his brother. It was tempered slightly by

174

jealousy: that Harry could care so passionately about the path he'd chosen for himself.

When Signora Docci finally retired upstairs, Antonella took it as her cue to head home. She couldn't be persuaded to stay; she had a week of hard work ahead of her. This wasn't what Adam wanted to hear, but he had to make do with a surreptitious squeeze of his arm when she kissed him goodnight – recognition of what had passed between them in the garden.

Thrown back on each other's company, Harry nodded over his shoulder at the villa looming above them.

'Must be a shocker to heat in winter.'

'Must be.'

'What happened to her face?'

'Car accident.'

'Are you screwing her?'

'No.'

'Mmmmm.'

'I'm not screwing her, Harry.'

Harry studied him with a sporting eye. 'I believe you.'

'That's a huge relief to me.'

'And Signora Fanelli?' asked Harry, fluttering his fingers in the air. 'At the Pensione Amorini?'

Adam felt a hand clutch at his heart. How the hell did Harry even know her name? Then he remembered; he had told Harry to go to the pensione and ask for directions to the villa.

'Don't be ridiculous.'

'She's bloody gorgeous. And I reckon you're her type.'

'Tell me, Harry, was it one or two minutes you spent in her company?'

'Aloof. Like her. Two dark horses. Cavorting together. Yes, I can see it.'

'Well, you're wrong. That famous sixth sense of yours must have deserted you.'

Harry weighed Adam's words. 'Maybe. Yeah. Come to think of it, imagine . . . it'd be like screwing Auntie Joan.'

'She's not *that* old.'

He realized too late that he'd stumbled into one of Harry's well-laid conversational traps.

'I knew it!' Harry trumpeted.

'Keep it down, that's Signora Docci's bedroom.'

Harry glanced up at the loggia. 'What, not her too!?'

'Harry . . .' hissed Adam.

Harry beamed. 'You little devil. She's gorgeous, dirty too, from the look of her.'

Adam wasn't going to be drawn on this.

'Come on – details.'

'No.'

'Something. Anything.'

'Has it been that long?'

Harry gave a short laugh. 'Quite a while, as it happens.'

Harry was curious to know if Adam intended to tell Gloria. Not for the first time, Gloria was referred to as 'the girl who likes killing animals'.

'Her family hunts and shoots.'

'And yours lives in Purley, otherwise known as the arse-hole of Croydon.'

'So?'

'So are you going to let her know?'

'She ended it.'

Harry nodded a couple of times. 'Well, I can't say I'm upset. I never liked her.'

'I know. You told her.'

'Did I?'

'You don't remember? She remembers.'

'Well, who cares now? She's out of your life. And you, Paddler, have finally slept with a good-looking woman.'

'Gloria was good looking.'

Harry heaved a weary sigh. 'It's like parents and babies. They're too close. They can't see just how ugly the little buggers are.' He lit a cigarette. 'Love isn't just blind – it blinds.'

'That's very profound. Who said it?'

'James Bond, I think.'

'In a rare moment of melancholy.'

Harry laughed, but Adam knew better than to relax his guard. Sure enough, Harry nudged the conversation back to Adam's other university friends.

'Come on, Paddler, face the facts – you're not one of them. They're all so bloody . . . well, rich.'

'They're still people.'

'They're people who like people like them. Oh, it's okay now, you're a good-looking boy with half a brain and half a sense of humour. But that bloke you hang out with, what's his name? Big ears, windpipe like a fireman's hose, father owns half of Herefordshire . . .'

'Tarquin.'

'Right, Tarquin – can't you see he's humouring you? You're his piece of entertainment, the middle-class boy made good.'

'You met him once.'

177

'I'm telling you, he'll drop you as soon as he's back in the real world, and you're selling insurance.'

'I'm going to work at Lloyd's.'

'Selling insurance.'

Adam struggled to control his temper. 'You know nothing about my relationships with my friends.'

'I've seen all I want to.'

'You can't just write off two years of my life like that.'

'Why not? You did.'

'Fuck off, Harry.'

Harry leaned forward and stubbed out his cigarette. 'I might just take you up on that. I haven't slept in days and I've got an early start.'

'You're leaving?'

'You wish. No, I thought I'd have a slog round Florence.'

Heading upstairs together, Harry asked if he could borrow some of Adam's clothes. He tried on some trousers, a shirt and a linen jacket. 'Christ,' he said, checking himself in the wardrobe mirror, 'it's little Lord Fauntleroy.' He also said, 'I'll need some cash.'

'I just sent you some!'

'Believe me, you don't want to know.'

'Believe me, I do.'

'The Swiss girl came back.'

'You're right, I don't want to know.'

As Harry was leaving his room, Adam asked, 'Why are you really here, Harry? In Italy?'

Harry hesitated. 'I'm not sure you're ready to hear it.'

'I say, Holmes, not the Giant Rat of Sumatra?'

Harry's blank expression broke into a smile. It was a private joke, a cause of much amusement to them as boys:

a reference to a Conan Doyle short story in which Sherlock Holmes makes passing mention to Watson of a terrible incident in his past involving 'the Giant Rat of Sumatra . . . a story for which the world is not yet prepared'.

'Demmit, Watson,' snapped Harry, 'I said never to mention the Giant Rat of Sumatra.'

18

True to his word, Harry was up early. In fact, he'd already left the villa by the time Adam awoke.

The prospect of a full day free from Harry's unpredictable presence was a big relief. He needed time and space to concentrate. His work on the garden had ground to an almost complete standstill in the past few days.

He had read deep into the night in order to finish *The Divine Comedy*, rising up through Paradise with Dante to the poet's final, blinding vision of the universe bound together by God's love. Adam had experienced no such epiphany, though, no Damascene revelation. As far as he could tell, there were no further associations between the poem and the memorial garden, aside from a brief mention of Apollo just after Dante and Beatrice have made their ascent from Purgatory to Paradise and Dante calls on the sun god to help him in the last stages of his journey.

Any hopes that he would see things differently in the morning soon vanished. After breakfast he read through his copious notes, searching for missed connections, but drew a glaring blank. Heading for the garden, he barged through the gap in the yew hedge and made a brisk tour, defiantly disinterested. This slightly curious logic – that if he treated the place with indifference it might be more inclined to speak to him – proved unsound. If anything, he found it more inert, more stubbornly unresponsive, than he'd ever known it to be. Even the statues seemed bored by their roles, like a troupe of jaded actors at the end of a long run.

Completing the circuit, he stopped at the grotto and entered. The low morning sunlight slanted through the entrance, dispersing the Stygian gloom. Apollo, Daphne and Peneus shone white as weathered bone against the rock-encrusted wall, a moment of drama trapped in marble by an unknown and rather heavy-handed sculptor.

Peneus seemed strangely uninvolved with the scene unfolding above him, quite content where he was, sprawled along the rim of the marble basin, cradling his water urn. His expression was hardly that of a man who has just answered his daughter's plea to turn her into a laurel tree. Rather, he wore a look of weary resignation, the sort of look worn by Adam's father when asked to perform some tedious domestic chore.

As for Daphne, her face suggested there were far worse fates to suffer than metamorphosis. She was frozen in the act of turning her head to look behind her at the pursuing figure of Apollo. Maybe her expression was intended as one of welcome release from unwelcome advances, but there was something ecstatic in the curl of her lips which implied she was actually enjoying herself.

He studied Apollo carefully – Apollo, his last remaining

link to *The Divine Comedy*. He was reaching for Daphne, but the gesture was hardly fraught with desperation and hopelessness, as it was in Bernini's famous sculpture of the same subject in the Villa Borghese. In fact, here in the grotto, they looked more like an amorous young couple playing tag in the woods.

His gaze dropped to the unicorn, its head bowed towards the empty marble trough. He ran his fingers over the stump of its missing horn, his mind turning to the drawing he'd come across in the papers gathered together by Signora Docci's father. It was a pen-and-ink sketch of the grotto executed in the late sixteenth century, therefore almost contemporaneous with the construction of the garden. The anonymous artist wasn't exactly overburdened with talent, but it was pretty evident that the unicorn had been missing its horn even way back then.

Was it possible it had never had a horn? If so, what did this mean? If a unicorn dipping its horn into the water signified the purity of the source feeding the garden, what did a hornless unicorn signify? Impure water, not fit to drink?

Instinct told him that nothing in the grotto had been left to chance, that each and every one of its peculiarities was a necessary part of another story buried away in the composition, according to Federico Docci's instructions.

The harder he strained to see it, though, the more it receded from him. In his frustration, he found himself talking to the sculptures, exhorting them to share their secret. He was still doing this when a shift in the shadows at his feet announced the appearance of someone in the entrance behind him.

Maria had been out gathering wild flowers. An unruly bunch of them lay in the shallow wicker basket hanging at her elbow. Her eyes ranged over the interior, establishing that – yes – Adam was alone. And – yes – he was obviously losing his marbles.

'Another beautiful day,' said Adam.

'Yes.'

'Not as humid as yesterday.'

'No.' Maria raised the basket. 'I have to put these in water.'

Adam winced as she left, a flush of embarrassment warming his cheeks, sweat pearling his forehead. He tried and failed to see the humour of the situation. Maria obviously experienced less difficulty, because a moment later he heard the dim but unmistakable sound of laughter.

He waited a while before creeping from the grotto, eyes screwed up against the glare. He lit a cigarette. It was his first of the day and he was hit by a wave of light-headedness.

He glared at Flora – twisted on her plinth, perched high above her kingdom – and he found himself thinking that she was to blame. The goddess had issued an edict of silence to her subjects; she had commanded them to shun his advances. Why, though? Why allow him to glimpse a part of the story then shut him out?

Only one answer presented itself to him.

Okay, he thought, let's do it your way.

He was nearing the villa, still working out how best to broach the sensitive subject with Signora Docci, when he saw her on the lower terrace, standing at the balustrade, looking out over the plunging olive grove. He wondered if Maria had told her about his solitary rant in the grotto.

Her face as he approached suggested she knew nothing of the incident. 'Good morning,' she said.

'Good morning.'

'Another beautiful day. Not as humid as yesterday.'

His exact words to Maria in the grotto.

Adam gave a weak smile.

'Are you feeling better?' she enquired.

'I was feeling fine then, and I am now.'

'I have a cousin – Alessandra – they took her away for the same thing.'

She was clearly going to have her moment of amusement at his expense, whether he liked it or not.

'Talking to sculptures?'

'Paintings.'

'Waste of time,' said Adam. 'They've very little to say for themselves.'

She laughed. 'Where's Harry?'

'He went into Florence.'

'He's a strange young man.'

'He had a difficult birth.'

'Really?'

'No. But he's always been like that, as long as I can remember. He doesn't care what people think of him. He just, well . . . is Harry.'

'Is he a good sculptor?'

'I don't know. I suppose. They asked him to stay on and teach when he graduated last year.'

'He must have something, then.'

'Yes, a strange desire to spend the rest of his life welding rusty pieces of metal together.'

184

It was a cheap swipe, revenge for Harry's assault on him the night before, but Signora Docci was amused.

'You remind me of Crispin when he was younger. He also made me laugh.'

It was the opportunity he'd been waiting for.

'I wanted to ask you about him.'

'About Crispin?'

'It's a personal question.'

'Oh.'

'Very personal.'

She took up her new cane, crossed to one of the benches and lowered herself on to it. 'On one condition – I'm allowed to ask you a personal question first.'

'Okay.'

'Are you falling in love with Antonella?'

'No,' he replied after a moment. 'I think I already have.'

'Why?'

'That's two questions.'

'I'll allow you two.'

'I don't know why. I hardly know her.'

'No, you don't.'

'It's inexplicable.'

'Physical attraction – that's inexplicable.'

'It's more than that.' Trying to pin it down in words was impossible. 'I can see myself being happy with her.'

'And if I told you she had made a number of young men quite unhappy?'

'I'd ask myself what your reasons were for saying it.'

'You don't believe me?'

'I didn't say that. But maybe I'm young enough to make mistakes and still survive.'

'Mistakes at any age can colour a life for ever. Just one mistake.'

'Emilio, for example?'

There, it was done now, there was no turning back.

'Emilio?' she said warily.

'Was he your son?'

'Of course he was my son.'

'I mean . . . with Professor Leonard.'

Signora Docci turned and stared off into the distance. When she looked back at him he saw that her eyes were moist with tears. Her voice, however, remained surprisingly level, devoid of emotion.

'I would like you to leave.'

'Leave?'

'Today.'

'You mean . . .?'

'Yes. I want you to leave the villa.'

Adam could hear the blood beating in his ears. It was about all he could hear.

'I'm sorry if I've offended you.'

She looked away. 'Just go.'

He shaped the snowdrift of papers on the desk in the study into ordered piles. It took three trips to carry everything upstairs to his bedroom. He did so in a daze.

He pulled his suitcases out from under the bed and began to pack. At a certain moment he had to stop. He went to the open window and smoked two cigarettes in quick succession, working through the consequences of his behaviour.

The Pensione Amorini was out of the question; too close

186

to home. He'd take a room in Florence, pick up his photos, maybe stay a day or two. Shit – Harry. He'd completely forgotten about Harry. He'd have to wait at the bottom of the driveway for Harry to return from town. What would he tell him? The truth? He couldn't tell him the truth: that they were without a bed that night because he'd felt compelled by a statue of a classical goddess to ask probing and impertinent questions about their hostess' dead son.

His only comfort was that, as explanations went, it wasn't so far removed from some he'd heard from Harry over the years. Harry would probably just shrug and ask him where the nearest bar was.

Maybe he'd go to Venice with Harry. Why not? They'd never been travelling together.

He was still groping for empty consolations when he heard a light knock at the door.

'Yes?'

It was Signora Docci.

She crossed to the armchair near the fireplace and subsided weakly into it.

'Emilio wasn't a mistake,' she said. 'I knew exactly what I was doing. Even if Crispin didn't.' She paused. 'We were in love. I can still feel the force of it. It was almost violent. What I did . . . what I allowed to happen . . . it made sense at the time, complete sense, in the way that things do to the young. And I was very young – your age. I don't expect you to understand, but Emilio was a gift to myself because I couldn't be with Crispin.'

'Why not?'

'Money, of course. He didn't have any, and Benedetto's

family did. A lot. The estate was in trouble at the time. My father felt bad, I know – he was very fond of Crispin – but he would not allow us to be together.' She lowered her eyes. 'Benedetto was a good man. I have not had a bad life.'

'Did he know?'

'No one did, not even Crispin. I never told him.'

'You never told him?'

She hesitated. 'I think it would have destroyed him. I had just got married when . . . well, when it happened. He was very upset. Ashamed. He liked Benedetto a lot. When Emilio was killed, I wrote him a letter. I tore it up. What good would it have done?' She drew a long breath. 'There, now you know, you have your answer.'

Adam could think of nothing to say.

'How did you guess?' she asked.

He told her about the family photo in the album and about Gregor Mendel and his gene theory of earlobes.

She nodded, impressed. 'I didn't know that,' she said, 'but I'm surprised Benedetto didn't.'

'Maybe he did.'

'If he did, he never told me.'

But maybe he told someone else, Maurizio for example. Maybe Maurizio knew that Emilio was not his true brother.

Signora Docci held out her hand. Adam walked over and took it.

'Don't go,' she said. 'I would like you to stay.'

He should have been relieved – and he was – but there was also a nagging voice in his head telling him to finish packing the suitcases on the bed, to leave Villa Docci far behind him while he still could.

'Are you punishing me now?' she asked, misinterpreting his silence.

'No.'

'I'm sorry; I should not have asked you to go away. I was shocked by your question.'

'And I shouldn't have asked it.'

She took his words as an apology when really they were a reprimand to himself.

19

Do you have everything you need, Signora?

Yes, thank you, Maria. You don't have to tuck me in, I'm not a child.

You've been crying.

It's nothing. Memories. Sentimentality. And you know how I hate sentimentality. Is Harry back from Florence yet?

Not yet.

I hope he's all right.

I don't think you have to worry about that.

No. He's very eccentric, isn't he?

He's too familiar.

You mean he's not afraid of you.

If you say so, Signora.

Oh, I do, Maria, I do. And I think you quite like that. I've had an idea.

Don't change the subject just when I'm beginning to enjoy myself.

They will both need evening wear for the party.

Harry's staying for the party?

That's what he told me at breakfast.

Oh, you had breakfast together, did you?

I was thinking that I could unpack Emilio's suits.

If the moths haven't had them.

I've checked. They haven't.

The legs will need to be taken up.

Not for Adam. A few centimetres for Harry. I'll see to it.

Yes, do that. Goodnight, Maria.

Goodnight, Signora.

Maria . . .

Yes, Signora?

It's a good idea.

20

Adam was woken by the light, the one that lived on his bedside table, the one that was now hovering directly over his head.

He twisted away. 'Jesus . . .' he mumbled into the pillow.

'Yes, it is I, my Son.'

'Fuck off, Harry.'

Harry flopped on to the bed. 'I'm in love,' he announced.

'What's his name?'

'Don't mock. She's Finnish.' He lit a cigarette.

'Finnish?'

'Swedish-Finnish.'

'Swedish-Finnish?'

'Apparently there are lots of them in Finland: Swedish Finns.'

'Oh, for God's sake, Harry.'

'What?'

'Was she related to the Swiss girl in Milan, by any chance?'

'She wasn't after my money.'

'*My* money.'

'Although I did buy her dinner.'

'Oh, that's what's on my jacket.'

'She was very grateful,' said Harry, blowing a perfect smoke ring into the air.

Adam checked his watch – almost two in the morning – and resigned himself to the fact that he wouldn't be going back to sleep any time soon.

'And what does she do, this Swedish Finn?'

'Pretty much anything you ask her to.'

For much of the following day the back of the villa was crawling with men. Electricians laid a giant spider's web of flex as discreetly as possible; an impressive marquee was erected on the lower terrace near the stand of umbrella pines; smaller tents sprang up elsewhere. Maurizio and Chiara had driven up from Florence. They spent much of their time in the company of Signora Docci, deep in discussion with caterers, florists and other official-looking types.

The sound of raised voices would carry into the study from time to time, whenever Signora Docci and Maurizio crossed swords over some detail, which was often, with Chiara doing her best to mediate. At a certain point, Chiara had had enough. Adam knew this because she said as much when she appeared in the study and monopolized an hour of his time. Whatever suspicions he might have harboured about her husband, he liked Chiara. She was warm, frank and irreverent.

'Every year they argue,' she said, lighting her first of many cigarettes. 'Why, I don't know. Everyone will come,

193

everyone will get drunk, and then everyone will go home. Men will meet the lovers of their wives and not know it; women will meet the lovers of their husbands and know it immediately. And lots of people will find new lovers.'

'Sounds like a romantic affair.'

'You are young, not a man still.'

'Not yet a man,' said Adam, correcting her English. 'Or not a man yet.'

'Exactly. Not a man yet. You believe yet.'

'You still believe.'

She gave a dismissive sweep of her arm. '*Ma questa lingua di barbari mi fa caggare.*' Which loosely translated as: This barbarian tongue makes me shit.

'What do I believe?' asked Adam, carrying a smile.

'In life. Love.'

'How do you know?'

'I see you,' she replied, pointing her cigarette at him.

'What do you see?'

'I see a boy like my son, but more intelligent. I see the way you look at Antonella.' Adam rolled his eyes in what he hoped was a convincing display of amused forbearance. 'Yes, I do. And I see that you are . . .' she couldn't find the English word '. . . *un osservatore.*'

'An observer.'

'Yes. You watch. And you think. You are always watching. But you are . . . *passivo.*'

'Passive.'

'Yes, passive.'

'You should meet my ex-girlfriend, you'd have a lot to talk about.'

She laughed, a deep and husky laugh. Adam wondered

if she was naturally blonde. It was hard to tell from her complexion.

'Ah, see,' she exclaimed. 'You are doing it now.'

'What?'

'Watching. What were you thinking?'

'Nothing.'

'Liar.'

'Okay. I was wondering if your blonde hair is natural.'

Chiara leaned across the desk and stubbed out her cigarette in the ashtray. 'I could prove it to you,' she said, 'but I don't know you well enough.'

There was something so matter-of-fact in her delivery that it stripped the statement of all flirtation.

This slightly bizarre exchange didn't colour the rest of their conversation, even if the image it conjured up never quite left Adam's head. Chiara talked about a trip she had once made to Scotland. She liked the Scottish, she said, they were hill-people, like the Italians. Hill-people were different. Hills had names, they had stories attached to them. Peaks and passes had been defended, battles had been fought in their valleys. You couldn't ignore hills, they seeped into your marrow, they became part of you.

Adam put forward a corresponding argument for the flat fenlands of Cambridgeshire, his father's childhood home, but Chiara refused to allow anything to tarnish her theory, tossing his case out of court.

She told him about the rugged countryside near Perugia, where she'd grown up, and where she still had a house. She told him about the other houses they owned, the one in Florence and the one by the sea.

'And how do you feel about moving here?' Adam asked, nudging the conversation his way.

'It is what Maurizio wants, and it is not so far from town.'

'You have your doubts?'

'I have never felt happy here.'

'It's a beautiful place.'

'Yes, I know, of course.'

'Maybe you'll feel better about it when you've re-done the top floor,' remarked Adam.

'Maybe.'

'Maria says you have plans.'

'Of course. It's not natural.' Her eyes flicked towards the ceiling. 'Do you think it's natural?'

'No.'

'It is like . . .'

'What?'

'*E come fosse sempre vivo.*' It's like he's still alive. 'It is not natural. I don't care what Francesca thinks.'

'Apparently it was her husband's wish.'

'Pah!'

It was a surprisingly eloquent utterance, as was the gesture that accompanied it – a dismissive flick of the hand.

'Benedetto was obsessed, everyone said it. *She* said it. Then, when he died, she did nothing.'

'Maybe he asked her not to.'

'That's what she says; before he died he made her promise. But he did not make Maurizio promise.'

'Have you ever been up there?'

'Only one time. When it happened.'

'You were here when it happened?'

'We all were, in the house by the farm.'

They had been celebrating, she explained, a big meal with lots of wine. Maybe a little too much wine, with hindsight – Emilio had a tendency to become belligerent when drunk. They had good cause to be happy, though. The Allies were at the gates of San Casciano and they'd received word from the German officer in command of the villa that he intended to disregard his orders and pull back to the next German line of defence, just south of Florence.

This wasn't cowardice on his part. He knew that to make a stand at Villa Docci would quite possibly result in the destruction of a building he'd come to love. He was a good man, said Chiara, a very tall and very cultivated man from Hamburg, and it was sad that he hadn't outlived the war. She still remembered the tears in his eyes as he was leaving, when Emilio told him that he would always be a welcome guest in their home once the hostilities were over.

They had survived the German occupation and were all in high spirits when the sound of gunfire shattered the silence of the night. They knew that a small detail of men had been left behind to finalize the withdrawal from the villa, and their first thought was that these soldiers had been surprised by an advance party of Allied troops. On rushing outside, however, they also heard the sounds of music and laughter coming from the villa.

It was Emilio's idea to go and investigate: a matter of pride to him. It was chiefly thanks to his subtle diplomacy that Villa Docci and its occupants had come through the various phases of the war unscathed. Despite what people now said – and what she herself had thought at the time – Emilio was never a Fascist, he was a pragmatist. He did whatever was required to protect his family and the estate, happy to don any mask that served this end, regardless of the damage to his reputation.

She had since discovered that on at least two occasions he had used his influence with the Fascist authorities in Florence to protect Maurizio from certain 'difficulties' – problems arising from his association with underground Socialism.

And just as Emilio had worked those men of importance in Florence, so he had won over the German officer sent to establish a command post at Villa Docci, sitting up late into the night with him, talking about art, literature, science and philosophy. Not a single artwork had been damaged or pillaged, not a single labourer on the estate ill-treated. It had been an entirely painless co-habitation. Then, just as it was drawing to a close, Emilio was presented with the sight of antique furniture – precious family heirlooms – being tossed from the top windows of the villa by a couple of foot soldiers.

Unfortunately, they were not men he knew well; they'd recently been assigned to Villa Docci, plucked from the hordes of German troops retreating northwards. Emilio and Maurizio had burst in on the pair as they were hefting yet another piece of furniture towards the window. They were reeling drunk, laughing, and some German song was blaring from the gramophone player. Emilio took in the room – the broken mirrors, the slashed paintings and the bullet-holes in the ceiling frescoes – then he drew his pistol and fired a shot into the gramophone, killing the music. For a few stunned moments the four men in the room just stood there in the deafening silence, a frozen tableau.

Tempers quickly flared. There was much gesticulating and shouting, the words lost on Maurizio, who didn't speak German. The Germans glanced at their own pistols, abandoned nearby. Emilio ordered them to move away from the weapons. And that's when Gaetano the gardener entered the room, drawn to the villa by the rumpus.

Chiara made Adam swear never to repeat this particular detail of the story, the precise and unfortunate timing of Gaetano's arrival, because in many respects poor Gaetano was unwittingly responsible for the death of Emilio.

As Emilio turned instinctively towards the door, one of the Germans snatched up his own pistol and fired twice, hitting Emilio in the chest and the head. He crumpled to the floor, dead. Gaetano dipped back outside the room, but with nowhere to flee, Maurizio found himself staring down the barrel of the German's gun. His life was saved by the other German, who persuaded his companion not to pull the trigger. The two of them then fled.

Chiara saw the room the following day. Emilio's body had been removed, although his blood still stained the floor near the fireplace, where he had fallen. Allied soldiers arrived in the afternoon, but they seemed less concerned with what had happened than in turning up any intelligence left behind by the Germans. As soon as they were gone, Benedetto closed and locked the doors at the head of the staircase. It was a few days before he announced that the rooms would remain just as they were. He gave no explanation and he refused to discuss the matter further. With time, everyone grew to accept this unusual state of affairs. It only became an issue again when, years later, Benedetto himself died and Signora

Docci announced her intention to leave the top floor sealed off.

'It is not right,' said Chiara, stubbing out her cigarette and getting to her feet. 'We have German friends. They will be at the party. It is an insult to them. It is not right. It is the past.'

There was more that Adam wanted to ask, but he'd already shown an undue interest in the episode, cajoling her with questions, extracting from her the closest thing to an 'official' account of the killing as he was ever likely to get. Somehow he couldn't see Maurizio being quite so forthcoming, not that he would ever have risked approaching him on the subject.

He accompanied Chiara outside on to the terrace, fleeing the fug of smoke that now filled the study. Amazingly, she immediately lit another cigarette before going in search of her husband and her mother-in-law.

Adam stood for a while at the balustrade, going over the conversation in his head, trying to make sense of it. He watched the workmen toiling away on the terraces below, and he saw just the place to call his thoughts to order.

The air in the chapel was surprisingly cool, almost damp. Alone this time, he surveyed the interior with a more critical eye. It was as plain and simple a place of worship as he'd ever been in. There were no false lines or proportions, no signs of excess – no writhing Baroque baldachins bolted to the wall, no fussy frescoes or elaborate carvings. It was as if the building itself had shunned these things over the centuries, successive generations of Doccis somehow sensing its dislike of such frivolities.

200

Standing there, breathing the building in, he was left in no doubt that the same deft hand that had fashioned an imposing villa for Federico Docci had also shaped this little house of God.

He had done some research: Signora Docci had been right; almost nothing was known about the reputed architect of Villa Docci, Fulvio Montalto. He appeared to have been an apprentice to the Renaissance sculptor and architect Niccolò Tribolo. A letter in the Tribolo archives alluded to a meeting between Federico Docci and Fulvio Montalto – the master being absent – at which the plans for a new country residence were discussed. Maybe Tribolo had conceived the plans himself but, given his onerous workload at the time – he was overseeing the construction of the Boboli Gardens for Cosimo de'Medici – it seemed more likely that he had simply handed the commission to his young charge. Fulvio Montalto had more than repaid the confidence placed in him, and it was unfortunate that he had then vanished from the map.

Adam found his feet carrying him to the spot near the south wall where Emilio lay. He thought of him there, down in the dank, dark earth. What did a body look like in a coffin after fourteen years? Liquefied? Mummified? Had the walls of the coffin given way? Were his bones already mingling with the rich Tuscan soil?

He dumped himself on a nearby pew, dejected. He knew the reason for his mood; it had begun to settle on him the moment Chiara mentioned Gaetano the gardener's untimely arrival at the villa on the night of Emilio's murder. This one small statement had crushed the seed of Adam's suspicions underfoot.

Everything he'd concocted in his head over the past days sprang from Fausto's claim that Gaetano had been inconsistent, that he'd changed his story about his exact whereabouts at the moment of the killing. Well, of course he had. Who wouldn't have changed their story in his position? His sudden arrival on the top floor had distracted Emilio, enabling the German to lunge for his gun and open fire. Gaetano must have been devastated, Maurizio sympathetic. It was easy to imagine them presenting an altered version of events to the world in order to spare Gaetano's feelings, just as it was easy to imagine local gossip-mongers like Fausto latching on to any inconsistencies in Gaetano's account and gleefully misinterpreting them.

It was clear to him now that he had brought a sinister conspiracy into being through a sheer act of will. He'd stretched the facts to fit his case and disregarded those that didn't – crimes he'd often been accused of in the past by Professor Leonard. Standing there before the altar, it also became clear to him why he'd allowed his imagination to run away with him. The memorial garden had denied him any further taste of intrigue, so he'd searched for it else-where – he'd manufactured it from his own frustration.

This recognition of his foolhardiness wasn't without its consolations. He was liberated, relieved of duties, no longer required to speculate about who and how and why, endlessly playing out imaginary scenarios in his mind, searching for the worst wherever he turned. He was free to enjoy the company of a man who had shown himself to be nothing but charming and civil.

❧

Harry had always scrubbed up well, which was fortunate, because when Adam went to wake him before lunch he was sprawled face down on top of the covers, still in his clothes. He was also dribbling. Remarkably, only twenty minutes later he sashayed on to the terrace fresh-faced, clean-shaven and sparkle-eyed. His hair even bore the traces of a half-hearted stab at a side parting.

He arrived as the rest of them were taking their places at the table on the terrace.

'Hi, hello, I'm Harry.' Maurizio and Chiara both seemed a little overwhelmed by the violence of the handshake, Signora Docci not entirely displeased with the kiss Harry planted on her cheek.

Chiara remarked on their close physical resemblance – the same dark colouring, the same jaw lines, same wide mouths.

'Adam hates it when people say that. He thinks he's better looking – taller and better looking.'

'He *is* taller,' said Maurizio.

'I slouch.'

Harry straightened in his chair to make the point. Maurizio looked sceptical.

'Okay, I also have bandy little legs. But at least they're not skinny. You won't ever catch Adam in a pair of shorts like these.'

'I can't deny it,' said Adam, 'I wouldn't be seen dead in a pair of shorts like those.'

The laughter set the tone for the meal. It was a pleasant affair, the conversation tripping along quite merrily, until Signora Docci asked Harry what he had thought of Florence.

'Disappointing.'

'Disappointing?'

'If I'm honest.'

'Don't feel you have to be,' said Adam.

Harry ignored him. 'I don't know what I was expecting, something more romantic, I suppose. It's so bloody . . .' he searched for the word '. . . masculine.'

'Masculine?' From Chiara, this time.

'Big, bold, brash . . . hard. I mean, take that cathedral . . .'

'The Duomo,' said Adam tightly, meaning *Shut up right now*.

'That's the one. Let's face it, it doesn't exactly have you reaching for a pen to scribble poetry.'

Adam noticed that Maurizio was smiling. Signora Docci and Chiara bristled defensively.

'Many poets have written about *il Duomo*,' said Chiara.

'Short poems, right?'

Maurizio laughed, drawing a sharp look from his mother. 'I know what Harry means,' he said. 'Florence is not like Siena, or Venice, or Padova. It is much more robust. I can imagine being disappointed.'

It was unfortunate that Chiara retaliated with mention of Florence's unrivalled artistic heritage, because on that subject Harry showed even less diplomacy. He had found the art a bit of a letdown, too.

'Really?' Signora Docci asked incredulously.

'A bit.'

This proved to be something of an understatement. In Harry's humble opinion, the Renaissance marked a low point in the history of Western art. As with most of Harry's theories, the originality of the hypothesis coupled with his passionate conviction almost made up for the glaring flaws in his argument.

He didn't deny that the painters and sculptors of the Renaissance had made great leaps in terms of representational realism, but he questioned whether this was progress, whether it made for better art. You could argue – and he did – that medieval art, with its distortions and disproportions and stylizations, was more real because it wasn't trying to trick the eye. Renaissance art, on the other hand, was devotedly illusionistic. In fact, the illusion had almost become an end in itself. The technical prowess of faking a sense of depth on a flat picture plane or rendering a human figure with near-photographic precision sometimes seemed more important to the artists than the subjects themselves, than the higher, sacred purpose their works were intended to serve. With a few notable exceptions, much of what he'd seen in the galleries and museums of Florence had left him cold. One of the exceptions was Michelangelo's statue of David in the Accademia.

That, he had hated.

A towering monument to man's mawkish fascination with himself, a triumph of form over content, style over substance, was how Harry described it. Where was the terror of a young shepherd boy about to take on the enemy's champion in single combat? The only sign of it Harry had been able to detect lay between David's legs. Fear, like cold, could do that to your penis, Harry explained considerately, for the benefit of the ladies. No, the 'snake-hipped Narcissus' looked more like 'some dim-witted teenager primping himself in front of a mirror before a big night out'.

Harry's views sparked a lively debate, just as he'd intended. There weren't many things he enjoyed as much as an intellectual scuffle. Unfortunately, red wine was one of them, and it was flowing freely throughout the main course – a potentially explosive combination.

Adam judged his moment carefully. At the first sign of beady-eyed belligerence, he dragged Harry away on the pretext of showing him the memorial garden.

No one seemed to mind when Harry asked if he could take his wine glass with him.

Adam experienced none of the usual anticipatory thrill as they made their way down the path into the valley. He had felt defeated by the garden even before the matter of Emilio's death had laid siege to his thoughts. He gave Harry only the barest background, mentioning little more than the fact that Federico Docci had cast his wife as Flora, goddess of flowers.

Harry stopped as they pushed through the gap in the yew hedge, the gloomy tunnel of trees stretching out before them. 'Jolly spot,' he said.

He didn't speak again until they reached the open ground at the foot of the amphitheatre. He looked up at the statue of Flora, the triumphal arch looming on the crest above her, then he turned, taking in the rest of the valley, the trees pressing in on the pasture.

'What are you thinking?' asked Adam.

'It's beautiful. But eerie.'

'What else?'

'Is this a test?'

'No.'

It wasn't a test, but he did want to see the place through Harry's eyes – afresh, for the first time. Maybe it would throw up something.

'I need help,' said Adam.

'From me?'

'I'm that desperate.'

Harry read off the inscription on the triumphal arch, pronouncing it incorrectly.

'Fiore,' said Adam. 'It's Italian for flower.'

'As in Flora.'

'Exactly.'

'And that's her – the statue?'

'That's the goddess.'

'Is it a likeness?'

'There's no way of knowing, there are no portraits of Flora. I think it might be, though.' It was a feeling that had crept up on him in the past few days. Her face didn't fit the template of the time. The features didn't quite accord with the bland, polished refinement of the late sixteenth century. The mouth was too strong, the nose too pronounced, the chin too square. She was too real.

They climbed the slope beside the amphitheatre, stepping on to the second level. Harry handed Adam his wine glass and lit a cigarette for both of them. He then proceeded to examine the statue from every angle.

'Well, it's not my kind of thing,' he said eventually.

'I guessed as much.'

'But it does have a certain quality.'

'You think?'

'Uh-huh.'

'What?'

'Well, she's hot.'

'Hot?'

'Horny. Look at her.'

Harry slid his hand up the statue's leg, just as Antonella had done at their first meeting. This time was different, though; Harry's hand kept going, working its way right up into Flora's groin.

'Yep, she's wet.'

'Oh for God's sake, Harry.'

'Well, look at her, see how she's twisted that way then back – all coy but not really.'

'It's a classic pose.'

'Oh, a classic pose,' mocked Harry. 'All I'm saying is I wouldn't mind being on the receiving end of that look.'

Adam glanced up at Flora's face, the slightly pursed lips, her wide-set almond eyes gazing off into the distance . . .

But where exactly?

Adam's head snapped round, then back to Flora. She was looking down the slope and across the vale towards the wood, with its towering trees and its dense undergrowth of laurel. They presented an impenetrable screen, but he had a pretty good idea of what lay beyond.

'Stay here,' he said.

He lost his footing as he hurried down the slope, stumbling badly, painfully. Gathering himself on the level ground, he called up to Harry. 'Tell me where she's looking.'

'What?'

'Where she's looking. Tell me exactly where she's looking.'

He hurried off, hobbling. He had done something to his ankle. It wasn't hurting yet, but he could tell it would be, and soon.

When he reached the tree-line he turned and shouted, 'Here?'

Harry gesticulated and yelled back, 'Up a bit. Bit more. That's right. No. Back a touch. I don't know. There. Yes. There.'

Adam stripped off his shirt and slung it over the nearest branch. Looking deep into the woods, he set his sights on a distant tree in direct line with the statue and his shirt. He kept his eyes tightly fixed on the tree as he pushed his way through the overgrown laurel. It was a struggle, like walking against the current in a lively river.

When he reached the tree, he turned. He could just make out his shirt hanging from the branch.

He had to be exact, which meant removing his trousers and hanging them from a branch. When he slipped his shoes back on he noticed that his ankle had already started to swell.

Singling out another tree that lay along the same axis, he set off through the laurel. The tight-packed bushes clawed at him, grazing his bare skin. Once or twice he received a sharp jab in the thigh or midriff, enough to stop him momentarily in his tracks, but he didn't take his eyes off the tree until he reached it.

Fortunately, he wasn't required to remove his underpants as another marker; the next tree was close enough to the border of the wood for him to judge the rest of the journey by eye.

He turned and gave one final check that he was still on

target with Flora's line of sight, and then he stepped into the open.

He was at the northern fringes of the glade of Hyacinth, and there – directly in his path – stood Apollo atop his high, conical mountain, his arm outstretched towards Hyacinth, prostrate on his plinth on the other side of the clearing.

It came to him suddenly, setting his pulse racing.

Apollo was the key that unlocked the mystery.

He closed his eyes and hurried round the garden in his head, each element of Federico Docci's design unravelling, taking on new meaning, telling another story, one buried just beneath the surface.

A couple of sharp expletives brought him to his senses. It was Harry emerging from the wood, barging through the laurel, holding his wine glass aloft. Impressively, he seemed to have spilled barely a drop.

Harry's gaze roamed the glade before coming to rest on Adam. 'Jesus, Adam, look at you, standing there in your underpants and your shoes, all scratched to fuck. Is this where a Cambridge education gets you?'

'You sound like Dad.'

'I'm beginning to understand how he feels.'

Adam seized Harry and hugged him close. 'You're a genius, Harry.'

Harry patted his back and said, 'There, there, the nice men in the white coats will be here soon.'

Adam laughed and released him. 'It's not a memorial garden.'

'No?'

'Or rather, it is.'

'Right.'

'Only, it isn't.'

'Okay, now I'm really quite worried.'

'It's both. It's a memorial garden *and* a confession.'

'A confession?'

'To murder. He killed her. Federico killed her.'

'Who?'

'Flora.'

'Not her – him. Who the fuck is Federico?'

'Her husband. He killed her because she was having an affair.'

Harry took a sip of wine and nodded sagely. 'Seems a little excessive.'

Harry wasn't too happy about being dispatched into the wood to recover Adam's trousers, but he perked up a bit when they arrived back at the amphitheatre and Adam pointed out the anagram on the triumphal arch and the nine circles of Dante's *Inferno*.

Harry was on board, a happy passenger, by the time they reached the grotto. In fact it was here, standing before the story of Daphne and Apollo, that Harry figured out Federico Docci's chosen method of murder: poison.

It took them more than an hour to complete the circuit, hampered by Adam's injured ankle as well as their protracted discussions.

They only left the garden when they were both satisfied that the new hypothesis held.

Nearing the villa, Harry stopped suddenly and turned to Adam. 'That's got to be the weirdest thing we've ever done together.'

'Weirder than when we nipped over the back wall to spy on Mrs Rogan?'

'Okay, second weirdest.'

Harry managed to make it through to the evening before reneging on his promise not to break the news about the garden.

Maurizio and Chiara were long gone by then, but Antonella had shown up for dinner, arriving directly from work with a leg of cured ham – a gift from her grateful boss, because of the lucrative order they'd just received from one of the American buyers.

Maria sliced ham from the bone and they washed it down with vintage champagne. Cases of the stuff had been delivered that afternoon and it was in need of 'testing' before the party, said Signora Docci. Even Maria permitted herself a glass.

Adam raised a toast to Antonella and the fact that her creations would soon be on sale in New York.

'But what if they don't sell?' she asked with a pained expression.

'That's easy,' said Harry, 'they won't order any more.' He then called for another toast. 'To Adam. He's also got some good news.'

'Do I?'

'You know you do.'

'Harry –'

'Stop bleating and tell them.'

'The garden . . .' guessed Antonella.

'There's more to it than meets the eye,' said Harry. 'Much more.'

Antonella was smiling at Adam. 'You solved the rest of it?'

Signora Docci leaned forward in her chair. 'The rest of it?'

Antonella turned to her grandmother. 'He told me a bit already.'

'Traitor.'

'I don't share everything with you, *Nonna*.'

'That's clear to me now.'

They turned their eyes on Adam, waiting.

'I couldn't have done it without Harry.'

'It's true,' confirmed Harry, 'he couldn't.'

Signora Docci raised her hand abruptly. 'Don't say. I want to be there when you say. In the garden.'

'*Nonna*, we're about to eat and it's getting dark.'

'Tomorrow then. Tomorrow morning before you go to work.'

'How will you get down there?'

Signora Docci slapped the top of her thighs. 'On these, of course. And I have two strong young men to help me.'

'But I want to know now.'

'Then you can ask – once I've gone to bed.'

But when Signora Docci made her way upstairs after the meal, Antonella didn't ask. She chose to live with the anticipation for a while longer. Harry assured her she wouldn't be disappointed.

The three of them took their glasses and made for the lower terrace. They lay on the grass under the stars and talked about films they had seen, books they had read, life in England, life in Italy, and even – until Adam told Harry to shut up – Crystal Palace Football Club's recent promotion to the newly formed national Division Four.

Adam felt good, stretched out there on the grass, basking in the soft night air and the conversation, the quiet satisfaction of the breakthrough on the memorial garden washing over him. Only now that it was lifted could he appreciate the true load he'd been shouldering since that first visit to the dark valley down the hill. The place had unsettled him immediately, infected him. It had consumed most of his waking hours, and many of his sleeping ones, too. Life had gone on, but it had unfolded around him in a half-haze. He had lived it at one remove.

Now that the spell was broken, things were falling back into focus. Even Antonella appeared different: sharper, crisper, more distinct. And more desirable than ever. He wished, a little guiltily, that Harry wasn't there, that he was on his own with her. He even flattered himself that she was thinking the same thing.

It was annoying that she'd arrived by car; it denied him the opportunity of walking her home. He hadn't forgotten that it was while strolling through the garden with her on just such a night that she had kissed him. He could still recall the soft cushion of her full lips against his own, and the way her hand had snaked around his waist and drawn him against her.

He reached for his cigarettes and caught sight once again of the chapel down the end of the terrace, lurking at the periphery of his vision, as it had been all evening. He had managed to put it from his mind before. This time he was less successful. While Harry prattled on to Antonella about the neglected heroines of early blues music, Adam found his thoughts turning to Emilio's bones sunk beneath the flagstone floor. A life cut short by two bullets – one to the chest, one to the head – Chiara had been very specific.

He couldn't help thinking that there was something unnatural about this level of detail. Chiara could only have heard it from Maurizio, but what kind of man would describe his own brother's murder with such clinical precision? And the other details, too: the shot fired into the gramophone player, the Germans glancing at their abandoned weapons. It smacked of a piece of theatre hatched in the mind of a playwright. Like a bad lie, it was weighed down with unnecessary information.

He had made the same mistake himself the summer before, when, driving too fast, trying to impress his friends, he'd lost control of his mother's car, crumpling the Morris' fender against a tree. He had told his mother that he'd swerved to avoid a Springer Spaniel in the road. 'Welsh or English?' she had enquired with that knowing look of hers.

Then there was Benedetto, Signora Docci's husband. What had induced him to preserve the site of Emilio's slaughter, obliging his family to live with the memory while denying them access to the scene itself? He had consulted no one on the matter, and had clearly felt no need to justify his decision. Even allowing for his grief-stricken state, there remained something uncharacteristic, unkind even, about his behaviour. It had the faintly fanatical whiff of an act of penitence, as if he were punishing himself. Or punishing someone else, perhaps?

Maybe Benedetto knew the truth of what happened that night.

It was certainly an explanation. And a good one. Yes.

Benedetto had somehow unearthed the truth but he had chosen to keep the discovery to himself. The best he could bring himself to do was close off the top floor, a constant reminder to Maurizio –

Adam caught himself in this act of folly – speculating about the guilt of a man he had already acquitted. Why couldn't he shake off his suspicions? They were still there, like a wind on his back.

'Well?' said Harry.

'What?'

'Off with the fairies, were we? I said what about another bottle?'

Antonella held up her hands in surrender. 'Not for me. Any more and I won't get home.'

'So stay,' said Harry. 'The place is a little pokey but I'm sure we can find you a corner to bunk down in.'

Antonella smiled. 'No, I must go.'

'I'll see you to your car,' said Adam.

'Adam will see you to your car, and you will remind him to come back with another bottle of champagne.'

Antonella kissed Harry on both cheeks. 'Goodnight, Harry.'

The moment they were lost to Harry's view behind a screen of yew, Antonella hooked her arm through Adam's. It was a simple gesture, somehow intimate and formal at the same time. It gave him the courage to ask the question he had just sworn to himself he wouldn't ask.

'Have you ever been up there?'

'Where?'

He pointed to the top floor of the villa. 'There.'

'No.'

'Aren't you intrigued?'

'Of course I am. But it's not possible.'

'What if I asked your grandmother?'

'She would say no.'

'How do you know?'

'Because I asked her. It was my eighteenth birthday. I thought it would make a difference. It didn't. I was so angry I almost took the key and did it anyway.'

'You know where she keeps the key?'

Antonella drew to a halt. 'Why are you so interested?'

'Same as you, I suppose. Curiosity. Morbid curiosity. It must be a weird sight. And it'll be gone soon, gone for ever.'

'And we'll all be happy when it is.'

Her car was parked at the edge of the courtyard.

'Are you okay to drive?'

'I think so.'

'Take it slowly.'

'I'm trying to,' she said, 'but it's hard.'

He could make out enough of her expression in the moonlight to know that he hadn't misunderstood her meaning. 'Then take it quickly.'

Her teeth shone pale behind her smile. 'Okay.'

They kissed more urgently than they had the first time. His hand strayed to her buttocks, his palm drifting over the firm, round contours, absorbing the information and sending it to his brain. She didn't attempt to remove his hand. Quite the opposite. Her fingers pressed into the muscles of his back in encouragement.

When they finally broke off, he said breathlessly, 'God, you have a beautiful . . . rear.'

217

'Thank you. So do you.'

He held her close and ran his fingers through her long hair.

'When are you leaving?' she asked.

'I don't know. Soon. That's why I didn't want Harry to say anything about the garden. I don't have an excuse to stay around now.'

'Were you right? Did something bad happen?'

He hesitated. 'Yes.'

They kissed again, briefly, and then she got into her car. Peering up at him through the open window, she said, 'I'll tell you where the key is if you promise not to get caught.'

'It's a promise.'

She told him. She also reminded him to grab another bottle of champagne for Harry. Then she fired the engine and pulled away.

It might have been a trick of the shadows, but he could have sworn he caught a flutter of movement behind one of the first-floor windows as the headlights swept the court-yard.

Harry had removed himself to a stone bench during Adam's absence. He was lying on his back, staring at the star-stained sky. Adam popped the cork and filled their glasses.

'Did you kiss her?'

'Yes.'

'Bastard. She's too good for you.'

'Thanks.'

'It's true,' said Harry. 'I mean, you're a bright young boy and everything –' He broke off suddenly, snapping upright and fixing Adam with an intense stare. 'My God, you *are* a bright young boy, aren't you?'

'What?'

'Yes, you are. I mean, I've always known it . . . but do you have any idea what you did today?'

'*We* did it, Harry.'

'Rubbish. You were there, half a step away. You would have figured it out.'

Unaccustomed to hearing kind words from Harry, Adam wasn't quite sure how to react.

'The first person in how many years?'

'Three hundred and something.'

'I thought it was more.'

'We can push it to four if you think it'd make a better story.'

Harry laughed. 'It's a great story. This is going to change everything.'

'Why?'

'Well, you can't go off and sell insurance after this.'

'Why not?'

'Why not!? Anyone can sell insurance. How many people can do that?' Harry thrust his hand in the general direction of the memorial garden.

'What if I don't want to do that?'

'You've got to.'

'Why?'

'Why!? Because you see things other people don't.'

'No I don't.'

'Yes you do. You always have. Even when we were kids. It's true, Paddler. You were always taking things apart, looking at them from the inside out. Mum always says:

the only baby she's ever known that tried to smash its rattle open. We still laugh about it.'

'Oh, I'm happy for you both.'

'You look at things differently, you see things differently.'

'Then how come I looked at Flora and I didn't see her? Not really. I saw books.'

'So you learned something. You'll be better next time.'

'There isn't going to be a next time, Harry.'

Harry grew serious, almost aggressive. 'Listen to me. It's not like the other night. I'm not talking about your friends, I'm not talking about the last two years of your life – I'm talking about the rest of it.'

'I know you are.'

'You can't become an insurance man.'

'I don't have a choice! Someone's got to, and you're not going to!'

The vehemence of his reply was almost as shocking to him as it was to Harry.

'Jesus, Paddler –'

'It's true. The moment you said no to Dad, it was always going to be me.'

Harry placed his palms together. 'Listen to me. It's your life, not his. Do you want his life? Well, do you? Living in a place like Purley with a couple of kids? Is that what you want, catching the same bloody train every morning, moaning about rationing, worrying about your pension . . . screwing your secretary because you don't love your wife any more?'

'Don't be ridiculous.'

'Screwing . . . your . . . secretary,' said Harry with slow deliberation.

'Dad's not screwing his secretary.'

'Isn't he?'

'You're drunk.'

'I wouldn't be telling you if I wasn't.'

Adam eyed his brother for a moment then laughed. 'That's good, Harry. You're still good, I'll give you that.' He'd fallen for enough of these in the past to know what was coming next.

'On Mum's life,' said Harry solemnly.

Adam sobered up fast.

'His secretary . . .?'

'Vanessaaaaa.'

Vanessa was very smart, very well spoken. Her father was a high-ranking civil servant, and she knew all the dates in the social calendar off by heart.

'The one who likes operaaaaa. You can just see it, can't you? Dad snoring his way through Wagner then running for the last train home.'

'How do you know?'

'Mum.'

'She told you?'

'I asked her. You must have noticed something – the house . . . her hair . . . shoes. She's let things go.'

Had he really been that blind?

'She was asking to be asked.'

Adam dumped himself dejectedly on the bench beside his brother.

'They've talked about it,' said Harry. 'He doesn't know what he wants to do.'

'Did he tell her or did she find out?'

Somehow it seemed important to know.

'What do *you* think?'

'Bastard.'

'You in thirty years, if you're not careful. He made the wrong choice too. Remember how he used to make us laugh? He was a funny man once. How long since he was funny? How long since Mum drew a happy breath?'

Adam lit a cigarette then turned to Harry. 'The Giant Rat of Sumatra?'

'Like I said, you're a bright young boy.'

21

❧

It wasn't surprising that he woke snarled in the sheet. What surprised him was the fact that he'd managed to sleep at all. At some ungodly hour of the night he'd given up even trying to, surrendering to the turmoil in his head.

He had never glorified his parents' relationship, never held it up to others or himself as a model marriage. But he had always expected it to be there, them to be there, together. It was one of those things you took for granted, like the passing of the seasons. Harry was of the opinion that it was something they had to work out for themselves. Adam's instinct was to head straight home and help in whatever way he could.

A few hours of welcome oblivion had taken the edge off his panic. It also helped that he had something else to think about from the moment he swung his legs off the bed.

He was the last to appear at breakfast. Even Antonella was already there. She was as eager as Signora Docci to get going immediately, although they did allow him to throw back a small cup of dense black coffee first.

His sprained ankle had ballooned grotesquely overnight, and it screamed in protest during the long slow walk down from the villa. His mind, however, was on other things, toying with how best to reveal the story. In the end he just told it the way it was, taking each component of the garden in turn and exposing both its faces.

Signora Docci fell silent when Adam pointed out the anagram of INFERNO on the triumphal arch, and she barely spoke from that moment on.

Dante's *Divine Comedy* was the key text, he explained, not Ovid's *Metamorphoses* with its tales of gods and goddesses and all their shenanigans. Ovid was a red herring. He was to be ignored.

The story of Daphne and Apollo in the grotto was little more than a front, a cloak, a disguise. The sculptural arrangement needed to be looked at as a snapshot of a purely human drama: a young couple frolicking merrily while an older gentleman brooded nearby. It had nothing to do with the ancient myth it purported to represent. It was a depiction of Flora and her lover and a disconsolate Federico Docci.

Harry had provided the breakthrough with his throw-away comment about the look on Flora's face. From her perch on the second level of the amphitheatre, the adulterous wife was staring longingly at the distant figure of Apollo in the glade of Hyacinth. Apollo's unmasking as Flora's lover was the key that unlocked the mystery, exposing the whole masquerade. There was another clue to the importance of the sun god in Federico Docci's hidden design: a literary clue buried in the text of *The Divine Comedy*, when, just after he has ascended into Paradise,

Dante calls on Apollo for inspiration, to help him in the final stages of his journey.

What else did the grotto reveal once its characters had been exposed as the three parties to a Renaissance love-triangle? There was Federico Docci – in the guise of Peneus – clutching an urn, filling the marble trough with water, which then overflowed into the gaping mouth of Flora, her face set in relief in the floor – no longer a river god providing sustenance to the goddess of flowers, but Federico giving his wife something to drink. What, though? If that symbol of purity, the unicorn bent over the trough, had never possessed its horn, as the sixteenth-century drawing suggested, then whatever it was it was undrinkable.

'Poison . . .' said Signora Docci quietly.

'I think so.'

'But you can't be sure.'

'There's another clue. We'll come to it.'

From the grotto they travelled clockwise around the circuit, stopping at the glade of Adonis, with its sculpture of Venus grieving over her dead love. There was no need to explain the arrangement to Signora Docci and Antonella now that the central conceit of Federico's deception had been laid bare. Ignoring the 'official' identities of the characters on show, it was a representation of Flora grieving over *her* dead lover.

'You think Federico killed him?' asked Antonella.

'It looks that way. In the myth, Adonis was killed by a wild boar.'

'Our coat of arms,' muttered Signora Docci.

'Exactly.'

Signora Docci appeared a little overwhelmed by the

revelation. She said nothing more, but she did pay Adam a heartfelt compliment with her eyes.

At the foot of the garden stood the Temple of Echo, in front of which lay Narcissus, peering into the octagonal pool: two youngsters, their love destined to fail, death their reward. If the correspondence was to be believed, Flora – like Echo – had died a slow and lingering death. That poison had been the cause of it was supported by the inscription running around the architrave beneath the dome – *The hour of departure has arrived, and we go our separate ways, I to die, and you to live. Which of these two is better only God knows.* The words were those of Socrates, spoken shortly before he took his own life, poisoning himself with hemlock.

The glade of Hyacinth, the final element in the garden, mirrored the glade of Adonis on the other side of the valley. But whereas the first glade they had visited portrayed the death of Flora's lover, this one told the death of Flora herself.

In many ways it was the most interesting part of Federico Docci's carefully constructed programme. It revealed the most about the man behind the murders, offering insights into his thinking. Because Federico Docci had found himself faced with a problem.

It was easy to imagine his predicament.

The disguise is perfect. The garden he has laid out in loving memory of his wife – the garden he wishes the world to take at face value – is thematically flawless. Flora is made to live again as Flora goddess of flowers. He sets her at the head of the garden, a queen surveying her subjects – Adonis, Narcissus, Hyacinth – each of whose tragic deaths was marked by the genesis of a flower. Tragedy, Survival, Renewal, Metamorphosis, Death and Resurrection: the themes weave together effortlessly. Only the story of Hyacinth presents a problem.

It is ideal for his purposes, and certainly too good to consider abandoning. Zephyrus, the west wind, driven mad by his jealousy of Apollo, kills the object of their mutual affections. It's perfect, except for the fact that Hyacinth was a Spartan prince, not a princess. There is a problem with the gender. Federico gets round it by placing Hyacinth face down in the dirt, his/her hair covering his/her face, his/her body draped in a bulky robe.

It's a cheat, not up to his usual high standards, and Federico knows it. He doesn't mind too much, though, because it obliges him to leave behind a clue – the unusual posing of Hyacinth – and he has to leave at least one clear clue in each section of the garden. That's obviously the challenge he has set himself. He wants people to know the truth, but only once there's little risk to himself. That is surely the reason he waits almost thirty years, till his own life has all but run its course, before laying out the garden.

There was nothing more for Adam to say, so he fell silent. Harry slung an arm around his shoulder and grinned at the ladies.

'Not bad, eh? For a young 'un.'

'No, not bad at all.'

Antonella was far more fulsome in her praise, proposing a celebratory dinner that evening in honour of Adam's remarkable discovery.

Adam and Harry assisted a flagging Signora Docci back to the amphitheatre, each of them gripping a bony elbow,

Antonella bringing up the rear. They speculated about the identity of Flora's lover, concluding that it must surely have been one of the many artists and writers who attended Federico's cultural gatherings at Villa Docci. A younger man, no doubt, more Flora's age than her husband's. Or why not a woman? This was wishful thinking on Harry's part, though not entirely misguided. Tullia d'Aragona, the Roman poetess and courtesan, had disappeared abruptly from the Florentine scene in 1548 – the year of Flora's death. Maybe there was a connection, after all. Adam kept these musings to himself.

Arriving at the amphitheatre, Signora Docci asked to rest a while on the stone bench. She also asked to be left alone.

From a distance they saw her gazing up at Flora, dabbing at her eyes with the back of her hand every so often.

It was ten minutes or so before she called for Adam to join her.

'Are you okay?' he asked, setting himself down beside her.

'You don't know what you've done.'

'What have I done?'

'Something extraordinary. Crispin will be proud of you. *I'm* proud of you.' She patted him on the knee. 'At my age you don't expect to learn anything new.'

Harry seized the opportunity of a lift with Antonella to make another foray into Florence, despite Adam's warning that he was taking his life in his hands by climbing into a car with her. As they pulled away, he made a sign of the cross, blessing the vehicle.

Returning inside, Signora Docci was nowhere to be found. He called her name. 'In here,' came the dim and distant reply.

She was in the study, standing to the left of the fireplace, examining the small portrait of her ancestor, Federico Docci.

'Please, call me Francesca.'

'Francesca,' he said, trying it on for size.

'I insist.'

'It doesn't sound right.'

'It never did. I was never a Francesca. I always thought of myself as a Teresa.'

'A little too saintly, maybe.'

For a moment he thought he had gone too far, but her face creased into a smile. 'Oh dear, you really do know far too much about me, don't you?'

She turned back to the portrait.

'I'm thinking about burning it.'

'But you won't.'

She shook her head. 'It explains a lot in his expression, don't you think?'

'I think we see what we want to see.'

'Goodness me,' she said, 'already talking like a wise old professor.'

Adam looked suitably chastened.

'I would like to go to the chapel,' she announced. 'Do you mind helping me?'

There were gardeners at work on the terraces, trimming hedges, raking gravel and sprucing up the borders for the party. Signora Docci greeted them but didn't stop to talk.

'Are you religious?' she asked as they approached the chapel.

'No.'

'Not even as a child?'

'I enjoyed the stories.'

He was dreading a metaphysical debate. It didn't happen.

'Yes, they're good stories,' she said simply.

She crossed herself on entering the building and made her way to the altar, the tap of her cane echoing around the interior. She must have sensed his hesitation, because without turning she said, 'I doubt he'll strike you down in his own house.'

He joined her at the altar, where she removed a candle from her pocket – a votive candle in a red glass jar. He offered her his lighter to save her fiddling with the box of matches.

'Thank you.'

She lit the candle and placed it in front of the triptych.

'Maybe now she can rest in peace.'

Her words caught him off guard. Had she felt the same unnerving presence?

'No one knows exactly where she's buried, do they?' he said.

'When we buried Emilio we found some bones, but that means nothing.'

'Why was he buried here?'

'Emilio?'

'I mean, how many Doccis are?'

'Most of us are in the cemetery at San Casciano. There is a place for me there, next to Benedetto.' She paused. 'It was Benedetto's idea. He insisted. He wouldn't even discuss it. He wanted Emilio here.'

She took a few steps and stood over the remains of her dead son.

'Old men make the wars, but they send young men to fight the battles. It doesn't seem fair. They should go themselves.' She smiled wistfully at the thought. 'I wonder how many wars there would be if it worked that way.' Only now did she look up at him. 'All those boys. Parents should not have to see their children die before them. It's not easy to live with. Benedetto couldn't. The moment it happened he changed. I thought he was losing his mind. He would not even allow Emilio to be buried with the bullets that killed him. They were removed.' She turned towards the wall. 'They are there, behind the plaque, with Emilio's gun.'

'Really?'

'No one else knows that. Only me. And now you.'

He tried to push the thoughts away, but they kept coming at him, buffeting him. There were only two plausible explanations for Benedetto's strange behaviour regarding the bullets and the gun. He already knew what one of them was: the poor man really had lost his marbles. The second explanation required testing, and that meant gaining access to the top floor, it meant getting his hands on the key in the bureau in Signora Docci's bedroom.

Annoyingly, she took to her room the moment they returned from the chapel, pleading exhaustion and requesting that Maria serve her lunch in the upstairs loggia. Adam shook off his frustration. If he had to wait a while longer for an opportunity, so be it. There was another matter he had to deal with anyway – after he had phoned home.

The moment his mother's voice came on the line he seemed to lose all power of reason and speech. This wasn't entirely due to her irritating habit of answering the phone with the words:

'The Strickland residence.'

'Mum, it's me.'

'Adam, darling. How are you?'

How could she muster such heartfelt warmth and enthusiasm in her condition?

'Fine. Good. Yeah.'

He wanted to tell her that he'd been blind, insensitive, self-absorbed. He wanted to say that he knew what she must be going through. He wanted to reassure her that it would all be all right in the end, whatever happened, that even if Dad left her she would always have him and Harry and a life worth living.

As it was, they talked chiefly about the weather and his laundry arrangements in Italy. When she raised the subject of his work on the garden, he brushed the question aside, not wanting to diminish her story with an account of his own small triumph.

After ten minutes or so, it was patently clear to him that he was never going to raise the matter of his father's infidelity. How could he? It wasn't a language they had ever spoken. They both lacked the vocabulary.

'Mum, I have to go.'

'Of course you do. Make sure you give Signora Docci something for this phone call. You won't forget, will you?'

'Mum . . .'

'Yes darling?'

'I love you, Mum.'

'Gracious me,' she chuckled, 'you must be having a terrible time.'

'I'll see you next week.'

'What day did you say again?'

'I didn't. I'll call and let you know. Bye, Mum.'

'I'll send your love to your father.'

'Yes, do that.'

'Goodbye, darling. And try to keep Harry out of trouble.'

He replaced the receiver on its cradle and made straight for the kitchen. He told Maria that he wouldn't be requiring lunch today; he was going for a bike ride.

There were two men zealously tucking into bowls of pasta on the terrace in front of the Pensione Amorini – stonemasons from the look of them, powdered white from top to toe. Signora Fanelli must have insisted they eat outside regardless of the heat.

She was inside, chatting to the only other customer, an overweight man sporting a dark suit and a loud necktie. She turned as Adam entered, a flicker of alarm in her eyes. She recovered quickly, though, smiling warmly as she wandered over to greet him.

'How are you?'

'Good.'

'How's life at the villa?'

'Good.'

'Do you want to eat?'

'No thanks.'

'Something to drink then? A beer?'

'Why not?'

His arrival had disconcerted her. Maybe she didn't want to be reminded of their tryst. Or worse still, maybe she thought he had dropped by in the hope of a replay upstairs.

Before he could set her mind at rest, she was gone, heading for the kitchen.

She really was very beautiful – more beautiful than he remembered – and he wondered, not for the first time, what on earth had induced her to share herself with him.

He took a sip of beer and pressed the chill glass to his cheek. It was good to get out, away from Villa Docci, to slip its grip for a while. That's what he told himself. He knew in his bones he'd done no such thing.

Villa Docci had not released him. If it had, he'd be wandering the streets of Florence right now, dipping into churches, galleries and museums with Harry. Why was Harry the one down there doing it? The Renaissance was *his* thing, not Harry's. All that seminal art right on his doorstep, destined to go unseen by him, masterpieces callously ignored. And in favour of what, exactly?

He tried not to think too hard about why he had allowed himself to be drawn back into the dark abyss of his suspicions. The reasons flew in the face of common sense, they violated the laws of logic by which he liked to think he operated. This was uncharted territory for him, instinct his only guide.

It occurred to him that he wouldn't be sitting there on a bar stool in the Pensione Amorini if that same instinct hadn't served him so well in the memorial garden. As ever, all things sprang from and returned to the garden.

Signora Fanelli served the lone gentleman his food then joined Adam at the counter. Was it significant that she had tied up her hair while in the kitchen?

'It's nice to see you.'

'I came to say goodbye. I'm leaving soon.'

'Before the party?' she asked.

'You know about the party?'

'Everyone does. The children here always go and watch – from a distance, of course. I used to when I was young.'

'I also want to say goodbye to Fausto, but I don't know where he lives.'

She drew him a map on a paper napkin. He'd forgotten that she was left-handed.

When he pulled some coins from his pocket to pay for the beer she said, 'Don't be silly, I don't want your money.'

She accompanied him outside to his bicycle. 'You won't tell him about us, will you? Fausto, I mean.'

'Don't worry, I'm too embarrassed.'

She smiled apologetically. 'I didn't mean that. But you won't, will you?'

'No.'

She cast a fleeting look at the stonemasons before kissing him on both cheeks.

'Goodbye, Adam.'

'Goodbye.'

'Hello.'

Fausto looked up, squinting. 'You?'

'Me.'

Fausto was mixing mortar in an old tin pail. He was stripped to the waist, revealing a wire-and-whipcord body. Wiping the sweat from his brow with the back of his forearm, he rose to his feet.

'You like it?' He nodded at the low, stone-built, tile-roofed structure he was working on. The building itself was finished; he was erecting the walls of a small yard out front.

235

'For the pig?'

'For a whole family of little pigs.'

'It's beautiful.' Adam looked around him. 'It's all beautiful.'

He wasn't being polite. The modest farmhouse was set among a run of terraces carved out of the wooded hillside just south of San Casciano. It was an isolated spot, accessed by a precipitous dirt track barely passable on foot, which probably accounted for the old US Army Jeep parked beside the farmhouse.

'Yes, it's not bad. Are you thirsty?'

'Yes.'

'Go and get a couple of beers from the fridge. I have to do this now or the mortar will set.'

As with Antonella's farmhouse, the living accommodation was on the first floor. Unlike Antonella's place, Fausto's home was stuffed to bursting with furniture, pictures, books and other curiosities. In the middle of the kitchen table was an upturned German helmet, painted pink and doubling as a flower pot, a bushy fern sprouting from it. The ramshackle shelves in one corner of the room were almost exclusively given over to books on warfare and historic battles. Knowing that to delay any more would mean he'd been snooping, he grabbed a couple of beers from the fridge and headed back outside.

As soon as Fausto was done slapping the mortar around a few more blocks of stone, he took Adam on a tour. They inspected the vines, the olive trees, the orchard, the maize and the sunflowers. There was also an extensive vegetable patch, as well as a large jerry-built coop with chickens busy turning table scraps into eggs. The crops were clearly suffering from the lack of rain, but it didn't seem to bother Fausto. 'Everything a man needs,' he declared with pride. 'Except a woman to share it with.'

They drank the next two beers in the shade of a vine-threaded pergola beside the house. Adam asked about the books on battles heaped up on the shelves in the corner of the kitchen.

'I'm interested, it's true. So much of who we are, what we are, comes down to a bunch of men fighting in a field.'

Adam smiled. He hadn't thought of it in those terms before.

'In 1260,' said Fausto, 'Florence and Siena went to war. September 3rd. It was a Saturday.'

Adam's Italian wasn't up to catching all of the details, but as he understood it, this was how things unfolded. Siena was already a divided city, and the Florentines weren't fools. They waited till the different factions were at each other's throats before sending in their messengers, two horsemen carrying with them a simple yet stark ultimatum: If the Republic of Siena didn't surrender at once to Florence, then the city would be razed to the ground. It wasn't an idle threat. The Florentine army massing to the east was more than capable of following it through.

The one thing the Florentines hadn't banked on was the Sienese burying their differences overnight. Sworn enemies gathered before the cathedral that same evening and greeted each other like brothers. Then they called on the Virgin Mary to help them in the forthcoming battle.

The two armies clashed the following day at Montaperti. According to eye-witness accounts, there was enough blood flowing at one point to drive four watermills. By far the greater part of it was Florentine blood. That field near Montaperti was home to a massacre, and it was years before any animals ever ventured near it.

'Imagine it,' said Fausto. 'The next day was a Sunday. That's when the Sienese army returned. They dragged the Florentine banner through the streets behind an ass. You think those bastard Sienese have forgotten that day? Of course they haven't. It's what they teach their children in school. It's in their eyes every time we play them at football.'

Fausto paused to light a cigarette.

'People think of Italy as an old country. It isn't. We're young, younger than the United States. We only united in 1870, not even a hundred years ago. We're not a country yet, and we won't be for a while. These things take a long time. No, those bastard Sienese haven't forgotten Montaperti. It's part of who they are. In the same way Hastings is part of who you English are. That's one of the great battles. You know why? Because a bunch of men fighting in that one field changed the whole course of your country's history.'

Fausto took a slug of beer.

'But you didn't come here to talk about this stuff. Am I wrong?'

'No.'

'So tell me.'

'I have a question. It's about Gaetano.'

'Gaetano?'

'The gardener who left last year.'

'I know who Gaetano is.'

'Where is he now?'

'Viareggio. By the sea. He owns a bar there, a fancy place – La Capannina.'

'You've been there?'

Fausto spread his arms to indicate his dishevelled appearance. 'What do you think?'

'How much does a fancy bar in Viareggio cost?'

'Apparently he inherited some money from his family down south.' There was a note of scepticism in his voice.

'You don't believe it?'

'How do I know? More to the point, what do you care?'

Adam gathered himself then took the plunge. 'The last time I saw you, you said Gaetano changed his story about what happened the night Emilio died.'

'Was I drunk?'

'You lied?'

'Why do you want to know?'

'Just tell me what you meant.'

Fausto sighed. 'Look, it was something Gaetano's uncle told my father the next day.'

'What?'

'He said he was almost run down by the Germans when they were leaving.'

'Gaetano said that?'

'To his uncle.'

Adam digested this news. 'He turned up later. He wasn't there when it happened.'

'It was a long time ago. Who knows what really happened? Who cares?'

'I do.'

Fausto leaned forward in his chair. 'Listen to me. The Doccis' business is their own. Who are you? You've been here – what – a week? You didn't know them before and you'll probably never see them again. Just leave it alone.'

'How do you know I didn't know them before?'

'What?'

'How do you know I didn't know the Doccis before?'

'You said.'

'No I didn't.'

'Yes you did.'

'No.'

'*Porca l'oca!* Look at you. Look at you! I'd chuck a bucket of water over you if the well wasn't dry. I warned you about that place. Didn't I warn you? Pull yourself together, this isn't normal behaviour, you're acting like a crazy man. Just leave it alone.'

Adam wanted to tell him that he'd tried to leave it alone – more than once – but he couldn't. He no longer had any choice in the matter.

'Did Maurizio kill Emilio?' he asked bluntly.

'I'm not going to answer that.'

'Why not?'

'Because how the hell should I know?'

'But you think it's possible . . .'

'Anything's possible.'

'Well, I think he did it.'

'What if he did?'

'I think I can prove it.'

'What if you can?'

'You don't believe in justice?'

Fausto gave a short, despairing laugh. 'This is madness. You should go now. I'm serious. Go. Leave.'

Fausto got to his feet to press home his point. He made no move to shake Adam's hand, so Adam turned and left.

22

Signora, are you awake?

Yes.

Shall I open the shutters?

Thank you, Maria.

Did you manage to sleep?

Not much.

Antonella called. She has bought fish for dinner this evening.

What kind of fish?

Does it matter? She knows I don't like cooking fish.

I'm sure she didn't do it to annoy you.

I'll mess it up. I always mess it up.

Maria, I've never known you to mess anything up.

Except the wild boar in chocolate sauce.

Yes, that was truly terrible. It was also twenty years ago.

Twenty-three.

It's good to see you've put it behind you.

Maurizio and Chiara have arrived.

Did they come by the villa?

No, I saw their car over at the farm.

We should invite them to dinner.

Antonella already has.

Oh, has she?

I like Chiara.

So do I, Maria. Where's Adam?

He went for a bike ride.

In this heat?

I was wrong about him.

Don't go soft on me now.

Signora?

In all the years we've known each other, I've never once heard you admit to being wrong about anything.

He's no fool.

No. But he's young, and therefore naïve.

He's twenty-two next month.

He told you?

I saw his passport.

I'm not sure it's acceptable to go rifling through the guests' belongings.

I was cleaning his room. It was on the sideboard.

Then you're forgiven.

I think I'll bake it.

Excuse me?

The fish, Signora.

23

Dinner was a trying affair.

It didn't help that the meal was billed as being in his honour. He had always struggled with that kind of thing. Some children glowed with self-importance at their birthday parties; others blushed, even when they managed to blow all the candles out.

It didn't help that he was seated directly opposite Maurizio down one end of the table. It didn't help that Harry and Antonella had returned from Florence the worse side of two cocktails each, giggling like love-struck teenagers. And it didn't help that he now knew for certain that someone – someone at the table, or the someone serving them – had been going through his papers in the study.

He knew, because he had laid a trap, stacking his notebooks in an apparently careless (yet very particular) fashion, laying his ballpoint pen on a pile of loose papers so that its tip pointed directly to the upper left-hand corner of the top sheet. Simple yet effective. The idea of lacing the bait with something had only occurred to him at the last moment. He had slipped a sheet among the papers. On it was written in big bold capitals: I KNOW YOU'RE LOOKING THROUGH MY THINGS.

Whoever it was had done a good job of covering their tracks. Not good enough, though. The notebooks were too neatly stacked, the pen slightly out of alignment. Thankfully, Antonella was beyond suspicion. He had set the trap after her departure for Florence with Harry, and it had been sprung before their return.

The ruse with the sheet of paper served him less well than he thought it might. In fact, about the only thing he learned was that it's impossible to second-guess someone who knows you're trying to second-guess them. He saw signs of guilt wherever he turned.

Maurizio and Chiara had moved into the house above the farmyard earlier in the day. They wanted to be around to help with the final preparations for the party, just two days off now. In an uncharacteristic display of selflessness – brought on, no doubt, by the brace of gin fizzes – Harry offered to vacate his room so that they could sleep in the villa.

Signora Docci sweetly acknowledged his noble gesture, while pointing out the obvious: that a lack of bedrooms was rarely a pressing concern at Villa Docci. No, it was a question of principle. 'It's their farmhouse, and they hardly ever use it. It's good for them to use it.'

'My mother's right. It's good for us to use it,' said Maurizio tightly.

'It'll be one of their last opportunities.'

Everyone looked to Signora Docci. She savoured the moment before continuing.

'I plan to be living there myself next month.'

'Mama . . .?' frowned Maurizio.

'That's right, I'm moving out of the villa. And you and Chiara are moving in, I hope.'

'Are you sure?'

'Of course I'm sure. Next month.' She lowered her eyes modestly and said in Italian, 'I'm sorry if it's taken longer than you thought.'

Adam despised what he saw in Maurizio's face: the spark of deep satisfaction behind the eyes, the struggle not to smile. He would soon be master of Villa Docci. The long years of waiting were over. Finally, there was a concrete, tangible purpose to his crime.

Maurizio must have sensed Adam studying him, because he shot a quick glance across the table and the look vanished from his face. It was the same sudden composure he had brought to bear in the memorial garden, when Adam had sprung on him the subject of fratricide in Dante's *Inferno*.

The mask was not allowed to slip again for the remainder of the meal. Even when it came time for Adam to detail his discoveries for Maurizio and Chiara's benefit, Maurizio's expression never faltered. He was not shaken by all the talk of murder and intrigue. Quite the reverse. He embraced it, heaping praise on Adam for his achievements and firing off questions to keep the discussion alive.

Adam was beginning to doubt the picture of the man he had painted for himself when he witnessed the one other wobble in Maurizio's performance. It occurred towards the end of the evening, just before Antonella left.

Signora Docci mooted the theory that Federico's murder of Flora and her lover, enshrined in the garden, had acted

246

as some kind of curse on the family, colouring the fortunes of the villa's occupants, consigning the Doccis to centuries of ill luck, violence and tragedy.

Her words cast a momentary pall over Maurizio's features, a sadness tinged with a telling self-pity. 'That's very interesting,' he said.

Chiara threw her husband a curious look and said in Italian, 'Since when are you superstitious?'

Since the moment it exonerated him of his own crime, thought Adam; since the moment it allowed him to view himself as a victim of some grander design set in motion by a murderous ancestor. Maurizio had leapt too readily at his mother's wild theory. That had been his mistake, and it shored up Adam's flagging suspicions.

Only as Antonella was leaving did Adam realize he'd paid her hardly any attention. She'd gone to a lot of effort to make the meal a special occasion, buying two magnificent fish which Maria had cooked to perfection, and he had barely acknowledged the fact. Worst of all, he wouldn't be seeing her again until the party. No one would. Something had come up at work. She hoped to get away early on Friday if at all possible, but she couldn't promise she'd appear much before the first guests arrived. These were about her last words before she disappeared into the night.

Maurizio and Chiara followed suit soon after. Adam noted that they stopped and kissed each other as they made their way across the parterre. When Signora Docci announced that she, too, was ready for bed, Harry told her to wait a moment: he had something for her. He disappeared inside the villa, promptly returning with his scuffed leather shoulder

247

bag. From it he produced something wrapped in a paint-bespattered piece of cloth. He laid the object carefully, almost reverently, on the table in front of him. It was about a foot long, not too thick – like a slender log.

'I was going to give it to Adam. But it's for you, a thank you. If you don't like it, give it to Adam. And if he doesn't like it . . . well, I'll shoot myself.' He let out a nervous laugh.

That's when Adam realized that one of Harry's own creations lay swaddled in the old rag. Maybe he should have guessed sooner, but he'd never seen anything by Harry on this scale. All the other works had been at least three or four times the size, considerably more in the case of the 'giant mechanical penis'.

This moniker, coined in relative innocence by Adam, had almost brought the two of them to blows right there in the Bath Academy sculpture studio at Corsham during Adam's one and only visit. Welded together from 'recovered pieces' – Harry's fancy phrase for scrap metal – the work in question was part building, part machine, and, in Adam's firm opinion, blatantly phallic.

For a horrible moment it occurred to Adam that the thing on the table, the thing about to be unveiled by Harry and handed to Signora Docci, might actually be a maquette for the same sculpture, a preparatory 'sketch' in miniature.

It wasn't. It was the first figurative piece by Harry that Adam had ever seen. And it was good. He knew it was good the moment he set eyes on it, because his very first thought was that it had almost been his, and now it never would be, not unless Signora Docci didn't like it. But he could see in her eyes that she did.

It was a creature, almost a man, but not quite. Mounted on a slate base, it had long spindly legs of welded steel which climbed to a thick barrel chest, redolent of an insect's thorax. There was no skin as such, just an irregular mesh of slender steel struts, each no thicker than a matchstick, which reached to the heart of the creature, leaving you in no doubt that it had been built from the inside out. The head consisted of two shapeless steel protrusions. The arms, like the legs, were skeletally thin, and were raised above this stumpy non-head and crossed at the wrists.

Somehow, the little insect-man was both robust and delicate, noble yet fragile, brave yet cowardly.

'It's made of mild steel. Do you like it?' Harry asked tentatively.

'Am I allowed to like him?' replied Signora Docci. 'I want to, but I'm not sure he wants me to.'

Harry beamed, happy with her reply. His head crept round to Adam.

'Well done.'

'Really?'

'Harry . . . really.'

Signora Docci held the sculpture up to the candlelight. 'He's so sure of himself but so frightened.' She paused. 'I see Mussolini at the end, before they strung him up with piano wire in Piazzale Loreto.'

'That's good,' said Harry.

'Maybe it's the way the arms are crossed above the head, but I see you and me in the Anderson shelter down the end of the garden in Kennington when the bombs were coming down.'

'That's good too,' said Harry.

'Thank you,' said Signora Docci. 'I love him and I will live with him for the rest of my life.'

Before carrying her prize off to bed with her, she told them that they needn't worry about what to wear to the party; something had been sorted out for them. She also told them that she'd be heading down into Florence in the morning with Maria for the final fitting of her dress. They both declined the offer of a lift, though for different reasons.

Adam knew that Maurizio and Chiara also planned to be away in the morning – they were dropping in on some friends who lived to the south. The timing was good. An opportunity for a snoop around the top floor of the villa was shaping up nicely.

'What's the matter?' asked Harry, the moment they found themselves alone together.

'Nothing's the matter.'

'Come on . . .'

'I wasn't lying, Harry, I love the sculpture.'

'That's not what I mean and you know it.'

'I'm fine, I'm just tired and a bit drunk.'

'It's Mum and Dad, isn't it?'

He felt bad snatching at the line Harry had thrown him, but it would keep his brother happy. And it did. They chatted some more about the situation at home. Meanwhile, Adam's head was on another matter altogether. He was thinking about the morning and how to shake Harry off before visiting the top floor.

The counter-intuitive solution came to him as they were making their way upstairs to bed.

'Do you want to have a look around the top floor?' he asked.

What could Harry say? Adam had already told him enough of the story for it to be an intriguing prospect. By the time he'd ladled on some of the more graphic details gleaned from Chiara, Harry was raring to go.

24

Signora Docci and Maria left for town soon after breakfast. Harry was all for making a move there and then, but
Adam was more cautious. It seemed like an eternity before
Maurizio and Chiara's top-of-the-range saloon car glided
past the front of the villa and down the driveway.

The key was exactly where Antonella had said it would
be: in a hidden drawer in the bureau in Signora Docci's
bedroom. It was smaller than Adam had imagined it to be,
but it worked. It fitted the door at the top of the staircase
and, with some judicious force, turned the mechanism.

The first impression was disappointing.

They found themselves in a stark, square hallway with
two corridors running off it. This was about all they
were able to discern until Harry applied his cigarette
lighter to the gloom. They found the light switch and
Adam twisted the ceramic knob. Nothing. Hopefully it
was just the bulb.

The flickering flame revealed a tall door leading off the
hallway towards the rear of the villa. It was locked, although

252

the key was in place. They located the light switch on the other side, but that didn't work, either.

'Shit,' said Adam.

'Shit,' said Harry, dropping the lighter and plunging them into darkness, 'I burnt my bloody hand.'

Adam could hear him groping around on the floor for his lighter. 'Let's just wait a moment, let our eyes adjust.'

Sure enough, out of the darkness three faintly glowing panels emerged: three sets of windows leaking light through their louvred shutters on the far side of the large room.

'We'll have to open one,' said Adam. 'Give me the lighter.'

The fluid was running low, but he made it to one of the windows, picking his way past furniture. He pulled open the centre window and forced the shutters apart. They groaned on their rusty hinges, and a desiccated bird's nest floated down to the terrace below.

The sunlight cut a rude swathe across the room. The first thing Adam noticed were his footprints in the thick dust coating the floor – evidence of an intrusion, not that there was anything to be done about it now.

Though not as lofty as those downstairs, the room still had a certain grandeur about it. There was an imposing fireplace of white marble, the walls were panelled up to the dado rail, and the ceiling was bedecked with frescoes.

'Jesus,' said Harry, 'what a mess.'

Broken and twisted pieces of furniture lay scattered around the room. There were rococo console tables, upholstered and gilded chairs, a delicate divan with shattered legs and a broken back.

An intricately carved frame was all that remained of the antique mirror above the fireplace. Its broken glass was strewn across the floor in front of the hearth, and in this debris lay the marble ashtray which one of the Germans had evidently hurled at the mirror.

'Paddler,' said Harry. He was staring up at the ceiling.

The frescoes were eighteenth century from the look of them: overblown and slightly suffocating, with lots of ballooning flesh and ruddy-cheeked cherubs on show. The centrepiece was a depiction of Diana and her hunting party, but it looked more like the aftermath of a bloody skirmish. Diana had been shot between the eyes. She also sported two bullet-holes instead of nipples. One of her attendants had been blasted in the groin and the cherubs had been picked off like hapless birds.

'Fucking Philistines,' murmured Harry.

Adam lingered when Harry wandered through to the adjacent rooms. The gramophone player on the table against the wall suggested that this was the scene of Emilio's murder.

According to Chiara, Emilio had fired into the gramophone to kill the music and attract the attention of the two Germans busy lobbing another piece of furniture out of the window. This detail of her account certainly appeared to be correct. There was a bullet-hole in the gramophone's wooden casing. It was deep, but not so deep that the bullet had passed clean through. Which meant it should still be there, embedded in the wood. Only, it wasn't. Someone had removed it with the aid of a knife or some other such implement. The mouth of the hole was scored with nicks and notches where someone had gouged it free.

'Look at this,' called Harry from the room next door.

He had thrown the shutters wide open. Adam peered

outside. The workmen hammering together a low wooden dais at the centre of the parterre were fully engrossed in their work, but he still drew the shutters back a touch.

'Hey,' complained Harry.

'You can still see.'

The room had obviously served as some sort of dormitory. There were four canvas cots still with their bedding, counterpanes folded down, pillows puffed up. They had made their beds, even knowing they'd be gone by nightfall.

'Nothing's been touched,' said Harry.

This wasn't quite true. There were a couple of wooden filing cabinets in the corner. Their contents had been searched, the papers hastily replaced on the shelves. A few stray files lay shrouded in dust on the floor, like flat-fish waiting for prey.

The next room was a corner room, and clearly the Germans' operations centre. There were metal desks and cabinets, and a bulletin board with cross-garterings was attached to the wall. A couple of typewriters had not made the last lorry out, and judging from the ashes heaped in the grate, a large amount of paperwork had ended up as smoke. Harry seemed more than happy to poke around, so Adam slipped away.

He returned to the scene of the shooting and tried to picture the events unfolding around him: Emilio and Maurizio coming through the door, the two Germans busy at the window, their backs turned, oblivious to the fact that they had company because of the music blaring from the gramophone player. He saw Emilio taking in the destruction around him – the broken mirror, the bullet-holes in the ceiling frescoes – before levelling his gun at the gramophone and firing.

It was easy to imagine an argument ensuing, as Chiara had described. What else had she said? That Emilio was standing near the fireplace when he was shot.

Adam wandered over. He examined the marble surround and the walls on both sides for evidence of a stray shot, but found nothing. That's when he noticed that the rug in front of the hearth was not centred. It had been dragged a few feet to one side. He crouched down and folded back the edge of the rug.

The stain was large and irregular. Emilio had bled a lot.

The pool of blood was still fresh when it had been covered up, judging from the mirror impression on the underside of the rug. This wasn't what attracted Adam's attention, though – it was the bullet-hole in the boards near the middle of the stain, easy to miss if it hadn't been for the slanting light.

He leaned closer, running his finger around the rim of the depression. As with the gramophone player, there were score marks in the wood where the bullet had been removed. This must have occurred some time after the event, or fresh blood would have seeped into the notches, whereas clean new wood showed through them.

The bullet might have vanished, but the grim truth remained: Emilio had not been fired on by the German from across the room; he had been executed at close range when already on the floor.

Hearing Harry returning, Adam folded back the rug and got to his feet.

❧

The rest of the day passed in a mist of distraction. Harry made a phone call then announced he was heading into town. It was his last chance to see the Swedish Finn. Her boyfriend would be back at the weekend, and Harry planned to leave for Venice on Sunday.

'A day to recover from the party, then I'm out of your hair. Tell me you'll miss me.'

'I'll miss you.'

'That was almost convincing.'

'It's true.'

'Then this might be the time to talk about you advancing me a small loan for the rest of my trip.'

'As soon as I've figured out what my own plans are.'

Which was easier said than done.

He felt numb, incapable of clear thought, after the discovery on the top floor. It was the closest thing to hard evidence against Maurizio – no, the *only* thing so far that approximated to any kind of evidence. The rest was speculation rooted in hearsay and intuition.

The bullet-hole in the floorboards changed everything. Emilio had been executed while on the floor. This was completely at odds with Maurizio and Gaetano's account of what happened that night, and pointed to their collusion in the killing. As for Benedetto, it was clear now that he had indeed discovered the truth. Who other than Benedetto had gouged the bullets free from the floor and the gramophone player? Torn between bringing down his only remaining son and doing nothing, Benedetto had opted for a third way – sealing off the top floor and burying Emilio in the family chapel, stark and close reminders to Maurizio of his heinous crime.

But Benedetto had not stopped there. His bizarre behaviour in the immediate aftermath of Emilio's death hinted at another agenda. In closing the top floor, he had preserved the scene of the crime, with its tell-tale clues. Why had he done this? So that someone else might one day decipher the truth? And why had he then taken Emilio's gun and secreted it behind the plaque in the chapel, along with the bullets? Because those relics of the murder offered hard, ballistic proof that Emilio had been killed with his own weapon? It seemed quite likely. It seemed more than likely.

This was all well and good, except for the fact that Adam now found himself caught on the horns of the biggest dilemma of his life. Should he act, or do as Benedetto had done: nothing? Why should he pursue the matter further, when the victim's own father had chosen not to do so? This was a serious business. This was murder. And it surprised him that the enormity of what he had embarked on hadn't occurred to him before.

His instinct was to make for the memorial garden. It was where he usually went to gather his thoughts. Not this time, though. If he was going to face some plain and hard truths, he couldn't risk exposing himself to its influence.

It was a preposterous notion, and not one he would have shared with any soul, but he still had the uneasy feeling that Flora Bonfadio, dead in 1548, was largely responsible for his current predicament. She had set him on his course, and she had been illuminating his path ever since. The flash of guilt in Maurizio's eyes, the revelation about Emilio's paternity – other insights, too – all had come to him while passing through her kingdom.

Nor could he rid himself of the sensation that she had

also exercised a similar control over matters relating more directly to her. She had nudged, cajoled and teased him, revealing her own tragic story to him piecemeal, as if by will. How could he be expected to enjoy a dinner in his honour when he had discovered nothing that she hadn't already chosen to share with him? And now that she had finally broken her centuries-old silence, why did he have the unnerving sensation that she expected something from him in return?

No, the memorial garden was not the place to head in search of clarity. He needed distance, and lots of it. Which was why he made for his bicycle and pedalled off into the hills.

The moment he saw the sign, he knew that's where he would go. Sant'Andrea in Percussina was not so much a village as a hamlet strung out along a country road, the sort of place you passed through without so much as a second glance or thought. But if Fausto was to be believed, it was here that Niccolò Machiavelli had written one of the world's most controversial and prophetic works of political science: *Il Principe*.

Fausto was right. The first person Adam collared directed him to the modest stone property that had once been Machiavelli's country residence. It lay dormant, the windows shuttered against more than the heat. He walked round to the overgrown garden at the back and tried to imagine Machiavelli strolling there, hatching his ideas, or hunched at a table, scratching away with a pen.

He knew the book well. It was short, to the point, uncompromising in its opinions – a manual for rulers on how to obtain and maintain political power. Machiavelli didn't shy from the more unpleasant realities of the political world. Anything was acceptable just so long as it served the primary goal: the survival of the state. This took precedence over all else. Even religious and moral imperatives were to be ignored by a ruler if they vied with his own interests.

Men of all political persuasions had bent Machiavelli's model of statecraft to their own ends over the intervening centuries, and Adam now found himself drawing guidance from *The Prince*, from the bald pragmatism which suffused the book.

Whatever Maurizio might or might not have done on the top floor of the Villa Docci fourteen years before, what was he, Adam, now going to do about it? Confront Maurizio with a direct accusation based on a few scraps of evidence? Run to Signora Docci and lay out his case? Of course not. He had taken the matter as far as he possibly could. Maurizio would no more be brought to justice than Federico Docci had been. Why pretend otherwise?

After this, his decision came easily.

25

Adam was woken by the sound of running water coming from his bathroom.

'Hello . . .?' he called groggily.

'Yours is brown too.'

He checked his watch. He'd slept for ten hours. He couldn't remember the last time he'd slept for ten hours.

'What?'

Harry appeared in the bathroom doorway. 'The water – yours is brown too.' He was unshaven and dressed in the same clothes he'd been wearing when he headed down into Florence.

'You just got back?'

'Uh-huh.'

'You stayed the night?'

'Are you always this sharp first thing? Yes, I stayed the night. And now I'm back and I want a bath and the water's brown.'

Adam rolled away on to his side. 'So complain to the management, demand a refund.'

Harry dumped himself on the mattress. 'Good evening, was it?'

'Hard to imagine, with you not there.'

'Want to hear about mine?'

'Not especially.'

Harry pointed to his cheek. 'The boyfriend came back early.'

Adam tried to focus. There was some discoloration at the side of Harry's mouth.

'He hit you?'

'I wish. He slapped me.'

'He slapped you?'

'It's humiliating, believe me, worse than you think, being slapped by a very small and very angry Italian man.'

'Why did he slap you?'

'Well, not because I polished off the milk in his fridge.'

'I thought she lived with two girls.'

'We went to his place.'

'Harry, why on earth would you go to his place?'

'The view. It's got a great view, right along the river, the Ponte Vecchio, everything. He wasn't meant to come back till today.'

'I give up.'

'That's what he said.'

'Huh?'

'When I had him by the throat: "I give up." He spoke good English.'

Harry's use of the past tense was more than a little worrying.

'You didn't kill him? Tell me you didn't kill him.'

'Of course not, but after that we couldn't exactly stay there.'

'You don't say?'

'We went back to her place. She was upset. She asked me to hang around, so I did. She just drove me back on her scooter. It's a Lambretta.'

'Harry, I don't care.'

'I think I'm going to get one for myself – a black Lambretta.'

'With what? You're broke. You're always broke.'

Harry turned on his side and grinned at Adam. 'I'm glad you brought it up.'

'How much do you need?'

'I don't know. Anything you can spare.'

'You can have it all.'

'Really?'

'I'm leaving on Sunday, same as you. You can have whatever's left.'

Harry took in the news. 'Why are you leaving?'

'I want to go home, I want to see Mum. That sounds pathetic, doesn't it?'

'No,' said Harry. 'Not if it means I get all the money.'

By mid morning a small army had descended on the villa. Lorries and vans jostled for space in the courtyard, disgorging everything from flowers to food, crockery to Chinese lanterns. There were even two pigs skewered on spits, ready for roasting.

The whole operation unfolded with military precision, co-ordinated by a handful of generals hired for the occasion, with Signora Docci and Maurizio acting as joint commanders-in-chief. She seemed much more inclined to involve him and allow him a say than she had the other day.

Maria bustled about in her efficient and rather formidable fashion, keen to exercise her authority over the outsiders – a category to which Adam and Harry clearly belonged in her view. They found themselves dispatched on numerous errands. It was on returning from one such menial mission that Adam found himself alone in the kitchen with Maria.

'*La Signora* wants to see you in the study.'

These were the first words of English he'd ever heard her speak. Her accent was thick, but the intonation perfect. He hoped that the slightly foreboding note in her voice was accidental.

Signora Docci was indeed in the study. She was seated behind the desk where Adam had spent so much of his time. And sitting in the middle of the desk was a bird's nest. Dusty and dried out, it was also dishevelled after its descent from the top-floor window. Adam cursed himself silently for the oversight.

'Maria found it on the terrace yesterday. There is only one place it could have come from.' There was no hostility in her voice, but there was a hard edge to her gaze, one he'd never seen before.

No point in playing dumb. Their footprints were all over the top floor. She had probably checked already.

'Did Antonella tell you where the key was? I hope she did. I don't like to think that you went through all my things looking for it.'

'It's not her fault. I kept pestering her.'

'Why?'

Adam shrugged. 'Morbid curiosity. An untouched murder scene. A frozen moment in time.'

All true, all things he had felt. He almost sounded convincing to himself.

'And was it worth it?'

'Worth it?'

'Worth risking our friendship over?'

Adam's mind shuddered to a halt. All he could think was: Christ, her English is good.

'I'm sorry,' he said feebly.

'I don't mind that you've insulted me, but you have insulted Benedetto. You knew it was his wish.'

'Yes.'

After a long moment she brought her hands together. 'Good. Well, let's not allow this to spoil your last week here.'

'I'm leaving on Sunday with Harry.'

'Oh.' She seemed surprised, even disappointed.

'I've finished my work on the garden.'

'I thought there were still questions.'

There were, not least of all: Did the garden hold a clue to the identity of Flora's lover? The library had yielded no more information on Tullia d'Aragona following her sudden disappearance from view the year of Flora's death. She was definitely emerging as a viable contender. The hunchback poet, Girolamo Amelonghi, seemed a less likely candidate, and many of the other names on the list were excluded by dint of the fact that they'd outlived Flora by many years. There were still a few individuals he needed to check up on, but that was something that required a far more extensive library than Villa Docci had to offer.

'Nothing we'll probably ever know the answers to.'

'No,' Signora Docci conceded.

❧

The first thing Adam did was go in search of Harry. He found him in the courtyard, where two tanker-loads of water were replenishing the villa's depleted well. Antonella was also there – she had just arrived – which meant he only had to have the conversation once.

'A bloody bird's nest?' said Harry.

'*Merda*,' said Antonella.

'She didn't seem too annoyed.'

Antonella wasn't convinced. 'We'll see.'

'I'm sorry, it was completely my fault.'

'I won't dispute that,' said Harry.

They all played their part in the transformation of the parterre into an alfresco dining area. Circular tables spread with white linen mushroomed around the fringes, and were soon adorned with bone china, silver cutlery and crystal. The party unfolded in the same fashion every year: drinks on the villa terrace, dinner on the parterre, then dancing on the lower terrace. A gradual descent into debauchery, Harry remarked. Apparently, he wasn't too far wrong. The event had acquired something of a reputation over the years.

The big test for Adam came when he found himself thrown together with Maurizio, deciding on the place-ment of the flares around the terraces. They spent a good half-hour in one another's company, and he was relieved to find that his resolve didn't falter once during that time. It wasn't even that he had to work at it. The matter of Maurizio's guilt or innocence had ceased to be a pressing concern, for the simple reason that all further specula-tion was ultimately futile. Besides, there was an innocent explanation for everything, even if you had to strain the laws of probabilities a little.

They chatted easily as they went about their business with the flares. There was even an intimacy in the way they ribbed each other. He suspected that his own shift in thinking wasn't solely responsible for this new familiarity. Some of the tension had also gone out of Maurizio since his mother's announcement that she would soon be vacating the villa, making way for her son.

The library and the study were designated as holding-areas for the cohorts of waiters, waitresses and bar staff descending on the villa. Adam was asked to clear out all his books and papers. When he carried them upstairs to his room, he found Maria setting out a dinner jacket on his bed, along with a dress-shirt, bow tie, studs and cuff-links. There was even a brand-new pair of patent leather shoes. These he could keep, Maria explained; they were a gift from Signora Docci. A quick glance into Harry's room revealed the same kit laid out on his bed.

Signora Docci brushed aside their thanks then retired to her room for a rest before the festivities kicked off. Antonella announced that she was heading home. Her brother Edoardo and Grazia were staying with her that night, and she still had beds to make, things to arrange. Adam walked her to her car, which she had parked in the farmyard, well out of the way. They took the track that led down the slope from the lower terrace. He had strolled through the farmyard on a couple of occasions, but he had never registered the high wooden doors set in the sandstone knoll on which Villa Docci perched.

'That is where the wine and the olive oil are made,' said

Antonella. When she proposed a quick tour, he didn't refuse. It was the first opportunity he'd had in a couple of days to be alone with her.

First came the dramatic drop in temperature. Then came the smell. Over the centuries the soft stone walls had soaked up the odours like a sponge. The huge vats where the grapes were trod and left to ferment were stained from past harvests and scrubbed spotless in anticipation of the next one, already ripening out there on the slopes.

They passed from the light heady scent of the *tinaia* to the thick musk of the *frantoio*. By the light of the bare overhead bulbs, Antonella explained how the olives were first crushed beneath a giant millstone turned by oxen, whose shod hooves had worn a circular furrow in the stone-paved floor over the centuries. The press resembled some medieval instrument of torture, with its giant turning screw and its beams clamped with iron. The whole operation was in need of modernization, Antonella explained, but Signora Docci was reluctant to throw out the ancient equipment as long as it still functioned.

'You must come and see it when it's working.'

'Is that an invitation?'

'You don't need an invitation.'

They made their way back through the underground labyrinth.

'*Nonna* says you are leaving on Sunday.'

'That's the plan.'

'It has gone quickly, your time here.'

'Too quickly.'

Antonella stopped at the door. 'I'm going to do this now because we can't later.' She took a step towards him and

268

kissed him, a fragile and lingering embrace. When she threw the light switch, plunging them into darkness, he assumed it was a prelude to something a little more intimate. But she slipped outside, playfully dodging his lunge.

He caught up with her as she was getting into her car. 'Don't be late,' she said.

'Late?'

'For *Nonna*'s special drinks on the terrace.'

He wasn't late, even though he lost ten minutes battling with his bow tie. In the end, Harry tied it for him, which was unexpected. The first thing they noticed on heading downstairs was that Harry's sculpture had ousted the bronze of a striding tiger from pride of place on the table in the entrance hall – an undoubted honour, but also a cause of some consternation for Harry.

It was a small gathering, immediate family and their partners. Adam recognized Antonella's mother immediately: the same lustrous black hair, the same almond eyes, the proud lift of the chin. She was a beautiful woman with an attractive whiff of danger about her. She was also older than he'd imagined, or maybe it was just the aura of a life lived to the full and fast catching up with her. Riccardo, her boyfriend, was her signal to the world that she was still a step or two ahead. A dark, lantern-jawed man in his thirties, he was improbably handsome. Against all apparent odds, he was also very cultivated and amusing. He was a cellist with an orchestra in Rome, although he was reluctant to talk about it. This was the first Friday night he'd had away from his work in months, and the last thing he wanted to do was discuss music –

he wanted to remember how sensible people spent their Friday nights.

When Antonella and Edoardo arrived, they both greeted their mother warmly. Neither had met Riccardo before, and while Caterina made the introductions Adam was able to admire the view.

Antonella's dress was made of shimmering midnight-blue silk which hung from her slender, tawny frame like liquid. The halter neck left her shoulders, back and arms bare, while the deep V neckline flirted tantalizingly with disaster. Her hair flowed freely about her shoulders but was pinned back off her forehead, brazenly revealing her scars.

He must have been staring at her like an idiot, because Harry leaned close and whispered in his ear, 'It's great when you catch God at his work, isn't it?'

It was an enjoyable event, helped along by attentive waiters forever topping up champagne flutes. Signora Docci looked magnificent in an emerald-green gown, its bright, bold colour matching her mood. Only Maurizio seemed a little out of sorts, and only when in Adam's company. He could feel the heat of hostility coming off Maurizio, melting the memories of the easy-going rapport that had marked their exchanges earlier in the day. There wasn't much time to dwell on this before Maria came through to the terrace with news that the first guests were arriving. Signora Docci went off to do her duty in the entrance hall. Her two children and four grandchildren went with her.

'It is time for the Doccis to smile and pretend to be a family,' said Riccardo – somewhat unfairly, it seemed to Adam.

The party's reputation proved to be a self-fulfilling

prophecy. It was clear from the start that people were bent on enjoying themselves. Most arrived well within the first half-hour, a steady stream of humanity soon filling the back terrace to overflowing. Some made for the parterre and the lower terrace. It was an idyllic sight: well-dressed couples strolling in the waning sunlight against the backdrop of the rolling hills to the accompaniment of the string quartet.

Taking Adam aside, Harry announced breathlessly that he'd just met the most amazing woman. The fact that she was married appeared to have no bearing on the matter, and Harry hurried off to make some alterations to the place settings.

Adam sought out Signora Docci, who was in discussion with a middle-aged couple. She used his arrival as an excuse to peel away, slipping her arm through his and leading him off.

'Where are we going?'

'Anywhere but there.'

Picking their way down the steps to the parterre, she explained that the man was a friend of Maurizio, a fellow partisan from the war. And like many partisans she had known, he'd been less set on fighting the Germans than on looting the factories the enemy destroyed while in retreat. Being first on the scene, the members of the Italian underground were often best placed to control the black market in any goods that survived. First it was shoes from Poggibonsi, then hats from Impruneta.

'He,' she said, with a slight jerk of the head behind her, 'came to our door with both. His prices were ridiculous.' She gave a little laugh. 'Our heroes of the struggle. Look at them now – no different.'

Adam had to ask. 'And Maurizio?'

'Let's just say, he never sold to us.'

She smiled and nodded at the leader of the chamber quartet as they negotiated their way across the parterre. They stopped at the balustrade, looking down over the lower terrace, the hills beyond already falling into silhouette.

'It's changing so fast.'

'What?'

She couldn't mean the view. Medieval peasants wouldn't have looked out of place in it.

'The world. Or maybe every age thinks just the same thing.'

'Maybe.'

'Big changes are coming. I can see it everywhere . . . music, theatre, films, art. Look at Harry's sculpture. Have you ever seen anything like it? Don't listen to the politicians, always look at the artists, they're the first to tell us where we're going.'

'Have you been talking to him?'

'Harry?'

'It's not the first time I've heard that line of argument.'

She laughed. 'Well, that one was mine.'

They were approached by a passing couple. A few pleasantries were exchanged, Adam was introduced by Signora Docci, but the couple soon took the veiled hint from their hostess and moved on.

Signora Docci ground the tip of the cane into the gravel, observing her handiwork for a moment before looking up.

'You have a gift, Adam, don't waste it.'

'You *have* been talking to him.'

'He's right. You sense things other people don't.'

272

'Or maybe I'm so ordinary that anything that isn't disturbs me.'

She laughed.

'I'm sorry you're leaving. I'm also sorry we only met at the end of my life. I think we could have been very good friends.'

Embarrassment left him mute. No one had ever spoken to him in such terms before.

'Remember those words,' she said.

'I will.'

She turned stiffly and surveyed the villa with an approving eye – the stir and hum on the terrace, the lowering sun skimming the roof.

'Now take this old lady back to her guests. It's time to announce dinner.'

Harry had engineered matters so that Signora Pedretti – the new love of his life – was seated between them.

'Make me look good,' said Harry, seeing her approach their table.

'How?' asked Adam.

'Just be yourself.'

Signora Pedretti was young, petite, impishly beautiful. Her delicate wrists glistened with gold, and her mouth was a startling splash of colour. She didn't appear nearly as surprised as Harry by the fact that providence had thrown them together again. Nor was she unhappy about it.

She proved considerably better company than the woman to Adam's left, who only came to life when he finally remarked on the jewels blazing at her neck. She was French, Parisian, married to the American gentleman holding forth on the far side of the table about the benefits of the fertil-izers and hybrid grains he sold to the Italians. God knows how much money he had made importing 'superior American product', as he termed it – quite a bundle, if his wife's necklace was anything to go by – but he talked like a man on a humanitarian mission. Italy was poor, ravaged by war, and desperately in need of being dragged into the twentieth century. He, of course, was proud to be playing his part in this mercy mission.

His words clearly rankled the Italians around the table, but, out of politeness, or maybe stupefaction, they held themselves in check. It took an English woman to light the touch paper. Adam had been introduced to her earlier in the evening – a tall, pale creature, gaunt and ascetic, with a bony high-ridged nose and heavy-lidded eyes that lent her a misleading air of boredom. It was a distinctive and familiar look, a particular brand of ugliness reserved for the English upper classes.

Those same lugubrious eyes now twinkled with mischief as she leaned forward, searching out the Italian faces around the table.

'I happen to know a lot of Americans,' she said with her cut-glass accent, 'and please don't think for a moment that they are all like Seymour.'

'Vera . . .' There was a note of friendly forbearance in Seymour's voice that suggested they were well acquainted.

'Can't you see they're only tolerating you? They find your views offensive. As do I.'

'I'm not trying to be offensive.'

'I know,' replied Vera with a wicked smile, 'it comes naturally.'

Seymour gave a hearty laugh. 'Touché.'

'If the United States is so worried about communism and Russia's interest in Italy, which is a questionable notion now that that funny little man Khrushchev is Premier, then you really should spend less time treating this country like a marketplace for your goods and more time making friends.'

The ensuing debate ran right through the starter of blue mullet and on into the spit-roasted pork stuffed with garlic and rosemary (which tasted as good as it had been smelling all afternoon). It was a lively and generally good-natured discussion about Fascists, Monarchists and democracy, poverty, over-population and America's desire to create the world in its own image. Even Harry and Signora Pedretti broke off from their quiet flirtation to chip in a comment from time to time.

Seymour fought his corner valiantly and with dignity, never losing his studied jauntiness, whereas his wife grew tetchy and spiteful. Her unquestioning belief in the redemptive power of economic prosperity bore all the hallmarks of religious zealotry. Her God was the one true God, and all unbelievers were doomed to damnation, or worse still: communism.

The discussion petered out over pudding, by which time the first stars were overhead, the torches had been lit around the parterre, and Adam was wondering just how much longer he could go without seeing Antonella. The moment the band struck up on the lower terrace, he downed the rest of his coffee and went in search of her.

People were rising now, making for the music. Through the building throng he saw her talking to Maria, who had abandoned the refuge of the villa. Maria was smiling – which in itself was a rarity – but it was her hands that seemed different. They made quick and expressive gestures as she talked. Her dark eyes lost some of their lustre when she saw Adam approaching, and she only stayed long enough to acknowledge his greeting.

'Poor Maria,' said Antonella.

'Is there a problem?'

'Only that she is a bit drunk.' She hooked her arm through his. 'Come, I want to meet someone.'

The elderly man in question was on the point of nodding off, his bald crown tracing a lazy circle in the air. The table where he was seated was deserted, except for a young couple on the far side, engrossed, pressed close in conversation, a picture of barely suppressed desire. When Antonella and Adam took a seat either side of the man, he started like a soldier called to attention.

'Rodolfo, this is Adam,' Antonella said in Italian.

Rodolfo's head snapped round. 'Adam?'

'And the garden . . .'

'Oh, the garden Adam. Does he speak Italian? Of course he does. Crispin wouldn't have sent him if he didn't speak Italian.'

'You know Professor Leonard?' asked Adam.

'Yes, yes, of course.' Rodolfo gripped his forearm surprisingly hard. 'Congratulations. I've known that garden almost all my life. What you have done is, well, exceptional. Have you told Crispin yet? Of course you have.'

'No.'

'No? Why not?'

'I don't know.'

'Well, you must, you must. He knew there was something in that garden. He knew it. He often said so. And it annoyed him that he couldn't identify it. We were young – your age – though of course we were both much better looking.' He found this extremely amusing. 'Anyway, we went there a lot with Francesca,' – he jabbed a crooked finger at Antonella – 'her grandmother. I should say that I hated Crispin then. You see, I knew I was only there for one reason – because they couldn't be alone together.'

'Why not?'

'It was a long time ago. It wasn't allowed. I, the boy who had always loved her, had to stand by and watch her lose her heart to him.'

This was clearly news to Antonella. 'Really?'

Her eyes flicked to Adam. He feigned an equal degree of surprise.

'Yes, but that's beside the point. The point is that Crispin sensed something right back then. Sometimes we would go there by ourselves, the two of us, him and me – that's when I grew to like him. He sensed it, you see?' Rodolfo patted Adam on the hand. 'You'll send me your thesis and I'll have it translated. I'll even see it published for you. Oh, nothing very exciting – a departmental journal at the university – but that's how it begins for all of us.' He gave a short and slightly demented snigger. 'And in sixty years if you play your cards right, you can be just like me – penniless, half-drunk at a party, and wondering what you've done with another man's cigar.' He searched around him.

Antonella pointed. 'It's in your hand.'

'So it is. Now, you two youngsters go and join the other

277

apes prancing in the cage.' He made to re-light the cigar. Antonella blew out the match.

'One dance,' she said.

'No.'

'I insist.'

'Persuade me.'

'It might be our last.'

'Good point. Help me up.'

It was a big band, with lots of brass, and it played big band numbers. Which was fine for those who knew how to dance to big band numbers, and not so good for those who didn't know how to dance to anything. To make matters worse, Rodolfo could dance – he could really dance. He also had remarkable stamina for a man his age, which gave Adam lots of time to dread the hand-over. When it finally came, he felt duty-bound to confess to Antonella that he had two left feet (one of which was still stiff and sore from his stumble in the memorial garden).

The alcohol helped, so did the excuse to lay his hands on her.

The band was set up on a tiered dais just in front of the stone balustrade. The dance floor consisted of a giant boarded circle at the heart of the terrace, with the marble fountain as a centrepiece. It was ringed by tall screens of tight-clipped yew strung with Chinese lanterns and flanked by flaming torches, which cast wild and restless shadows. Penned in by the hedges, the music was all-engulfing.

'Did you enjoy dinner?' asked Antonella as they fought for their patch on the crowded floor.

'Yes.'

'*Nonna* said you would. Vera is very . . . *provocativa.*'

'She certainly is.'

'She is a lesbian, you know?'

'Odd, she didn't say.'

Pressed close by the crush, Adam allowed his hand to stray.

'You're not wearing any underwear.'

'I can't with this dress.'

'How does it feel?'

'It feels good. You should try it some time.'

He hoped the ambiguity was deliberate.

'God, you're beautiful,' he said, his head thick with desire.

'Thank you.'

'I want to kiss you.'

'We can't.' She gave a theatrical flick of the wrist. 'The scandal . . .'

'I don't care. Tomorrow's my last day.'

'I know. That's why you're invited to lunch. In Siena. You said you wanted to see Siena. They're friends of Edoardo's. Harry can come too. It's all organized.'

'I want to be alone with you.'

She pressed her lips to his ear. 'Then it's lucky I have a plan.'

She refused to elaborate.

A short while later, he lost her to a string of competitors, beginning with her brother Edoardo. Adam received Grazia in exchange. He hobbled his way through a couple of numbers with her, then she too was taken from him, at which point he renounced the dance floor for the bar nearby. He was waiting to be served when Harry stalked up to him.

'Her husband's not here.'

It took a moment for Adam to realize he was talking about Signora Pedretti. 'I know, she said over dinner.'

'But a bunch of his friends are.' Harry lit a cigarette and glared about him.

'Harry, are you seriously trying to seduce a married woman?'

'I think so. Yes. Why? You think it's a bad idea?' He hesitated. 'Shit, it's a bad idea, isn't it?'

'Is it enough to know she would – under different circumstances, I mean?'

'Maybe.'

'So ask her.'

'Ask her?'

'Yes. Then you'll know. And then her husband's friends won't have to kill you.'

There was a simple logic to the suggestion that Adam suspected would appeal to Harry. It did. Harry tripped off in search of Signora Pedretti, greeting Antonella's mother as he went. Caterina approached Adam with the controlled steps of someone who knows they've strayed beyond their limit.

'Where's Riccardo?' he asked.

'Talking to my mother.' She gave a sardonic smile. 'I think she approves.'

'He's great.'

'So is Antonella.' She nodded towards the dance floor. 'I saw you dancing with her. You like her, don't you?'

Something in her voice brought out a defensive streak in him.

'Is that so hard to understand?'

'Of course not, I am her mother.'

'Yes, I like her.'

'Men do. That is never a problem for her.'

Intentionally, or otherwise, her words placed him somewhere in a long line of foolhardy suitors, and he was happy that the barman asked him for his order at that moment.

'One of those, please,' he said, pointing to Caterina's cocktail glass.

It was unpronounceable. And almost undrinkable.

'Did she tell you what happened to her face?'

The directness of the question threw him momentarily.

'Your mother did.'

'I was driving.'

'I know.'

'And Antonella was the one asking me to go faster. Did my mother tell you that?'

'No.'

'No, of course she didn't. No one remembers that.'

He looked at her and saw a drunk and guilt-ridden mother still groping for excuses many years on.

'You don't believe me? It's true. She was . . . *selvaggia*. Not like Edoardo. *Una piccola selvaggia*.'

A little savage.

He could feel his hackles rising now. Looking to dilute her responsibility was one thing; harbouring a hateful grudge against the daughter she'd disfigured seemed downright unreasonable.

'Were you drunk when it happened?' he asked, biting back a more aggressive riposte.

'Is that what you heard?'

'No.'

The tension went out of her frame. After a moment she

281

said in a lowered voice, 'Yes, I was drunk. Emilio was dead . . . just two months before.' She glanced away. 'I loved my brother.'

Yet another junction in the cat's cradle of cause and effect: Emilio's murder and the scars on Antonella's face.

Adam turned to the dance floor, where Antonella was spinning in the arms of some new admirer. 'Look at her,' he said. 'Look at the way she is. She doesn't mind. Why should you?'

Caterina seemed on the point of mouthing a response, but she walked away without speaking.

A moment later Harry came striding up to him.

'Great idea, Paddler.'

'What?'

'She said yes.'

'Who?'

'Who do you think? I asked her and she said yes she would, if circumstances were different.'

'Good, so now you know.'

'No,' said Harry, 'now I have to go and wait for her in the olive grove.' He slapped Adam on the back. 'Great bloody tactic.'

'Harry . . .'

Harry didn't turn; he just waggled his fingers in the air as he slipped away through the crowd.

'Oh shit,' muttered Adam.

He twisted back to the barman and asked for a bottle of mineral water.

Not long after, the numbers started to thin out. The champagne caught up with Grazia, who lost the ability to stand, let alone dance, at which point Edoardo and Adam bundled her into the car. Antonella drove. She said she'd be back to pick up Adam and Harry at eleven o'clock, which was less than eight hours off. Adam made a futile search for Harry. Then he headed for his bed.

Maurizio must have been watching him, tracking his movements, biding his time. He intercepted Adam at the head of the steps leading to the parterre.

'Do you have a cigarette?' he asked, his voice a gentle drawl.

Adam reached inside his jacket for his cigarettes and lighter.

Maurizio's hand shot out. 'I thought so,' he said, indicating the label sewn near the pocket. 'It's my brother's suit.'

'Is it?'

Maurizio took hold of Adam's shirt cuff, exposing the cuff-link. 'And these are his too.' The voice was calm, the eyes coldly attentive, but his fingers trembled with a barely suppressed rage.

'I didn't know.'

'No?' Maurizio took a cigarette from Adam's pack and lit one. 'And when you stole the key from my mother's room, did you know what you were doing then?' He smiled thinly, relishing Adam's discomfort. 'Maria told me. She thought I should know.'

'I've apologized to your mother.'

'And what were you looking for up there?'

'I was just curious to see.'

'And what did you see?'

'A lot of dust and some German desks.' Maybe it was

Maurizio's hectoring tone, but he found himself adding, 'I also saw where Emilio was murdered.'

Maurizio's face seemed strangely pale in the lambent light of the flares.

'Near the fireplace,' Adam went on, emboldened. 'But then, you know that – you were there.'

Maurizio recovered his composure, a pursed smile stealing over his features. 'It's good that your work is finished and you are leaving.' He handed back the cigarettes and lighter. 'Thank you.' Turning on his heel, he made his way down the stone steps.

Adam was filled with a sudden flood of anger. He wanted to run after him, to seize him, shake him, scream at him: You fool! Don't you see? I was happy to let it go, I *wanted* to let it go, to walk away. But now I can't. All you had to do was say nothing till I was gone.

As he fumbled a cigarette between his lips, his gaze dropped to the terrace below – to the dark mass of the chapel lurking beyond the moonlight in the shadow of the sandstone bluff. And in that moment it struck him that he was wrong. Maurizio was not to blame. He was no more in control of matters than Adam was. They were simply actors playing out a drama, their roles already written for them.

26

Harry sat up front with Antonella, shouting at her over the music blaring from the car radio. Adam lay sprawled across the back seat, pretending to doze. He had in fact slept surprisingly well; he just wanted a private moment to work through the details of the scheme he'd hatched.

Every now and then he would sneak a peek at Antonella, her hair tied back in a ponytail, revealing her small ears. Harry was remarkably perky, given that he'd waited in the olive grove for well over an hour before falling asleep at the base of a tree, waking with the sun on his face. He still clung to the belief that Signora Pedretti had come looking for him, despite Antonella's insistence that the woman was a notorious and mischievous flirt.

Antonella spurned the new road to Siena in favour of the old Via Volterrana, which twisted through the hills. It played to her recklessness behind the wheel – another good reason for Adam to have his eyes closed. They stopped briefly at San Gimignano, its ancient towers a testament to the competing vanities of its medieval merchants. Not so very different to what was going on in London right now, Adam observed. Harry told him to stop showing off.

Siena silenced them both with the rise and fall of her sinuous streets, the curving façades of her palaces, and her main square, the Campo, not a square at all, but a shell-shaped hollow at the heart of the hilled city. Siena was everything Florence wasn't – soft, curvaceous, feminine – and it was easy to see why her citizens had formed a special attachment to the Virgin. While Florence proclaimed its power, Siena exuded a quiet, contained strength. Buried in her coiling thoroughfares and her warm brickwork was a sense that she could absorb whatever was thrown at her. She might bend a bit, but she would never break.

Lunch was had in the walled garden of a large ground-floor apartment. Edoardo and Grazia were already there, as were ten or so other guests. Their host was a genial and unassuming little law professor. Adam never got a chance to speak to him. As soon as the pasta bowls had been cleared, Antonella announced that she was taking Adam off to see the 'Crete Senesi'. He had no idea what she meant, but he didn't protest. Harry said he'd stay behind, grab a lift back to Florence with Edoardo and Grazia.

'I told you I had a plan,' said Antonella as they stepped from the apartment building into the deserted street.

'Where are we really going?'

'Oh, I wasn't lying.'

The Crete Senesi turned out to be the vast sweep of un-dulating hills south of Siena – a ridged ocean of high, rolling pastures melting away into the far distance. Bleak and bald, it was an altogether different landscape from the one they'd travelled through that morning.

Adam saw from the map that their route took them close to Montaperti, the scene of the fierce battle so vividly described by Fausto. A detour was out of the question, though; they were on a tight schedule.

They hurtled south along dusty tracks, through straggling little villages. Fortress-like farms brooded on cypress-crowned hilltops, reminders of a time when you didn't just have to store your grain, you had to guard it against marauders. The vistas were endless and not a cloud broke the monotony of the clear blue sky.

To Adam it was a cheerless and uninviting world. Even more so in late summer, Antonella explained, when the crops were in and the patchwork slopes had been ploughed into a uniform desertscape. She rhapsodized about the area. It didn't want to be loved, she said, but that wasn't a reason not to love it. Adam only began to understand what she meant when they arrived at their first destination.

The abbey of Monte Oliveto Maggiore was perched precariously on a spur among crumbling sandstone canyons. For the white-robed monks it was a life lived on the edge of the abyss, literally and metaphorically. The colourful frescoes in the main cloister depicted the life of Saint Bernard. The cycle was sprinkled with pouting, firm-buttocked young men, leaving little doubt as to how the Sienese painter Giovanni Antonio Bazzi had come by his nickname: *il Sodoma*.

Twenty hair-raising minutes south lay Pienza, her back to the high ground, the Crete lapping at her feet. The small town's perfect Renaissance piazza was all that remained of a Sienese pope's dream to relocate the Holy See to his own part of the world. Way to the west, beyond the corrugated hills, the impressive mass of Monte Amiata stood out in bold relief against the clear sky – a conical parody of a volcano, now dormant.

They dropped back into the Crete, making for Montalcino on the other side. They never arrived. Ten minutes out, while barrelling along a hard white track, Antonella slammed on the brakes. The car slewed wildly before coming to a halt.

'I almost missed it.'

Dust swirled around the vehicle. Adam was still gripping the dashboard.

'What? You hit it? What was it?'

Antonella laughed. 'The turning.'

A rutted track cleaved a slope of towering sunflowers, falling sharply towards a bowl in the hills, and an oasis of dense, dark trees.

'Follow me,' said Antonella, abandoning the car at the tree-line and setting off on foot.

He smelt it first, another odour fighting with the sharp, sweet scent of pine sap. It was the smell of decay, of something dead and done for. Antonella walked on, threading her way through the trees. He was a few paces behind her when they entered the clearing.

'Wow,' he said quietly.

The walls of the rectangular pool were made of travertine blocks, some of which had been dislodged by the roots of encroaching trees. A narrow flight of steps led down into the water, which was chalky white, somehow both clear and opaque at the same time. Bubbles rose lazily to the surface at intervals, and the smell of sulphur hung heavy in the air.

'From Monte Amiata,' explained Antonella. 'There are lots of thermal springs in the area. But this one is special. It's very old, probably Roman.'

Her uncle Emilio had shown it to her and Edoardo when they were younger. He had told them they could only share the secret with one other person, one person each. He had made them swear. She appeared a little embarrassed by this confession.

'Am I really that person?'

Antonella gave a sheepish smile. 'Actually, you're the fourth.'

He laughed, taking her in his arms and kissing her gently on the lips. 'Well, thanks anyway.'

'Let's go in.'

She kicked off her shoes then turned her back on him, pulling her long hair aside. 'Do you mind?'

His hand was trembling slightly as he undid the zip of her dress. She eased it from her shoulders, allowing it to fall to the ground. She wore matching underwear – plain, simple, startlingly white against her amber skin. She stood all but naked before him, surprisingly unabashed.

'You're staring.'

'I don't think I've ever seen anything quite so beautiful.'

She removed her bra and stepped out of her panties.

'Okay, so I was wrong.'

She smiled. 'Your turn.'

His fingers fumbled with his belt buckle. The sulphurous vapours coming off the pool no longer stung his nostrils; they washed over him in heady waves, intoxicating.

When he was done, and his clothes lay bundled at his feet, she stepped towards him and pressed her lean body against his, dark skin against pale. They kissed, hands roaming, growing in courage as the same restless urge consumed them. She gripped his wrist and guided his fingers to the warm cleft of her thighs, the hair already matted with moisture. She let out a long, low moan as he eased a finger inside her. Her hips moved, setting the rhythm for him.

'Don't stop,' she purred, 'I'm very close.'

A few moments later, she came, shuddering against him, their mouths locked together, stifling her cries.

She hung limp and drained in his arms. 'Thank you. You're very gentle.'

'Am I?'

'Yes.'

She kissed him tenderly, her long fingers briefly closing around him, caressing him. Then she took his hand and led him silently to the pool. The stone steps stopped just below the waterline, and they lowered themselves down till their feet sunk into the soft, viscous mud coating the bottom. The water was hot, but not uncomfortably so.

They swam in slow circles, heads bobbing on the milky surface, stopping every so often to stand in the shallower parts. The therapeutic waters would cure him of every ailment known to man, apparently, although everything seemed to be in working order, she added, reaching for him beneath the surface. She didn't let go. They kissed hungrily. He raised her up, dipping his head to kiss her breasts. She hooked her legs around his waist and reached behind her, guiding him into her. That's when he lost his footing and they both went under. They came up laughing.

The steps offered the perfect support. She carried her weight on her elbows, facing him, her eyes never leaving his. At first he just stood there, relishing her tight, oily grip, the primordial sludge oozing between his toes. Then he began to move slowly, his hands clasping her narrow hips. Whorls and eddies spiralled off around them. She spurred him on with breathless words until he was driving into her.

She came again, just before he did. His own release hit him so hard that he had to seize the steps behind her to steady himself.

Later, bumping along back up the track to the gravel road, their clothes clinging to their damp bodies, Antonella turned to him. 'You're very quiet. Say something.'

'Whenever I smell sulphur I'll always think of you.'

She punched him in the arm.

There was no time to see Montalcino, or anywhere else for that matter. Antonella had promised her grandmother that she'd have him back at Villa Docci by eight o'clock for his farewell dinner.

'It might not be my farewell dinner,' offered Adam tentatively.

He told her he wanted to see the Piero della Francesca frescoes in Arezzo before leaving Italy, and that he planned to catch a train there when Harry boarded his to Venice. He could leave his suitcases at Villa Docci. It would mean at least another night together when he came back to pick them up.

He felt bad lying to her. He felt worse when she offered

291

to drive him to Arezzo herself. He turned down her offer, mumbling some lame excuse which she didn't contest, although it threw her into a silent little sulk. She seemed to have shrugged it off by the time they pulled up at her farmhouse. In fact, he assumed he had not only been forgiven but was about to be invited upstairs to her bedroom. Why else hadn't she driven directly to Villa Docci? Because she wanted to walk there, she explained.

They took the path that snaked down through the olive grove, the same one they had walked less than a week before at almost exactly the same hour. Adam was struck by how much had happened in that brief time. When they last trod the route together they hadn't yet kissed, Harry had yet to show up, the mystery of the memorial garden was still unsolved, and his suspicions about Maurizio's role in Emilio's death were no more than that: vague instincts unsupported by evidence.

He now had the foundations of a case against Maurizio, and with any luck he'd soon have the proof. What he would do with it, he didn't yet know.

They made their way up through the memorial garden, through the thickening shadows, his arm around her shoulder, hers around his waist. Antonella stopped at the foot of the amphitheatre and looked up at Flora.

'What?' he asked.

'It's a beautiful sight.'

'It is.'

He made to leave, but Antonella held him tight, refusing to budge. 'Wait,' she said.

At first he took it for the wind. It sounded like a light breeze rustling fallen leaves. Only when she pointed did he realize it was the sound of running water. Reflecting the steel-blue gleam of the twilight sky, they looked like two streams of mercury, girding the amphitheatre in a shimmering belt and flowing into the long trough at their feet, which, he now noticed, had been cleared of debris since his last visit.

He turned to Antonella.

'It's for you,' she said. 'A gift.'

'From you?'

'And *Nonna*. She paid for the two lorries of water.'

'They're up there?'

'It wasn't easy.'

'You set me up?'

'With a little help.'

She nodded up the slope. Signora Docci, Harry, Edoardo and Grazia appeared on the crest above.

'Don't just bloody stand there,' called Harry.

Signora Docci wagged her cane impatiently. 'Quick, go and look, it won't last long.'

The trough was filling fast, and they hurried down the steps to the grotto.

The water poured from Peneus' urn, filling the marble basin, overflowing into the gaping mouth of Flora set in the floor. It was beautiful, and it was an act of murder on open display.

They ran hand in hand through the pasture towards the Temple of Echo. The water was already flowing down the channel that scored the ground between the temple and the octagonal pool. Soon Narcissus would have a reason for staring so longingly into vacant space.

They set themselves down on a bench in the temple, shoulders pressed close, trying to suppress the sound of their laboured breathing. Beneath the iron grille in the middle of the floor, the water fell into some kind of shallow receptacle. That's what it sounded like – a sound warped by the chamber beneath the floor then hurled up through the grille towards the domed roof, scattering, echoing, filling the space, making the temple whole again.

Antonella had described the sound as being like whispers. She was right. But they were urgent whispers.

'It's different,' said Antonella.

'What?'

'The sound.'

'How?'

'I don't know.'

It didn't matter. Flora had spoken, and Adam could hear what she was saying.

Maurizio wasn't at dinner. He sent his apologies with Chiara – he wasn't feeling well after the previous night's festivities. Adam tried to imagine the look on his face when Chiara returned with the news that Adam had delayed his departure. Signora Docci seemed more than happy that the purpose of the dinner had been undermined. Harry pointed out that *he* really was leaving for good in the morning, so the dinner had lost none of its true purpose.

The only farewell of Harry's that couldn't be postponed till the morning was the one with Antonella. He insisted on escorting her back to her farmhouse. Adam went along with them.

Antonella produced a bottle of cheap brandy, half of which they drank on the mound beside her barn, sprawled on cushions set around a couple of guttering candles.

When they finally left, Harry made the most of his goodbye hug with Antonella to get to know her body a bit better.

Picking their way back down through the olive grove, Harry said to Adam, 'You can stay if you want.'

'It's okay.'

'Which means you did the dirty this afternoon.'

Adam said nothing. Harry barged against him playfully.

'You're not getting anything out of me.'

'Give up now, you know I will.'

'Harry, what are you doing?'

'Chinese burn.'

'Well it's not working.'

'Shit,' said Harry, releasing Adam's wrist.

27

Signora Docci sent them off in style in her navy-blue Lancia. They were driven by Foscolo, a man of few words. One of them was '*Arrivederci*', which he mumbled sullenly when he dropped them off at Santa Maria Novella station in Florence.

Adam bought a ticket to Arezzo to keep up appearances. He could exchange it later, once Harry was gone. There was an hour to kill before the train to Venice. They headed for the station bar, where Harry proposed they drink their way through the colours of the rainbow – a trick he'd picked up from the Swedish Finn.

'She lives just round the corner,' said Harry wistfully.

'She's got a boyfriend.'

'I doubt it, not any more.'

'You hardly know her. You're getting on that train.'

'Okay. But the reds are on you.'

Harry wasn't leaving empty-handed. The old tan leather suitcase, a gift from Signora Docci, was stuffed with many of Adam's clothes (which Maria, on her own initiative, had washed, dried and pressed in the space of one day). The only thing that Harry lacked was money. But when Adam handed him the greater part of his remaining cash, Harry produced a generous bundle from his own pocket, fanning it in the air.

'A commission.'

'A commission?'

'From Signora Docci. She wants another sculpture. I guess she wasn't just being polite after all.'

Adam leaned forward in his chair. 'Harry, listen, she's a sly old bird, she knows she's getting you cheap.'

Harry tilted his head in a strange fashion. 'That's got to be about the nicest thing you've ever said to me.' He lit a cigarette. 'I didn't say before, didn't want to, and I can still pull out . . .' His voice trailed off.

'What?'

'There's a gallery in London, a good gallery, the Matthiessen Gallery . . . they want me to do a show.'

'That's fantastic, Harry.'

'It's set for April. Will you come?'

Adam winced. 'April's bad, I'll be revising for my finals.'

'Since when did you ever have to revise for exams?'

'Of course I'll come!'

'I'm scared, Paddler. No – crapping myself.'

'Of course you are. If it's a flop, you're ruined as a sculptor.'

'Arsehole.'

Judging from her expression, the middle-aged woman at the neighbouring table was an English-speaker.

They only got as far as green before Harry had to head

for his train. He secured a seat for himself in a compartment then joined Adam on the platform for a farewell smoke.

'Weird times were had,' said Harry.

'They were.'

'And much fun.'

'Yeah.'

'We needed that, you and me.'

'You're right, we did.'

'She's a great girl, Paddler.'

'She is.'

'You look good together – I mean, she looks better than you, but you still look good together.' He paused. 'Don't mess it up.'

'Why would I mess it up?'

'I don't know.' He glanced off, then back at Adam. 'Something's going on, I don't know what, but I reckon you would have told me if you wanted to, if you wanted my help.'

'Harry, nothing's –'

Harry waved him down. 'Don't, it's insulting. I'm offering you my services.' He gave a short laugh. 'Not much of an offer, I know. Just say yes or no. I don't have to get on this train.'

'No.'

Harry scrutinized him closely then nodded. 'Okay.'

'But thanks for asking.'

The loneliness hit Adam the moment Harry's train edged out of the station. The kaleidoscope of Italian liqueurs mingling in his belly didn't help, nor did the fact that he missed the train to Viareggio by a matter of seconds, and with it being a Sunday he then had to wait two hours for the next one. He distracted himself with a gossipy magazine devoted to Italian cinema. He fought the urge to doze, fearful of what his unfettered thoughts might bring.

He lost the battle soon after the train cleared the depressing outskirts of Florence. Strangely, sleep proved to be a peaceful diversion. There was no warped and worrying analysis of what he was embarking on – this fool's errand – just momentary oblivion, his face pressed to the window, fields and farms sliding by outside.

Viareggio was an impressive town, its promenade backed by grand hotels, its beach a clean line of sand, the sunshades of its private lidos a colourful banded ribbon stretching off into the distance. It was high-season and hot, and the place was alive, a definite whiff of wealth in the air. The women were beautiful, their men paunchy and confident, and Adam's immediate instinct was to head straight back to the station.

He found himself a cheap room well back from the sea front, beyond the large pine wood that cut through the town. He paced his room, smoking, building up courage. Then he headed outside into the blinding sunlight.

He remembered the name of the bar. There'd been no need to write it down. It had etched itself on his brain the moment Fausto mentioned it. Maybe he already knew then, sitting in the yard at Fausto's farmhouse, that he would find himself here in Viareggio, asking for directions to La Capannina.

If Gaetano the gardener really had come into some family money, then it was evidently a large legacy. La Capannina proved to be a two-storey building in a prime spot on the front. It wasn't as imposing as the buildings that flanked it, but it was an architectural gem, a little art nouveau masterpiece. Set some distance back from the pavement, it had a terrace out front, fringed with exotic palms. A stone staircase climbed majestically to the main entrance, and the façade was stepped, allowing for a balcony terrace on the first floor running the full length of the building. The sea air had taken its toll on the place, but the scaling paint-work lent it an appealing air of shabby elegance.

Adam didn't venture beyond the front terrace, there was no need to, he would be returning later. He gathered from the waiter who brought him his drink that the first floor was given over to a restaurant. He made a reservation on the upper terrace for dinner and was about to ask if the owner was around, when he checked himself. He mustn't do anything to jeopardize his role as an innocent tourist, a simple bird of passage who had alighted on this perch by pure chance.

Thanks to Harry's unexpected windfall, he could afford to indulge himself a little. He bought a beach towel and a pair of swimming trunks then secured himself a patch of sand at a lido across the way. It came with a sun lounger, a beach umbrella and an unctuous waiter who kept trying to foist overpriced refreshments on him.

He lay there, staring at the jagged peaks of the moun-tains backing the narrow coastal plain – the same moun-tains that had offered up the gigantic block of white marble from which Michelangelo had hacked his 'snake-hipped Narcissus'. Harry's wonderfully dismissive phrase brought a smile to his face. It also brought to mind the aching void left by his brother's departure.

300

He hired a pedalo and struck out for the horizon, leaving the beach far behind. But even then, the empty seat taunted him. He saw Antonella's lean legs pumping the vacant pedals beside him. They should be here together, a couple, like all the other couples, the ones he'd been seeing all day, the ones his eyes kept settling on. Instead, he was alone, working through the details of some reckless plan in his head. He drew consolation from the possibility that Gaetano was away on holiday, or that he was an absentee boss who rarely showed his face at La Capannina, and certainly never on a Sunday.

As he sat there bobbing on the light Mediterranean swell, a more pleasing picture began to fashion itself for him. He saw a fish dinner eaten in peace under the stars, followed by a stroll along the beach and a good night's sleep. He saw himself boarding the train back to Florence in the morning, secure in the knowledge that he'd given the thing his best shot.

'Eh, Gaetano, how's it going?'

They weren't the first words Adam heard on entering the bar of La Capannina several hours later, but he had yet to order his first drink when the fat man in the fawn linen suit uttered them. The fat man raised a pudgy paw. The thin man sitting with friends at a booth table in the far corner returned the gesture, giving a slight nod of his tanned head as he did so.

Gaetano was bald and had trimmed what remained of his hair close to his skull. He wasn't at all what Adam had expected. He was handsome, well dressed, composed. It was hard to imagine that he owed everything he was to his complicity in a murder. In fact, it was near impossible to keep any faith at all with the idea.

Adam had run imaginary conversations in his head, toying with ways of steering their exchange. He hadn't thought about the difficulties involved in actually getting to meet the fellow in the first place. He took a table and pondered the problem.

Gaetano hadn't moved from his booth in the corner by the time he went upstairs to eat.

It was a perfect night, the cooling sea breeze a welcome change from the windless humidity of the hills. Overhead, the stars cast a dirty stain across the sky. The smell of grilling fish mingled with the soft scent of pine trees and the earthy spice of cigar smoke wafting up from the terrace below. The white wine was crisp and dry, his shellfish starter a revelation. Under any other circumstances he would have lingered over his meal. Instead, he wolfed it down, eager to get back to the bar.

'Good evening.'

Adam turned, saw Gaetano standing over him and froze in the act of raising the fork to his mouth. Was Maurizio that far ahead of him? Had he predicted Adam's next move and furnished Gaetano with a detailed description of the meddlesome Englishman?

'Are you enjoying your meal?' Gaetano enquired.

The clothes might have been discreetly elegant, but the hand which Adam shook spoke of a life spent working the soil.

'Yes. Thank you.'

Gaetano nodded approvingly. 'The best fish stew in Viareggio.'

'Yes, it's excellent.'

'Good. I'm pleased.'

It was only as Gaetano moved on to the next table that Adam realized he'd been doing no more than performing his patronly duty, checking up on his customers, ensuring that all was well. He cursed himself for missing the opportunity to strike up a conversation.

Maybe the tour of the diners was Gaetano's last act before breaking for the night and heading home, because he was nowhere to be seen in the bar when Adam headed back downstairs. The two men Gaetano had been sitting with were still in the corner booth, slouched and nonchalant in their short sleeves, and they had been joined by an elderly man and a young woman, both of whom had evidently taken too much sun that day. A faint ray of hope came with the sight of a fifth wine glass on the table in front of them.

Adam was at the bar, waiting to order, when Gaetano appeared from a door behind the counter with a box of cigars. He exchanged a few words with one of the barmen, who set up a bottle of malt whisky and some glasses on a tray.

The moment a table came free, Adam pounced. He immersed himself in his book, happy to bide his time, ready to be the last to leave, if that's what it took. A while later, a woman placed her hand on the back of the chair opposite and asked in a sultry voice:

'Can I?'

She was tall, fine featured, very attractive.

'Of course,' said Adam, assuming that she wished to take the chair to another table. Instead, she lowered herself into it.

'Are you alone? Apart from that boring-looking book, I mean?'

'Er, yes.'

'American?'

'English.'

'On holiday?'

'Studying.'

The woman slowly pulled a cigarette from her packet. 'Is it your first time in Viareggio?'

'Yes.'

'Where are you staying?'

'A pensione over there.' He waved his hand vaguely in the direction of the bar.

'Oh, that one.' She flashed a smile. 'I'm Alessandra.'

'Adam.'

'You have lovely eyes, Adam.'

'Thank you.'

'Do you also have a light?' She waggled the unlit cigarette between her fingers.

'Sorry. Excuse me.' He fumbled for his lighter on the table.

'Leave the young man alone, Alessandra.'

It was Gaetano.

'Oh, do I have to?' she pouted up at him.

'I'm afraid so.'

Alessandra looked back at Adam. 'The boss,' she said with a mocking tone. 'I think he wants you for himself.'

'Very funny, Alessandra.'

Alessandra leaned across the table, smiled sweetly, and raised the cigarette to her lips. Adam lit it for her. 'Spoil sport,' she muttered to Gaetano as she sashayed off.

The only explanation Adam could come up with was that she worked in the world's oldest profession, and the management didn't want her plying her trade under their roof. He was wrong.

'Alessandra used to be Alessandro,' Gaetano explained.

It took Adam a moment to assimilate the news. The timbre of the voice had been the only give-away.

'Really?'

Gaetano smiled at Adam's incredulity. 'There have been . . . difficulties with some of the customers.'

It was now or never.

'Can I offer you a drink? As a thank you, I mean.'

Gaetano hesitated. 'Sure,' he shrugged.

Adam opted for a twelve-year-old single malt scotch. Gaetano nodded his approval and followed suit.

He sensed he had just the one drink in which to hook his fish or Gaetano would be off, back to his booth. He'd already settled on flattery as his opening gambit, and the tactic worked. Gaetano thanked him for his compliments about La Capannina, and was disarmingly humble in his reply. The building provided the great atmosphere, the chef the great food – he was just the owner. Some of this humility deserted him when he went on to explain that he had reversed the sliding fortunes of the place in under a year, and to such an extent that the previous owner was now kicking himself over the sale price. He had even approached Gaetano on the subject of buying back a stake in the business.

It was the book that clinched it, though, just as Adam thought it would. It was a big work on Italian Renaissance sculpture, loaded with pictures, and it didn't go unnoticed by Gaetano. When Adam explained that he was an art history student, Gaetano confessed to knowing a little about sculptures from that period. He mentioned a garden he knew – a garden attached to a grand villa near Florence. He talked about it as if stumbling across such a thing was one of the hazards you faced when mixing in the sort of circles he did. He certainly didn't say that he had spent a sizeable chunk of his life cutting the garden's grass and pruning its laurel.

When Gaetano offered up a detailed and impressively vivid description of the garden, Adam found himself experiencing a strange sympathy for the man. The slightly desolate look that stole into his round, simian eyes suggested that years of exposure to the garden's unsettling atmosphere had also taken their toll on him.

Remembering his role, Adam reacted with enthusiasm, especially to the news that Flora, the goddess of flowers, was the linchpin of the cycle. He told Gaetano about Edgar Wind's new theory, published earlier that year, that Flora didn't just figure in Botticelli's *Primavera* and his *Birth of Venus*, but that her pairing with Venus was essential to the allegory of love buried in both paintings.

He had to hold himself in check when Gaetano quizzed him about the other sculptures in the garden. It was too easy to shine, too easy to give himself away. He shared a few further insights, just enough to impress. It seemed to do the trick. It was Gaetano who ordered the next round.

The bar had started to empty by the time the third round hit the table, and they were deep in a discussion about the war. It was Adam who had steered the conversation this way, looking for a tear in the tissue of lies that shrouded

306

Gaetano's account of his life. He claimed to have been a partisan, which might or might not have been true, although it seemed unlikely. When he said he had witnessed bad things, Adam pressed him further. Gaetano wouldn't be drawn on the subject, except to say that war made monsters of men – good men, men of standing, men you thought you knew – he'd seen it with his own eyes.

Adam said he'd hardly witnessed anything of the war other than the odd plane overhead – the privilege of growing up on a remote farm, he lied. Casting himself as a country boy had the desired effect. Gaetano confessed to being one too, and he had a storehouse of tedious anecdotes to prove it. This new turn in their conversation also allowed him to hold forth on his favourite subject: land.

He was obsessed with it. Land equalled power. History proved it. And if land was the past, then it was also the future. Italy was changing. The ownership of land was being opened up to a wider constituency. Only a fool could fail to appreciate the opportunities this presented.

'I'm going to give you some advice,' said Gaetano, leaning across the table, his eyes dimmed with drink. 'You know the real reason you should buy land?' He paused for effect. 'Because they can't make any more of it.'

The man's boorish self-satisfaction was almost unbearable, but Adam managed to look impressed by the statement. 'I hadn't thought of it like that.'

'That's why I'm telling you.'

Adam saw his opening and pounced. Land brought heavy responsibilities, he countered. It also incited passions, not all of them good. He'd seen it with his own family. Ownership of the farm had split his father's generation,

307

dividing siblings, turning them against each other. On one occasion it had even come to blows between his father and his uncle.

'Blows?' snorted Gaetano. 'I've known brothers kill over it.'

Adam feigned a doubtful look.

'It's true. You don't believe me?'

'Really?'

'Murder. All because of a big house and some land.'

A heavy silence followed. Gaetano clearly felt he had said too much, and Adam didn't need to hear any more. He had his confirmation.

The arrival of two more whiskies helped them draw a line under this chapter of their conversation, with Gaetano more than happy to return to the subject of his plans for world domination. He prattled on drunkenly about a big hotel just down the road that he had his eye on. It was ripe for improvement, the only problem being that his reputation now preceded him, and the owner was therefore likely to ask the fullest possible price for the place. He had toyed with the idea of purchasing it through an intermediary in order to throw the fellow off the scent. He had also set his sights on a villa estate in the hills above Pisa. It belonged to an old family who had fallen on hard times, but he would probably hold off for a bit. Better to build up the business first. Estates were thirsty, they required a steady flow of cash, he knew that from experience. Then there was marriage. Marriage was good for business and he had held out long enough. Maybe it was time to throw in the towel and make an honest woman of some young creature.

This unpalatable mix of astonishing self-importance and craven insecurity was almost too much for Adam to stomach, but he still managed to joke that when he next returned to Italy he expected to find Gaetano married and master of his very own Villa Docci above Pisa.

Gaetano didn't react immediately. When he did, it was to excuse himself for a moment. He needed to relieve himself.

Adam only realized his mistake as Gaetano stepped away from the table. Earlier in their conversation Gaetano had talked at some length about Villa Docci, but he had never mentioned it by name.

Or had he? Maybe he had. Maybe Adam was just being paranoid. A quick glance confirmed that he wasn't.

It wasn't exactly a nod, just the merest tilt of the head, but something about it suggested the uncontrollable reflex when the eyes have just made an urgent gesture all of their own. Adam couldn't see Gaetano's eyes, but he could see the two young men in short sleeves get up from the corner booth and follow him towards the back of the room.

Adam fumbled some notes on to the table in settlement of the drinks bill and, cursing himself for the precious moments his manners had cost him, hurried for the main doors. The front terrace was all but deserted, so was the boardwalk across the way. Sunday night was not the night for losing yourself in a crowd.

He turned right, picking up the pace as La Capannina fell behind his shoulder. He turned right again into the first street, heading away from the sea. His mind was racing. It was telling him he should have turned into the second street. The first street was so bloody predictable. He started to run, casting a wild look behind him. His ankle, stiff and sore, had not fully recovered from the fall in the garden. Walking was fine, a sprint something quite different. Fortunately, the safety of the park and its dark pine woods lay no more than a hundred and fifty yards off. He slowed to a walk as he neared the end of the street, checking over his shoulder. All clear behind still. He was safe.

He glanced left and right before crossing the broad street to the park. He was checking for traffic. What he saw was two men in short-sleeved shirts career from the mouth of the adjacent street. They spotted him immediately.

He sprinted across the road and was swallowed up by the shadows.

The ground beneath the trees was uneven, sandy, treacherous, and the broad canopies of the umbrella pines allowed almost no moonlight to filter through to it. He stumbled and fell twice in quick succession. The second time, he pitched forward into a dry ditch, winding himself. He heard his pursuers closing from behind, communicating in urgent tones. They had the advantage over him – this was their home turf.

He changed tack, cutting left, staying low, one hand in his pocket to stop the coins jangling, the other clutching the book on Renaissance sculpture. He thought about abandoning it but decided it might come in handy as a weapon, a last resort, something to hurl at them.

He had always prided himself on never having spent a minute more on a playing field than had been absolutely required by the various schools he'd attended. Staggering around a frozen rugby pitch or having small and very hard balls hurled at you had never been his idea of fun. He had spent much of his youth faking injuries or a staggering ignorance of the rules – anything that might see him ejected from the field of play. Play? That wasn't play. It was mortification of the flesh. He didn't mind tennis, especially doubles, when he could take up a position at the net and swat at anything that came his way. Nothing that involved over-exertion or, God forbid, stamina.

All the disparaging comments about sporty types came back to haunt him now. His lungs sucked greedily at the warm night air, blood beat a wild tattoo in his ears, and his legs felt strangely distant. Only the fear drove him on. It was a new kind of fear, one he had never experienced before, except in nightmares. It was the kind that prickled the skin of your thighs and your shoulders. Run or stand and fight, your body seemed to be saying to you: a stark and alarming choice.

At a certain point he had to stop, he could go no further. He dropped into some shrubs, pressing his face into the sandy soil, his fingers groping in the darkness for a better weapon to wield than a learned tome on Renaissance sculpture. He felt stripped bare, every action base and primitive, inborn. The same body that had let him down now came to his aid, helping him to control his laboured breathing, sharpening his hearing.

All he could pick up was the muted drone of distant vehicles. That was good, because the ground was spongy with pine needles and fallen twigs, impossible to move across without generating some kind of noise. He must have given them the slip. He waited five minutes, waited another five for good measure, then he crept from his lair.

Stealth suited his style. It also blunted the blind, head-long panic of before. He moved cautiously, sticking to thick vegetation, stopping every so often to listen for tell-tale sounds, avoiding any areas where the moonlight cleaved the darkness. When obliged to cross a path, he would halt, wait, checking first that the coast was clear.

He travelled a fair distance like this before reaching the clearing. It was large and ovoid, and through the dense belt of trees just beyond it he could make out the lights of the buildings on the north side of the park. He thought about skirting the open space. If he had, he would have walked straight into the arms of the enemy. Because it was from the tree-line off to his left that the man exploded the moment he began padding across the clearing in a low crouch.

'I've got him, he's here, I've got him!'

Adam surprised himself with the burst of speed he put on, the pain in his ankle forgotten. He might even have made it to safety if he hadn't collided with a tree.

He reeled backwards, stunned. He was aware of the book falling from his hand, and of the fact that it had cost him four shillings from a dusty shop just off the Charing Cross Road. Then something hurtled into him from behind, driving the air from his lungs and sending him sprawling.

The man wasn't big. He didn't need to be. He was brutal. He kept Adam subdued with a few well-placed kicks until his companion arrived. Together, they hauled him to his feet.

'Who the fuck are you?'

'What?' he said groggily, in English.

He was jerked, spun round, and hurled against a tree.

He cracked the back of his skull against the trunk, staggered but didn't fall. This meant that they didn't have to pick him up before seizing him by the arms and running him headlong into another tree.

For a moment, the world receded from him. When it flooded back in, he found himself on the ground, clutching his head, his palm sticky with blood.

'Who the fuck are you?' spat one of the shadows looming over him.

He cowered, raising his arms protectively above his head. 'No,' he said pathetically, tearfully, convinced now that he was pleading for his life, that they would keep piling him into trees until he was nothing but pulp.

He never got to know if that really was their intention.

There was a sound like the snapping of a branch and the shadow on the left pitched forward on to him. By the time he had scrabbled out from beneath the dead weight, it was almost all over for number two. He was on the ground, yelping in pain as blows rained down on him. The assailant had some kind of instrument in his hand, hard to make out in the darkness, and with blood sheeting into his eyes.

Suddenly, there was silence. He heard his rescuer breathing heavily.

'Go,' snapped a gruff voice. 'Get lost!'

He didn't require any more encouragement; the first man was already beginning to stir.

Stumbling off through the trees, he heard the sound of a couple more blows finding their mark. He also became aware of the dampness between his legs.

28

Signora Olivotto at the Pensione Ravizza proved to be something of a saint. She took him into her apartment and cleaned and dressed his wounds. When she suggested he remove his trousers so that she could clean them, she mentioned the dirty stains at the knees, not the wet patch around the crotch. She even pretended to believe his story that he'd tackled two men who had tried to pick his pocket.

'Well, you're going to have a scar to remember your bravery by,' she said archly.

The cut in his eyebrow was not so long, but it was deep. When it refused to stop bleeding, a doctor was summoned. He shaved one part of the eyebrow, administered three stitches and two aspirin, and then categorically refused payment. Signora Olivotto must already have solicited the doctor's discretion, because he never once asked how Adam had come by his injuries.

The pain in his head and ribs made for a terrible night's sleep. So did the thought of two men lying bludgeoned to death in the park by his mysterious saviour. What would have happened if the shadowy stranger hadn't come to his rescue? And who was he? Was it possible that he was connected in some way? Or had he simply stumbled upon the fracas and done the right thing by the weaker party? They were imponderable questions. There was also the matter of his book on Renaissance sculpture, abandoned at the scene, his name scrawled on the flyleaf. A calm and reasoned assessment of his predicament threw up only one solution: Get out of Viareggio as quickly as possible.

Signora Olivotto had washed his trousers and left them out to dry overnight. They were still damp in the morning, although they quickly dried off in the early sunlight. He took breakfast in his room so as to avoid the stares of the other guests, his left eye now badly swollen.

Realizing that he couldn't leave town without knowing for sure, he slipped out of the pensione and hurried to the park.

He wasn't able to identify the exact spot, but he made a thorough sweep of the patch of woodland where the confrontation had occurred. There were no dead bodies and no police cordons sealing off a crime scene. He didn't find his book, but he did feel his spirits lift a little as he limped back to the pensione.

Signora Olivotto ordered a taxi to take him to the station. The moment it pulled away, he redirected the driver to the first stop down the line. He wasn't going to risk boarding the train in Viareggio itself. If Gaetano had any sense, he'd be waiting for him there.

It was a small station, and the train that stopped at it also stopped at every other small station between Viareggio and Florence. This was fine by Adam. It gave him plenty of time to think.

Rattling along through the shimmering heat of the Arno Valley, it dawned on him that his one night in Viareggio had changed everything. The search for the truth behind Emilio's death was no longer a private affair, one to be pursued in secret. He had lost the initiative. Gaetano must surely have contacted Maurizio by now. He had to assume, therefore, that they'd worked out exactly who he was and why he'd travelled to Viareggio.

At first he chided himself for the silly slip of the tongue that had led to his exposure. His thinking had changed by the time the train pulled into Santa Maria Novella station.

So what if they knew? What if things had gone according to plan? He would be stepping off the train, his suspicions confirmed, and wondering just what the hell to do next. He had been naïve. Discovering the truth was never going to be enough of an end in itself. There was always going to be a confrontation of some sort with Maurizio. Viareggio had simply hastened the inevitable.

29

Maria was the first to set eyes on Adam. The moment she did so, her hand shot to her mouth. She took him to the kitchen and listened to his (now embellished) account of the set-to with the pickpockets. She insisted on removing the bandage and examining the wound in his eyebrow. The doctor's needlework was decreed 'adequate', although an extra stitch wouldn't have gone amiss. She rested a consoling hand on his arm and asked him if there was anything he wanted. She made him a coffee then dispatched him upstairs with instructions to have a bath and change his clothes before lunch.

As he stood staring at himself in the bathroom mirror, three thoughts occurred to him in quick succession: he looked truly terrible, dirty and damaged; it was good to be back at Villa Docci; and Maria had shown him more warmth in the last fifteen minutes than she'd managed to muster during his entire stay.

He wasn't surprised to find Maurizio seated at the table

on the terrace when he came down to lunch. Maurizio's reaction was no less predictable. It matched his mother's for horror and surprise and furrow-browed sympathy. Adam spent much of the meal trying to reach Maurizio, to extract from him a look, something, anything that suggested they both knew that his story of pickpockets in Arezzo was a ringing lie.

It was a faultless performance by Maurizio. Adam was able to spend much of his time admiring it, because he never doubted for a moment that it *was* a performance. As the meal wore on, however, he began to worry. Maurizio would have quizzed Gaetano closely; he would know that Gaetano had not let slip Maurizio's name to Adam. All Maurizio had to do was brazen it out, make no reference at all to Viareggio, and Adam would be hamstrung, left with nothing more than a broken chain of circumstantial evidence.

This is what Maurizio should have done, so Adam was surprised when he showed up in the study soon after lunch. He entered from the library, shutting the door behind him. He also closed the French windows leading on to the terrace.

Adam was at the desk, reading. He hadn't absorbed one word of the book. He had been praying for Maurizio to make just such a blunder.

Maurizio lit a cigarette. 'Gaetano sends his apologies.'

Silence seemed the best tactic.

'Who was the man in the park?'

So that was it. Seeking Adam out wasn't a blunder on Maurizio's part; it was an act of necessity. He needed to know if Adam was working alone. He needed to know just what he was up against.

'I don't know. It was dark, I didn't even see his face.'

Maurizio's eyes narrowed, studying him closely. 'I believe you.' He wandered to the fireplace and flicked some ash into the grate. 'I don't know what you think you know, but let me tell you how it is. I know Gaetano, of course I do. We all do. When he left last year he asked me to help him in his business.' He gave a wry smile. 'No, he asked to borrow some money. I said no, and then I saw La Capannina and I said yes. I thought it was a good invest-ment. And it is. The arrangement between us is very compli-cated. I'll be honest, it is not exactly legal. This makes him very sensitive. It makes us both very sensitive. I'm sorry you suffered because of it. But that's all it is – a business arrangement.'

He had to hand it to Maurizio, it was a nice try, offering up an explanation that would allow Adam to walk away from the affair with a clean conscience.

But he was beyond that now. He had changed. They had hurt him. They had scared him. No, they had made him piss himself with fear, thinking he was about to die.

'You're lying,' he said. '*I* know you're lying, *you* know you're lying. You killed Emilio, and when Gaetano saw what you'd done, you had to buy his silence. Maybe you're still buying it. Did Gaetano tell you about his plans? He has big plans – money no object – *your* money, I imagine.'

He was surprised it hadn't occurred to him before that the relationship was one of ongoing blackmail, that Gaetano had raised the price on Maurizio with La Capannina. It was a gratifying thought that Maurizio really had been paying for his crime for the past fourteen years.

Maurizio's expression hovered somewhere between pity and amusement. 'Is that really what you think? That I killed my own brother? Are you mad?'

He tossed his cigarette into the fireplace and approached the desk. He was no longer amused.

'You come here and you tell me this? You dare to tell me this? I was there.' He stabbed his finger against his chest. 'I was there. I saw that German shoot Emilio. I saw him walk up to him and shoot him again in the head.' He made a pistol of his fingers and 'fired' at the ground. 'And I did nothing. Nothing. I watched. If doing nothing means I killed him, then yes – I killed him.'

It wasn't the tears welling in Maurizio's eyes that unsettled Adam, it was the pistol-fingers he had pointed at the ground. That explained the bullet-hole in the floor upstairs – a detail of the shooting Chiara had failed to mention to him, and which Adam had blithely taken as proof of Maurizio's hand in his brother's death.

It was the cornerstone of his case – his only piece of hard, physical evidence – and Maurizio had whipped it away with one simple gesture. The whole ramshackle structure of the conspiracy he had built now came crashing down around his ears.

'Well . . .?'

'I'm sorry,' Adam replied quietly.

'You're sorry!?'

'Yes.'

Maurizio spun away from the desk, exasperated. 'Is that all you can say?'

'I'll leave.'

'Yes, you will.'

'Now?'

'Tomorrow morning, as you planned. I don't want to make a scene for my mother.'

Adam nodded. Maurizio shot him a contemptuous look and stalked out of the room.

He made his way upstairs in a daze, shaky and lightheaded. He tried to marshal his thoughts but they scattered off in all directions like a rioting mob, leaving him to poke around in the ruins of his argument.

He found himself in his room, unpacking then repacking the suitcases he'd prepared before leaving for the coast.

Why couldn't he think straight? The close chain of his reasoning was usually the one thing he could rely on. Maybe he was in shock. Yes, that was it. Or concussed. The doctor in Viareggio had warned him he might be.

He was right about one thing: Viareggio had indeed brought matters to a head, forcing a confrontation with Maurizio. He gave a quick and manic laugh. It was about the only thing he *had* been right about.

At least it was over now, done with. He was in no condition to take the thing any further, even if he had wanted to. Which he didn't. He wanted to leave. He would have phoned for a taxi there and then, but even that seemed like a task too far.

He lowered himself into the overstuffed armchair near the fireplace, wincing as he did so. They had really worked him over beneath the pines in Viareggio. Something was badly wrong with his ribs. There was a sharp and unfamiliar edge to the pain, worrying. And as for the throbbing in his skull, the aspirins barely brushed the surface of it.

He was a wreck, inside and out. He had never been brought this low in all his life. Like Dante, he had finally reached the ninth circle of Hell.

No. It was a false comparison to draw. Because Dante's journey had not ended there, deep in the abyss. He had risen up through Purgatory and on into Paradise, guided by the ghost of his dead love, Beatrice.

He dwelt on this thought for a while then heaved himself up out of the armchair and made for the door, every step a discomfort.

Something told him to turn back before he got there. It was exactly this – his cockeyed belief in his own spectral guide – that had brought him to his current predicament. Strangely, though, it no longer mattered to him if he was the dupe of his own diseased fancy. He was too far gone to care.

He felt oddly calm as he edged his way through the gap in the high yew hedge. In fact, it was the first time he had ever entered the memorial garden free of any apprehension or disquiet, he realized. Maybe it was the pain racking his body. It was certainly the closest thing he had ever experienced to what she must have felt at the end.

Whatever curious affinity he had cooked up for himself and Flora, she was having none of it.

She offered no solace, just a blank and stony stare.

He told himself not to lose heart. She had done this to him before, rebuffing his advances then allowing him close. Antonella and Harry had both sensed it in her – she liked to tease. She was exactly as Federico had cast her in stone all those centuries ago.

He walked the circuit slowly, aware that it was the last time he would ever do so. He waited and hoped. In vain. Half an hour later he found himself back at the amphitheatre, dejected, rejected, his final tour complete.

He ran his fingers over the inscription on the stone bench: ANIMA FIT SEDENDO ET QUIESCENDO PRUDENTIOR. The Soul in Repose Grows Wiser. Yet another clue left by Federico Docci. How many had he left in all? Just the right amount for his crime to go undetected for almost four hundred years. It was an impressive piece of judgement on Federico's part – worthy of admiration, even – and it was easy to picture Federico applying the same rigorous subtlety to the murders themselves. Why else had he not been brought to book? He saw Federico nursing his ailing wife till the bitter end, the distraught husband, perfectly in character. And he saw Maurizio, the distraught brother, squeezing out a tear to deflect the suspicions of a stranger.

That's how good you had to be to get away with it.

He was alert now, in the grip of a new clarity, the implacable logic tightening around him.

Maurizio knew for a fact that Adam had visited the top floor, because Maria had told him so. He might well have assumed, therefore, that Adam had discovered the bullethole in the wooden boards and that he'd recognized it for what it was – the linchpin of a case against Maurizio. All Maurizio had to do was remove the pin and the wheel would fall off.

Maurizio was still in character, playing a role. Short of

killing Adam, what else could he do other than talk his way out of suspicion? There was to be no confession, not even the slightest admission of guilt.

An innocent man would not have shown up for dinner. Offended by the wild accusations levelled at him, he would have snubbed Adam on his last night at Villa Docci.

Adam waited, baited his hook, and when an opportunity presented itself, made a last desperate cast. This he did in the cellar, where Maurizio had gone to select the wine for the meal, and where Adam joined him moments later.

'I'm sorry.'

Maurizio turned. 'Yes, you said.'

'I just have one more question, though.'

'Don't do this.'

'What happened to the gun?'

'What gun?'

'Emilio's gun.'

'My father destroyed it.'

'Really?'

'That's what he said.'

'Did you see him do it?'

He wasn't afraid to push; a guilty man couldn't afford to push back. And Maurizio didn't. He examined the label of a dusty bottle and made for the door. 'I think we should join my mother,' he said flatly.

'*She* knows what he did with the gun. And with the bullets he took from the body.'

An innocent man would have carried on walking, not stopped and turned at the door.

'That's right, he had the bullets removed. They're behind

the plaque in the chapel – Emilio's plaque – along with the gun. Your father put them there. Your mother thinks it was the act of a man losing his mind. I think he knew. I think he worked out what happened up there.'

Maurizio's eyes were impossible to read, sunk in two pools of shadow cast by the bare overhead bulb.

'You say *you* did nothing. *He* did nothing. Not then. But he did leave clues. And he did leave proof – ballistic proof that Emilio was shot with his own gun.' He paused. 'If you don't believe me, ask your mother.'

'Oh, I believe you,' said Maurizio evenly. 'If she told you they are there, they are there. But why do I care? I don't. I only care that you leave this place.'

Dinner, inevitably, was a living hell. The worst thing was the abrupt farewell with Antonella, who clearly wanted to make more of their last evening together. What could he do, though? He had no choice. The moment Maurizio excused himself and headed back to the house by the farm, he too was obliged to call it a night. It wasn't hard using his injuries as an excuse, but it was hard enacting an emotional farewell with Antonella when his mind was on other matters altogether.

They kissed by her car, resolved to write to each other, and that was it – she was gone.

30

He has to come. He has to come.

It was an annoying and persistent little mantra. He would shake it out of his head only for it to barge its way back in again a few minutes later.

After fighting it for three hours, he wasn't just bored, he was exhausted. And hurting. The aspirins were wearing off. It didn't help that he was hunched in a tight recess at the back of the altar.

He unfolded himself from his hiding place and lay flat on the stone floor, arms at his side. It struck him that he was not alone, that both Flora and Emilio lay close by, stretched out in exactly the same fashion, and it gave him comfort.

He stared at the roof, barely discernible in the faint light from the lone candle on the altar – just a dim mesh of beams and crossbeams. He imagined it being built, men high overhead on wooden scaffolds, hammering the structure into being, the blue vault of a summer sky above them.

He closed his eyes, picturing it, and felt himself drifting off to sleep. He snapped upright, shunted himself back beneath the altar, huddling on his haunches, knees against his chest.

He has to come. He has to come.

Maybe he's already been then gone away again. Maybe he saw the ladder lying on the ground against the wall of the chapel, the one pushed over by Adam after he'd clambered through the window. It had been an awkward manoeuvre, but a necessary one, Maurizio being unlikely to enter the chapel unless the door was locked from the outside, the key safely beneath its rock.

Christ, he wanted a cigarette. He couldn't remember the last time he'd gone so many waking hours without one. There was that production of *Hedda Gabler* at the Cambridge Arts Theatre, over three hours of excruciating student overacting unbroken by an interval, although the blonde girl from Newnham playing Hedda had been very easy on the eye. What was her name again? She had a brother at Corpus Christi with a claret-stain birthmark on his neck . . .

He was woken by a rasping noise. He recognized it immediately as the mechanism of an old lock groaning in protest. He stiffened, straining his ears. He heard the creak of hinges. And then whispers.

He hadn't come alone! He'd brought someone with him. Or something. Something shuffling, scampering. A dog padding around, getting its bearings, sniffing out the dog-history of the place. Not good. Bad.

A male voice hissed a command, calling the animal to

heel. But for how long? A torch beam cut through the darkness, making a quick sweep of the interior, casting the shadow of the altar against the back wall.

Adam cowered. He hadn't entered the chapel through the door, so there was no scent for the dog to pick up on, not unless it went wandering. He knew the dog – a collie with a bunch of other stuff thrown in, young and skittish, but hardly an attack dog. He could remember being pleasantly surprised that Maurizio and Chiara didn't feel the need for a pedigree animal.

Another sound now, off to his left. A bag of tools being laid on the ground. A hand rummaging inside. Then silence. Followed by a scraping noise. Maurizio working away at the join around the plaque. Best to wait a while before surprising him.

The dog had other ideas.

He didn't see it until it appeared right in front of him, wagging its tail and panting. Good game but I found you, it seemed to be saying.

He tried to push it away. It licked his hand and let out a small yelp.

'Ugo.'

Definitely Maurizio's voice.

Ugo gave a couple of merry barks and the torch beam swung round to the altar.

Adam cut his losses and crawled out from his hiding place, squinting into the torchlight. He turned on his own torch and fired it at Maurizio's face, blinding him back. After a moment's stand-off they both lowered their torches towards the floor.

Adam stroked Ugo's head, a gesture intended to give the

impression that he was relaxed and in control. Maurizio's body was braced as if for a fight, his face as pale as ashes. The screwdriver in his hand looked far from innocent.

'Why are you here?' he asked darkly.

'I don't know.'

'Why?' insisted Maurizio.

'I didn't have a choice. I had to find out.'

Maurizio turned suddenly and used the screwdriver to prise the plaque free of the wall. His torch revealed nothing behind other than bare, raw stone. There was certainly no gun, and no bullets.

'Very clever,' muttered Maurizio. 'Very clever.'

Instinct told Adam to keep his own confusion to himself. Where the hell was the gun?

Maurizio sat himself down on the end of a pew. There was something defeated about his body language that Adam found hard to square with the man, so he kept his distance.

'Well, now you know.'

'Why?' asked Adam. 'He was your brother.'

'It happened. I don't have to explain to you.'

'Because of all of this . . . a house, some land?' He wanted to believe that something else had played a part – a clash of ideologies, anything other than simple greed.

Maurizio didn't reply; he stared at his hands, as if they alone had been to blame for his actions.

'Where was Gaetano?'

'He arrived as the Germans were leaving. He was coming upstairs when he heard the shots.' Maurizio raised his face and added flatly, 'There's nothing you can do.'

'I can tell your mother.'

'Yes. And she will do nothing.'

'How do you know?'

'Because I won't permit her to.'

'Oh really?' scoffed Adam.

A slyness crept into Maurizio's smile. 'You're an intelligent boy – work it out.'

Even in the half-light Adam could make out the cold and creeping cunning in his eyes. Maurizio seemed to be saying he was ready to add matricide to fratricide, if that's what the situation called for.

'It's your decision.'

Ugo's sudden bark sounded like a triumphant cry, applause for the brilliance of his master's devilish strategy.

'*Zitto*,' spat Maurizio. But Ugo had no intention of remaining silent. He barked again, bounding towards the door of the chapel.

Maurizio moved with impressive speed, but the door still swung open before he got there.

Maria stepped into the chapel, shielding her eyes from the glare of Maurizio's torch.

'Maria . . .'

Maria pulled the door shut behind her, her face set in stone. 'I heard everything.'

Maurizio's eyes flicked back and forth between her and Adam, searching for a connection. Adam could have told him there was none, if Maurizio hadn't figured it out for himself.

'What are you doing here?'

'Listening.'

'Who for? My mother?'

Maria didn't reply, but her silence seemed to speak to Maurizio. 'Who then?' he asked. 'Antonella?'

Again, Adam saw nothing in Maria's face that constituted an answer. Maurizio clearly knew how to read her better. 'Of course . . . she knows it will come to her if I don't get it,' he said, his tone suggesting that the pieces were now falling into place for him.

Adam, on the other hand, was struggling to keep up, his mind reeling, trying to process the information.

He gave up the fight when Maurizio added, 'Whatever she's giving you, I'll give you more.'

'She's giving me a lot.'

'It's nothing.'

Maria took her time before replying. 'I want a house of my own. Not an apartment. And I want money.'

'How much?'

'Enough so I don't ever have to worry again.'

'It's yours,' said Maurizio.

Adam didn't intend to speak. The English words just exited his mouth. 'Maria, what are you doing?'

She glanced at him, her expression ashamed but resolute. 'What about him?' she asked Maurizio.

'What can he do? He's leaving tomorrow. He already knows he has no choice.'

Maria nodded again and made for the door.

'Maria . . .' pleaded Adam.

She stopped and turned. 'What? Who are you? What do you know? You know nothing.' She thrust a finger towards the villa. 'All my life my father worked for her, and what did he get? Nothing. What will I get? Nothing. That is the way it is. All I want is to die beneath my own roof and pay for my own funeral. Is that so much to ask? Well, is it!?'

331

Maurizio made a calming gesture with his hands.

'Who are you?' Maria went on. 'You're a child. You know nothing.'

In the silence that followed her departure, Adam reached out a hand to steady himself against a pew. It wasn't enough. He had to sit down.

Maria was right. He knew nothing. He was entirely out of his depth. He looked up to see Maurizio standing over him, nothing triumphant in his look, just a quiet certainty.

They left the chapel together. Maurizio locked the door and placed the key in his pocket. He raised his face towards the stars then turned his gaze on Adam. 'I meant what I said about my mother. It's your decision.'

Sleep was out of the question. He didn't even try. He sat on the terrace and chain-smoked. Bewilderment and an over-whelming sense of his own naïvety battled for possession of his head. He was unable to absorb what he'd witnessed. He knew there had been a trade – Maria had sold her silence for a hefty price – but what was all the talk of Antonella?

She knows it will come to her if I don't get it.

He hadn't misunderstood Maurizio's words. Or Maria's response to them. He ran their exchange over and over in his head – feverishly testing it, challenging it – until the creeping dawn light had dimmed all but the brightest stars. Then he got to his feet.

Nearing the farmhouse, he stopped briefly to admire the new sun stretching its pale fingers over the hills. If he hadn't delayed for that moment, he would have been walking across the yard, caught in the open, when the door at the top of the outside staircase swung open and Fausto stepped from the farmhouse.

Adam dipped out of sight behind the corner of the barn. Fausto! It wasn't possible. He resisted the urge to check, certain that his eyes hadn't deceived him, wishing that they had. What was Fausto doing creeping from Antonella's house at dawn?

He hurried round the back of the barn. From the corner of the farm buildings he had a broken view through a cluster of cypresses of the track leading to San Casciano. Fausto passed along it, grave and pensive, slightly stooped. Adam followed, sticking to the trees.

Fearing detection, he was obliged to fall behind when Fausto reached the outskirts of San Casciano. Twice he almost lost him in the labyrinth of streets. The third time, he did lose him, but by then he had a pretty clear idea of where Fausto was headed.

The Pensione Amorini wasn't yet open for business. The shuttered windows of the ground floor allowed him to skirt the building undetected. He slipped into the back garden through the door in the stone wall. The kitchen was at the rear of the building, its windows giving directly on to the garden.

He could hear voices and the clatter of crockery. Peering cautiously around the window frame, he saw Signora Fanelli loading up a tray with plates and bowls. Her back was to Adam, which meant he had a clear view of Fausto's left hand resting lightly on her arse. Signora Fanelli turned her head and kissed Fausto briefly on the lips.

He walked to the bar in the Piazza Cavour as if in a trance. His head throbbed, his ribs pulsed with pain, and he was jittery from lack of sleep. Unsurprisingly, the coffee didn't help.

He picked over the evidence of his own eyes, desperate to find fault with it. He couldn't. Antonella had claimed not to know Fausto, yet she clearly did know him. Signora Fanelli and Fausto's relationship had appeared to be one of vague acquaintance, yet there was obviously much more to it than that.

Slowly, strand by sticky strand, the web they had spun to ensnare him came into focus. He couldn't see all of it, but he could see enough of it. Fausto was the key. It was Fausto who had first fired his suspicions about Maurizio with an apparently throwaway comment two weeks before. Fausto had backtracked, yes, but just enough to remove suspicion from himself while keeping Adam's interest alive. La Capannina in Viareggio had come from Fausto, just as the key to the top-floor rooms had come from Antonella. Christ, she had played it well, refusing him once before offering it up. And why had she offered herself up to him at the thermal spring? Because she thought he was leaving the next day? Because his work wasn't done yet, and she needed him to stay? The answer was obvious, impossible to ignore.

Maria, too, had played her part, fuelling tensions with Maurizio, raising the temperature. There had been no need to tell Maurizio about Adam's visit to the top-floor rooms, but she had done so. According to Signora Docci, it had also been Maria's idea that Adam wear Emilio's dinner jacket to the party, the cause of yet more antagonism with Maurizio.

The evidence stacked up by itself. Almost every memory he turned to supported the case against them. Even his seduction by Signora Fanelli could be made to fit, and he felt sick to the pit of his stomach when he thought about it. He had been guided and steered since his very first night in San Casciano.

But why him? He had figured it out by the time he'd drained another cup of coffee.

Maurizio needed to be exposed, dethroned, if Villa Docci was to pass down Antonella's branch of the family. She had evidently set her heart on the place, but all she had to work with were her suspicions about Maurizio's involvement in Emilio's death. She also knew that Maurizio was far too wary to fall into a trap laid directly by her. So she'd used a puppet. She had pulled the strings and Adam had danced. And everything had gone according to plan until the very last moment.

This was the only consolation in the affair – Maria's betrayal. Antonella hadn't banked on Maurizio outbidding her as the hammer came down. She had underestimated him. Maria, older and wiser, hadn't.

He carried this pleasing thought with him as he strode briskly along the track back to Antonella's farmhouse.

She wasn't there. Nor was her car. Both were gone. It was no bad thing. He would only have screamed at her. Or worse.

He made do with snatching up a rock from the roadside and hurling it through her kitchen window.

The farewells were absurd, Signora Docci the only unrehearsed actor in the farce. Knowing the stakes were high, Adam played his part to innocent perfection. So did Maria. Her eyes even misted with tears as she kissed him goodbye on both cheeks. Maurizio sweetly offered to drive Adam to the station himself.

They sat side by side in silence for most of the journey. Time was on their side, and Adam asked if they could swing by Piazza Repubblica to pick up his photos of the memorial garden. Maurizio accompanied him inside the shop. He also insisted on staying with him until the train departed. His last words were to the point.

'You have a good brain. Use it. Somewhere else. Not here. Don't ever come back here again.'

As the train jerked out of the station, he reached for the photos of the garden. He skipped over the ones of Flora, not because they were any worse than the others – he was a hopeless photographer, they were all second-rate – but because he felt ashamed. He felt as if he had let her down.

There was to be no justice for the man who slept alongside her beneath the stone floor of the Docci family chapel.

31

England was in the grip of a heat wave, which meant there had been four whole days of uninterrupted sunshine. Adam woke to the sound of the rain hammering against the window on the morning of day five, his first morning back.

His mother's opening words to him when he headed downstairs were, 'I told him he should have taken his umbrella to work.'

It was a familiar phrase; he'd heard her utter it many times before in that gently reproachful way of hers. This time, though, it grated, it remained lodged in his brain while the coffee percolated and his mother sang the praises of the new pop-up toaster they'd purchased while he'd been away. The cat had also been neutered in his absence, he discovered.

He didn't blame her. He knew he was party to the petty exchanges that constituted life at home. He had shared nothing of any significance with his parents over dinner the night before, aside from some impressions of

Italy and an account of his work at Villa Docci. His father's reaction to the news of Adam's unmasking of the garden could be described, at best, as one of grudging respect. Just as predictably, his mother had waited until she was alone with him before offering some heartfelt words of congratulation. Publicly, she always took her lead from her husband – a state of affairs that had irritated Adam in the past, but which now seemed wholly unacceptable.

'Sit down, Mum.'

'Darling?'

He carried the cup of tea he'd just made for her to the kitchen table, leaving her little choice but to join him.

'It's lovely to have you back, darling.'

He waited till she had settled herself down. 'Mum, I know about Dad.'

'About Dad?' she asked, a slight note of anxiety jarring with the cheery innocence.

'Harry told me.'

Her gaze faltered. 'He shouldn't have done that. I asked him not to.'

'Mum –'

'He promised he wouldn't.'

'Mum –'

'I'm very angry with him.'

'Mum.' He reached across the table and took her hand.

She bowed her head and stared at her cup of tea. He couldn't see her face behind the curtain of hair, but he could see her shoulders start to convulse. The first faint sobs built quickly in volume.

He slid from his chair and skirted the table. He wrapped

his arms around her from behind and held her tight while she bawled.

Later, after they had talked, it was she who suggested they treat themselves to lunch at the Grey Friar – an old coaching inn set in a fold of the North Downs beyond the urban sprawl. It was known for the quality of its cooking and its exorbitant prices, and they only ever went there on special occasions. This felt like one. His mother certainly seemed to think so. She sank two sherries before the meal and even smoked one of Adam's cigarettes. They both ordered the trout, which they ate at a table in the garden now that the rain had stopped and the clouds were clearing.

He told her everything that had happened to him in Italy. The only details he spared her were those of a more intimate nature. She rarely interrupted, allowing him to unburden himself.

When he was finished, she said, 'Well, you young people certainly do lead colourful lives.'

It was exactly the sort of thing she *would* say – exactly the sort of thing he had prayed she wouldn't say.

'Oh, for goodness sake, Adam,' she snapped, 'I was joking.'

The considered questions she now began firing at him suggested she'd been listening extremely attentively. She searched for an alternative interpretation of events, something that would remove the hurt of Antonella's deceit. When she failed to find anything, she consoled him – in the way that only a mother can.

❧

Adam's father was late home from work, but he returned bearing 'extremely good news'. His acquaintance at the Baltic Exchange had reiterated his offer of unpaid (but invaluable) work experience. Adam was welcome to start whenever he wanted.

'I don't think I want to do it, Dad.'

'You don't think you want to do it?' scowled his father.

'That's wrong. I *know* I don't.'

The inevitable argument ensued. At a certain point his father lost his temper. 'As long as you're living under my roof and at my expense, you'll do as you're told.'

The sheer volume caught them both off guard.

'How dare you!?' erupted Adam's mother. 'How dare you talk like that!? You have no rights here. Not any more.'

His father was struck utterly dumb, and Adam found himself transported to a small side-chapel in a Florentine church. Something in the shapeless anguish of his mother's mouth recalled Masaccio's Eve at the moment of her expulsion from the Garden of Eden.

Silence continued to reign. Adam's father glanced at him and realized immediately that his secret was out. He had not anticipated this and he hung his head.

'Tell him,' said his mother. 'Tell him what really happened in Italy. Tell him what they did to you.'

For a man who set great store by logic and cold fact, it was natural that his father should show more interest in the mechanics of Maurizio's crime and its discovery than in the human cost to Adam. However, he did find it in himself to say, 'If that girl ever darkens this doorstep . . . well, I don't know *what* I'll do.'

❧

A week later, he found out.

He asked her to wait on the doorstep while he went in search of Adam.

It was a Saturday afternoon, and Adam was mowing the lawn while his mother weeded the borders. He was still in his tennis gear, having played a couple of sets with some friends that morning.

His father appeared from the house, looking shaken. 'There's a young woman to see you. I think it's . . .' his fingers fluttered around his forehead '. . . from Italy.'

'Antonella . . .?'

'Possibly. Yes. From what you said.'

'Didn't you ask, Charles?' called his mother from behind a hydrangea.

'No, I didn't bloody ask, okay? I was too shocked.'

Antonella wasn't alone. Fausto hovered sheepishly at her shoulder.

Wild joy fought with anger. His instinct was to slam the door in their faces. Politeness prevailed, assisted by a big dose of curiosity.

'Come in,' he said coldly. 'You too,' he added to Fausto in Italian, using the formal *lei* instead of *tu* to make a point.

His parents had appeared behind him in the entrance hall, defiant, protective, and looking completely ridiculous in their tatty gardening clothes.

'It's okay,' he said to them, 'we'll go into the garden.'

As they stepped on to the back terrace, Antonella pulled an envelope from her pocket and handed it to Adam. It was thick and heavy.

'What is it?'

341

'Read it. It's okay.'

She touched him reassuringly on the arm.

He had spent many hours shaping her into a demon, a valuable life lesson at best, and it shocked him just how easily one feather-light touch could dismantle all his good work, melting the stony desolation of the past week.

'I don't know . . . I'm not sure I can . . . What is it?' He could feel tears starting to prick his eyes.

'It's okay,' she said.

'Go on,' said Fausto gently.

He took his cigarettes from the terrace table and made for the bench at the end of the garden.

Villa Docci

My dear Adam,

I hope this letter finds you well. I suspect it doesn't, and I don't doubt that I am to blame for that.

Maybe Antonella has already told you something of what has gone on, in which case much of what I write will come as no surprise to you. Either way, you must believe me when I tell you that Antonella had no hand in what happened – none whatsoever. She, like you, is entirely innocent. The rest of us are not. Please try not to judge Maria and Fausto too harshly. They only did what I asked of them, and not always willingly.

I have used you, Adam. I used you before I met you, I used you while you were here, and maybe I am still using you now. I don't expect you to forgive me for this, but I hope that one day you will come to understand my reasons. As Virgil says to Dante at the beginning of *La Divina Commedia* – which, thanks to you, I have read again – 'The way out is the way through.' That is how it was for me. Finding myself in a dark place, I saw only one way out of it.

My son killed my son. I suppose I have always known it, from the moment Benedetto first locked the door, closing off the top floor. It was not like him to do such a thing. His nature was to look forwards, never backwards. He gave his reasons, of course, and I chose to believe them. The alternative was unthinkable.

I am now certain that Benedetto worked out what really happened that night, and leaving those rooms just as they were was his punishment for Maurizio. He wanted Maurizio to live with the memory of what he had done. I have visited the rooms only twice. When Benedetto died I went looking for what he had found up there. A part of me was relieved when I failed. I now know what he discovered because I have followed your footprints across the dusty floor, I have seen where you stopped near the fireplace and folded back the carpet. I have seen the bullet-hole in the wooden boards stained with Emilio's blood. You found what Benedetto found, as I hoped (and feared) you would.

The only certainty in life is death. This is something I have always accepted, that is until death paid me a visit last Christmas. Even then, it was not death itself I feared, but the prospect of seeing Emilio again, of standing before him, both of us knowing that I had let him down, that I had done nothing. I swore to him then that if I lived I would get to the truth, however painful it might be. The moment that oath was made I knew I would survive, because I now had a reason to. So it was that one sickness replaced another.

My plan was simple but I required help. That is when I contacted Fausto. I have known him many years. His grandfather was a fine man, his father was not. I'm sorry if I speak ill of the dead, but they seem to me as fair a target for criticism as anyone. Even as a small boy, Fausto was exceptional. Benedetto and I took an interest in him for the sake of his grandfather. Fausto was not to know, but he found out that we had helped with his education over the years. And when I needed help he was there for me. These few lines do not do justice to our friendship or to the respect I have for him.

It was Fausto who went south for me earlier this year to the village near Rome where Gaetano comes from. It was Fausto who discovered that Gaetano's story of a family inheritance was untrue. And it was Fausto who helped me work out how to get to the truth. As you now know, I think, he has an interest in tactics and strategies.

Your role in this affair was mapped out many months ago: a young student, intelligent and inquisitive; the seeds of a mystery planted in his head by Fausto and nourished by me. If Maurizio suspected for a moment that I was behind the thing, he would never have shown himself. The threat had to come from someone else, an innocent. And you are, Adam.

344

It is not your fault. Your age is to blame. A more experienced man would have read the signs. He would have seen that he was being led by the hand.

Almost every step you took was determined in advance. Not all. Some things were impossible to anticipate. Three stand out. I steered you towards the photo albums in order to bring Emilio to life, to make him matter more to you, but I never imagined that you would see the truth of his parentage in those old images. I underestimated you (not for the first or the last time). I am glad now that I did. It has forced me to be honest with Crispin, as I should have been many years ago.

How do you tell a man that the son he never knew he had is dead? It is not easy, but it is finally done. If you have not been able to contact Crispin since your return it is because I have asked him to make himself unavailable to you until you have received this letter. Needless to say, he is extremely angry with me for the way I have treated you, almost as angry as Antonella, although that would take some doing. I have never been spoken to by anyone as I have been by her in these past days.

The other great surprise, impossible to predict, was your work on the garden. There was nothing false about my praise. What you achieved is extraordinary. What it means, I still don't know. As I told you once, I am not superstitious, but I want to be, I want to believe that you have lifted the curse on this place, on our family – the curse of Federico Docci, murderer, the same curse that drove my son to kill his brother.

345

To believe this is to spare Maurizio some of the blame, and myself some of the pain.

Then there is you, Adam. I did not think for a moment that I would come to care about the boy Crispin sent me. But I did, more than you can ever know. Twice I was close to telling you all. On another occasion Maria threatened to do the same. I persuaded her not to. If she showed you no affection while you were here (and I know she did not) it is only because she hated herself for the part she agreed to play. She did not wish to become attached to you.

Maria came late to our team, after your arrival. She was my eyes and ears, my spy. She went through your papers to see how your suspicions were developing, and whenever she could, she stirred Maurizio against you. If Antonella had not told you where the key to the top floor was hidden, then Maria would have done so. She was brilliant. On your last night here she even showed genius, when she was discovered by Maurizio's dog at the door of the chapel.

As you are now aware, there is no gun behind the plaque in the chapel. There are no bullets. Benedetto destroyed them all. The lie I fed you was the bait to draw Maurizio out. It was planned this way. It was also planned that, on hearing Maurizio's admission of guilt, Maria would come straight to me. The dog was not planned.

Exposed, what could Maria do? She had just heard Maurizio threaten my life. She could not allow him to think there was any connection between her and me. So she lied. She made him believe (and you, too, I think) that she was there for Antonella. Just how convincing she was, you know better than I do. It was certainly enough to fool Maurizio and buy me time to arrange matters at my end. We are a large family, the Doccis, and any action taken by me was always going to require the support and sanction of certain relatives. This has now been received.

It is not possible in Italy to disinherit a child, but a child can choose not to receive their inheritance. This is what Maurizio has done, in exchange for my silence. I shall never see him again. How he explains this change of circumstances to his wife, his children and his friends is his business. It will be difficult for him, but I don't doubt that he will find a way. Maybe his excuse will be that I have decided to remain in the villa, which is true, and he can no longer tolerate his mother's indecision.

Is this justice? No. Is there enough evidence to convict Maurizio of Emilio's murder? There never was. But at least the truth is finally out. It is enough. It has to be enough because that's all there is, that's all there was ever going to be. I knew this from the start, before I even met you.

There it is, Adam. I wish you weren't a part of it, but you are, and you only have me to blame. Fausto and Maria acted out of loyalty to me, and I expect you to find it within yourself to forgive them. I expect no such thing for myself.

I cannot imagine what you are thinking right now, but let me say this. I lied to you, I used you, I even placed you in physical danger (although you were more closely protected than you are probably aware). All of these things are true, I don't deny them, but most of what passed between us was good and honest. I meant what I said to you just before we sat down to dinner at the party. I asked you then to remember my words. Do you? I hope so, because they are as true as any I have ever spoken.

You fell foul of an old woman looking to do the right thing by her dead son. It may seem enormous to you now, but time and the weight of experience will compress the painful memory of your stay at Villa Docci until it is just one slender stratum in the bedrock of your life. Try not to forget that.

With great affection,

Francesca

Adam read the letter twice, steeping himself in the words.

When he returned to the terrace, he found his mother serving tea. She saw from his face that all was good and gave a small smile as she withdrew.

'I thought you were the one behind it all.'

'I know,' said Antonella. 'Maria had to make Maurizio believe it.'

'It wasn't just that. I saw Fausto leaving your house that last morning.'

Antonella exchanged a look with Fausto. 'He came to see me, to explain. We argued, but he persuaded me to play along. He said it wasn't for long. And it hasn't been, although it feels like it.'

She reached out and gingerly took his hand.

Fausto slid a book across the table. It was Adam's book on Renaissance sculpture, the one he had lost in the park in Viareggio.

Adam fingered the tome. 'That was you?'

Fausto nodded.

'You followed me there?'

Fausto nodded.

Adam's eyes remained locked on Fausto's.

'I'm sorry, Adam. Really.'

'Really?'

'Really.'

'Okay.'

'Good,' said Fausto with a beaming smile. 'That's very good.'

Their bags were collected from a small hotel near Purley station. They had taken rooms there, not knowing how things would go. This displayed 'an admirable lack of presumption' according to Adam's father, who had started to thaw a little. Fausto was assigned Harry's room, Antonella the guest bedroom at the far end of the corridor.

Adam took them off to the Stag and Hounds for a drink before dinner. Fausto had never seen darts played before and muscled in on a game, shamelessly filching cigarettes from his new and slightly bewildered friends.

It was the first time Adam had been alone with Antonella since her arrival, and it felt good.

'Hello,' he said.

She smiled and stroked his thigh beneath the table. 'How are you feeling?'

'Numb. Relieved.'

'Thanks for the present.'

'The present?'

'The rock in my kitchen.'

'Sorry, I didn't have time to wrap it.'

She laughed.

He glanced over at Fausto. 'Was Signora Fanelli involved?'

'Signora Fanelli?'

'I followed Fausto after he left your place. He went straight to see her at the pensione.'

'So?'

'Well . . . they're close. I saw them kiss.'

'I think that is a new thing, after you arrived. *Nonna* says they used to be very close, but there was some problem. She is very happy about it.'

'I'm sure she is.'

'Why are you smiling?'

'Nothing.'

Given what he now knew about Signora Docci's *modus operandi*, it wasn't so surprising that she'd even found time for a bit of match-making along the way. There were any number of pensiones in San Casciano she could have placed Adam in.

It was warm enough to have dinner on the terrace. His mother excelled herself in the kitchen; his father cracked open a couple of bottles of vintage claret he'd been saving for Adam's graduation. They raised a toast to Harry. When they speculated about some of the scrapes he must surely have got himself into by now, it was good to hear the sound of his father's laughter again.

Inevitably, some hours later, Adam found himself tiptoeing down the corridor towards the guest bedroom. Antonella was waiting for him, already naked beneath the sheets. The need for silence only heightened the intensity of their love-making. When it was over and they were lying tangled in each other, he cried, overwhelmed. Antonella licked away his tears and held him.

Later, out of the darkness beside him, she said, 'My grandmother thinks she knows who Flora's lover was.'

'Huh?' he grunted, from a delicious half-sleep.

She repeated herself.

Now he was awake. 'Who?'

'She wouldn't tell me. She will only tell you, in person – *faccia a faccia*.'

'Does she ever stop?'

'Stop?'

'Playing games.'

He tried to summon up anger at this latest piece of manipulation, but it was a struggle. Signora Docci might think that responsibility for her behaviour stopped with her; he wasn't so sure. He had re-assessed many things over the past week, but he hadn't quite been able to shake the conviction that someone else had been controlling matters all along.

He couldn't remember the last time he'd seen his parents both in their dressing gowns in the kitchen. His father was seated at the table with Fausto; his mother was frying bacon at the stove.

Adam shuffled up to her in his pyjamas and gave her a kiss on the cheek. 'Morning.'

'Is Antonella awake?'

'I don't know. I didn't look in on her.'

She slipped him a knowing look. 'Well, why don't you take her up a cup of tea anyway?'

'Good idea.'

He filled the kettle, glancing over at the table as he did so. Fausto was explaining something to his father in rapid-fire Italian while shifting pots of jam, cutlery and other objects around in some kind of demonstration.

His mother leaned close to him and whispered, 'We think it's the battle of Hastings.'

32

❦ ❦

It had rained in his absence, enough to swell the grapes on the vines and raise hopes of an acceptable harvest. There was even a faint tinge of green to the scorched pasture below the grotto, although this was about the only noticeable change in the memorial garden.

Adam opened the book Signora Docci had given him. It was his for the keeping, a gift: a leather-bound edition of Ovid's *Metamorphoses*, old and rather precious, he suspected. She had made him promise not to read the dedication on the flyleaf before reaching the garden.

It was short and very touching, and tucked into the same page was a small piece of paper on which she had written:

Metamorphoses 1:316

He found the line in the text and smiled. She intended to make him work for the answer.

It hadn't come to him by the time he reached the glade of Hyacinth. Standing before the statue of Apollo, he opened

353

the book again at the relevant passage. It dealt with the story of Deucalion and Pyrrha, the lone survivors of the great flood, whose raft grounded itself on Mount Parnassus. The line itself read:

Parnassus is its name, whose twin-peaked rise
Mounts thro' clouds, and mates the lofty skies.

He looked up at Apollo perched atop Parnassus, his mountain home – only, it wasn't Mount Parnassus, because it rose to a lone and very pointed peak. It was unlike Federico Docci to deviate from Ovid without a reason; his attention to detail was too meticulous.

He worked his way through the other options – Mount Olympus, Mount Helicon – but again he turned up a blank. That's when he realized he was coming at it all wrong.

He wasn't looking at Apollo; he was looking at Flora's lover in the guise of Apollo. Which meant that he wasn't looking at Mount Parnassus; he was looking at, well, just a mountain, one that climbed to a high, sharp peak.

A tall mountain.

'Montalto,' he said quietly.

It was a direct translation.

Fulvio Montalto, the young architect of Villa Docci. No wonder he had disappeared from the historical record. Federico Docci had made sure of that.

The circle was complete. And so was Flora. This final revelation, this last piece of the puzzle, somehow rounded her off, made her whole. Because it allowed her love to live again. Stopping to gaze up at her as he left the garden, he saw it burning in her eyes, just as Fulvio's love for her still smouldered in the effortless beauty of the villa he had designed for her. No doubt there was more of their story yet to be uncovered, maybe even a record of Fulvio's death buried away in some dusty archive. But her job was done. She had handed him the baton. It was up to him what he did with it now.

Threading his way back up the overgrown path to the villa, he cast his thoughts back to that sun-struck May day in Cambridge – where it had all begun – and asked himself whether he would have done anything differently, knowing what he now did.

It was not a question easily answered.

He barely recognized himself in the carefree young man cycling along the towpath beside the river, bucking over the ruts, the bottle of wine dancing around in the bike basket.

Try as he might, he couldn't penetrate the workings of that stranger's mind, let alone say with any certainty how he would have dealt with the news that murder lay in wait for him, just around the corner.